JEFFREY F̶O̶ ̶A̶N̶D̶ ̶H̶I̶S̶ ̶ ̶ ̶ ̶ ̶ ̶VEL

THE PORTRAIT OF MRS. CHARBUQUE

"Ford has created a masterpiece. . . . A marvelous, elegant book."
—*Austin Chronicle*

"A strange and affecting tale of obsession, inspiration, and the supernatural, with a dash of murder thrown in. . . . The twists and turns of Mrs. Charbuque's commission keep the pages turning."
—*New York Times Book Review*

"A standout literary thriller." —*Publishers Weekly* (starred review)

"Art history, Hitchcockian suspense and Pynchon-esque augury in equally bizarre measure, *Portrait* is a portrait of the artist at work as well as captivating intellectual fluff." —*Sun* (Baltimore)

"Jeffrey Ford is a fascinatingly unconventional writer." —*Locus*

"Eccentrically satisfying. . . . Ford's union of fantasy, science, mysticism and art is set in a Victorian Gotham that recalls an Edith Wharton novel, only with furtive, menacing shadows lurking behind the hansom cabs." —*Salon.com*

"Smart [and] spellbinding." —*School Library Journal*

"Chillingly surreal." —*Kirkus Reviews*

"Well-crafted, funny, charming, grotesque, bulging with arcane Victoriana, *The Portrait of Mrs. Charbuque* is a deliciously quirky thriller." —*Montreal Gazette*

The

GIRL IN THE GLASS

The

GIRL IN THE GLASS

JEFFREY FORD

An Imprint of HarperCollins*Publishers*

THE GIRL IN THE GLASS. Copyright © 2005 by Jeffrey Ford. All rights reserved. Printed in the United States of America. No part of this book may be used or reproduced in any manner whatsoever without written permission except in the case of brief quotations embodied in critical articles and reviews. For information address HarperCollins Publishers, 10 East 53rd Street, New York, NY 10022.

HarperCollins books may be purchased for educational, business, or sales promotional use. For information please write: Special Markets Department, HarperCollins Publishers, 10 East 53rd Street, New York, NY 10022.

FIRST EDITION

Dark Alley is a federally registered trademark of HarperCollins Publishers.

Designed by Nicola Ferguson

Library of Congress Cataloging-in-Publication Data

Ford, Jeffrey, 1955–
   The girl in the glass / Jeffrey Ford.—1st ed.
     p. cm.
   ISBN 0-06-093619-3
   1. Swindlers and swindling—Fiction. 2. Spiritualists—Fiction.
   3. Depressions—Fiction. 4. Mediums—Fiction. 5. Seances—Fiction. I. Title.

PS3556.O6997G57 2005
813'.54 2004065644—dc22   2004065638

05 06 07 08 09 ❖ / RRD 10 9 8 7 6 5 4 3 2

For Jack, with all my love and respect.
It's your move.

The

GIRL IN THE GLASS

A MEDIUM TO TRUTH

Some days ago I sat by the window in my room, counting the number of sedative pills I've palmed over the course of the last three months. Even though my fingers tremble, I've discovered that the erratic action can be a boon to tricks involving sleight of hand. In the midst of my tabulation, I happened to look outside at the beautiful summer day. A breeze was blowing through the trees that bordered the small courtyard, and their silver-backed leaves flashed in the sunlight. It was then that I noticed a bright yellow butterfly flutter past and come to rest on the head of the weathered concrete Virgin that sits amid the colorful zinnias that nurse Carmen had planted in the spring. The orange dot on its lower wings told me it was an alfalfa, *Colias eurytheme*.

The sight of this beautiful creature immediately reminded me of my benefactor and surrogate father, Thomas Schell, and I was swept back to my youth, far away in another country. I sat that day for hours, contemplating a series of events that took place sixty-seven years ago, in 1932, when I was seventeen. Decades have since died and been laid to rest, not to mention loved ones and personal dreams, but still that distant time materializes before me like a restless spirit at a séance, insisting its story be told. Of course, now with pen in hand, I have no choice but to be a medium to its truths. All I ask is that you believe.

ECTOPLASMIC PRECIPITATION

Every time the widow Morrison cried, she farted, long and low like a call from beyond the grave. I almost busted a gut but had to keep it under my turban. There could certainly be no laughter from Ondoo, which was me, the spiritual savant of the subcontinent.

We were sitting in the dark, holding hands in a circle, attempting to contact Garfield Morrison, the widow's long-dead husband, who fittingly enough had succumbed to mustard gas in a trench in France. Thomas Schell, ringmaster of this soiree, sat across from me, looking, in the glow from the candlelight, like a king of corpses himself—eyes rolled back, possessed of a bloodless pallor, wearing an expression straight from a nightmare of frantic pursuit.

To my right, holding fast to the gloved dummy hand that stuck out of the end of my jacket sleeve, was the widow's sister, Luqueer, a thin, dried-out cornstalk of a crone, decked with diamonds, whose teeth rattled like shaken dice, and next to her was the young, beautiful niece (I forget her name), whom I rather wished was holding my prosthesis.

On my other side was the widow herself, and between her and Schell sat Milton, the niece's fiancé, your typical scoffing unbeliever. He'd told us during our preliminary meeting with the widow that he was skeptical of our abilities; a fast follower of Dunninger and Houdini. Schell had nodded calmly at this news but said nothing.

We didn't have to sit there long before Garfield made his presence known by causing the flame on the candle at the center of the table to gutter and dance.

"Are you there?" called Schell, releasing his hands from those of the participants on either side of him and raising his arms out in front.

He let a few moments pass to up the ante, and then, from just behind Milton's left shoulder, came a mumble, a grumble, a groan. Milton jerked his head around to see who it was and found only air. The niece gave a little yelp and the widow called out, "Garfield, is it you?"

Then Schell opened his mouth wide, gave a sigh of agony, and a huge brown moth flew out. It made a circuit of the table, brushing the lashes of the young lady, causing her to shake her head in disgust. After perching briefly on the widow's dress, just above her heart (where earlier Schell had inconspicuously marked her with a dab of sugar water), it took to circling the flame. The table moved slightly, and there came a rhythmic noise, as if someone was rapping his knuckle against it. Which, in fact, someone was: it was me, from underneath, using the knuckle of my big toe.

Ghostly sobbing filled the dark, which was my cue to slowly move my free arm inside my jacket, reach out at the collar for the pendant on my neck, and flip it around to reveal the back, which held a glass-encased portrait of Garfield. While the assembled family watched the moth orbit closer and closer to fiery destruction, Schell switched on the tiny beacon in his right sleeve while with his left hand he pumped the rubber ball attached to a thin hose beneath his jacket. A fine mist of water vapor shot forth from a hole in the flower on his lapel, creating an invisible screen in the air above the table.

Just as the moth ditched into the flame, which surged with a crackle, sending a thin trail of smoke toward the ceiling, the beam of light from within Schell's sleeve hit my pendant, and I adjusted my position to direct the reflection upward into the vapor.

"I'm here, Margaret," said a booming voice from nowhere and everywhere. Garfield's misty visage materialized above us. He stared hard out of death, his top lip curled back, his nostrils flared, as if even in the afterlife he'd caught wind of his wife's grief. The widow's sister took one look at him, croaked like a frog, and conked out cold onto the table. The widow herself let go of my hand and reached out toward the stern countenance.

"Garfield," she said. "Garfield, I miss you."

"And I you," said the phantom.

"Are you in pain?" she asked. "Are you all right?"

"I'm fine. All's well here," he said.

"How do I know it's really you?" she asked, holding one hand to her heart.

"Do you remember that summer day by the sound when we found the blue bottle, and I told you I loved you?"

"Oh," cried the widow. "Oh, yes. I remember."

The ghostly image slowly disintegrated.

"Remember me," said the voice as it started to fade. "I'm waiting for you . . ."

Milton, who was well shaken by the visitation, said in a faltering voice, "I believe it's raining in here."

Schell spoke from the side of his mouth, "Merely ectoplasmic precipitation."

The widow's sister came around then. The niece called, "Uncle Garfield, I have a question."

Unfortunately Uncle Garfield had taken a powder. He spoke no more, but a few seconds after it had become obvious he was gone for good, a dead rat fell out of the darkness above and onto the table right in front of Milton, who gave a short scream and pushed back his chair, standing up.

"What does this mean?" he yelled at Schell, pointing at the razor-toothed corpse before him. His eyes and hair were wild.

Schell stared straight ahead.

Milton turned to look at me just as I was in the process of stowing the fake hand in the pocket inside my jacket. If he wasn't so upset, he might have noticed that my left sleeve was empty.

"My exalted Mr. Milton," I said in my best Bombay-by-way-of-Brooklyn accent, "the dead speak a strange symbolic language."

He turned away and walked directly to the light switch. I slipped my arm into the sleeve, and the lights came up. The group was silent as they employed handkerchiefs.

"We've made progress, Mrs. Morrison," said Schell.

"Thank you so much for bringing him to me," she said. "How can I ever repay you?"

"I ask only my fee."

And a hefty one it was at that for half an hour's work. As we stood by the front door of the mansion, Schell stuffed the wad of bills into his coat pocket while lifting the widow's hand to kiss the back of it. I stood patiently, ever the assistant of the great man, but inside I was itching to get home and wash that dead rat residue out of my hair.

"You must come back," said the widow.

"It would be my express pleasure," said Schell.

I'd noticed that while we stood gathered in the foyer that Milton tried to put his arm around Morrison's niece, but she shrugged his hand off her shoulder. Apparently she had no problem interpreting the strange symbolic language of the dead. Milton ignored this brush-off and stepped up to Schell.

"Most uncanny," he said. "I too would like to employ you for a séance."

"I'll consider it," said Schell, "although, usually, I make my services available to only a *certain quality* of individual."

Milton seemed to take this as an affirmation.

I delivered my Ondoo nightcap, one of my favorites from the

Rig-Veda, "May he whose head is flaming burn the demons, haters of prayer, so that the arrow slay them," and we left. It was our practice to always walk in single file with Schell first and myself behind, moving slow and measured, as if in a stately procession.

Antony Cleopatra was waiting beside the Cord, dressed in his chauffeur uniform and cap, holding the door. Schell got in the front, and after closing the door, Antony came around and held open the other door for me. Once we were seated, he got in the driver's seat, squeezed his hulking mass behind the wheel, and started the engine. As we traveled down the long, winding driveway toward the road, I lifted the turban off my head.

"How'd it go?" asked Antony.

"That widow held more gas than a zeppelin," I said.

"Or didn't," said Schell. "I was afraid to light the candle."

"How'd you come up with the bit about them on the beach and the blue bottle?" I asked.

"Passing through the parlor, on the way to the dining room where we had the séance," said Schell, "there's a lovely photograph on the fireplace mantel of the widow and poor Garfield, standing on a beach. In her hand is the bottle."

"But the color of it?" I asked.

"It was of a distinct shape most commonly used to hold an old curative elixir, Angel's Broom, now outlawed for its alcoholic content. These were sometimes made of brown glass but more often blue. I simply played the odds on the color."

I laughed in admiration. Thomas Schell possessed more flim-flam than a politician, a poet, and a pope put together. As Antony often put it, "He could sell matches to the devil."

THE BUGATORIUM

The world was on the skids, soup lines and Dust Bowls, but you would never have known it from the polished brass banisters and chandeliers of Mrs. Morrison's Gold Coast palace. The Depression wasn't our concern either as the three of us sat in Schell's Bugatorium (Antony's name for it), sipping champagne in celebration of a job well done. The air was alive around us with the flutter of tiny wings, a hundred colors floating by, like living confetti, to mark our success. An orange albatross, *Appias nero*, the caterpillars of which had arrived from Burma some weeks earlier, lighted on the rim of Schell's glass, and he leaned forward to study it.

"I'm positive the widow will have us back," he said, "and when she does we'll have to give her a little more of a show. She's a vein we've only begun to tap."

"Maybe Antony could pose as Garfield, you know, a flour job. We'll ghost him up," I said. "I noticed a window there in the dining room. If we could direct her to the window, he could be standing out in the garden in the shadows."

"Not a bad idea," said Schell, coaxing the butterfly off his glass with a gentle nudge of his pinky.

"I hate being dead people," said Antony.

"You're a natural," I said.

"Watch it, junior," said the big man.

We waited a long while for Schell to jump back in the conversation, but he didn't. Instead he merely sighed, took one more sip of his drink, and set his glass on the table. "Gentlemen, I'm through," he said and stood up. "Nice work this evening." He stepped around to where I sat and shook my hand. This had been the protocol since I was a child; never a hug at bedtime, only hand shaking. He then moved on to Antony and did the same. "Remember, no smoking in here, Mr. Cleopatra," he said.

"Whatever you say, Boss," said Antony.

We watched Schell leave the room, moving wearily, as though carrying some invisible burden. A few minutes later, the muffled sound of Mozart's *Requiem* came to us from down the hall and through the closed door.

Hearing the sad music in the distance, Antony poured another drink for himself and said, "Funeral time."

"What's wrong with him these days?" I asked, holding out my glass for a refill.

"No more booze for you tonight," he said.

"Come on."

"When you're eighteen."

"Okay," I said, knowing not to test his patience. "But what about the boss?"

"The boss?" he said, taking a pack of cigarettes and a lighter out of his shirt pocket. "His feelings are on unemployment."

"Well put," I said.

"You better believe it," said Antony, lighting the cigarette he'd placed between his lips.

"Why, though?" I asked. "We could be out there scrounging for a crust of bread, but business has never been better."

"This shit can get to you after a while. Bilking people, scamming old ladies." He leaned back and blew a big smoke ring. A beautiful blue morpho flew right through the center, dispersing it.

"That's what he does, though, and he's the best at it," I said.

"He's a fucking artist, for sure, but it's not really right."

"The widow looked pretty pleased to see her husband again tonight," I said. "How much do you think that was worth to her?"

"Yeah, yeah, I know the arguments, but I'm telling you, he's caught the funk from it," he said, standing to lean across the table and grab Schell's glass. As he sat back down, he flicked his ash into the remaining champagne, and it fizzed.

"What makes you so sure?"

"Back when I worked the carnivals, wrestling palookas and bending iron bars with my teeth, I saw all manner of shills. These guys, some of them were champs, you know, made a healthy living at it. Some of them would con their old ladies for a quarter if they could, but some a them actually had a conscience, and after a while, even if they never thought about it up front, underneath, the unhonestness of it ate them away."

"Schell . . . a conscience?" I asked.

"If not, why'd he take you in? I told him back when first he brought you home, I said, 'Boss, the last thing you need's some spic brat running around your life.' He said, 'Too late, Antony, he's ours and we have to raise him.'"

"And then you grew to love me," I said.

"Yeah," he said. "But, the boss, he's caught between a shit and a sweat."

I shook my head, unable to conceive of Thomas Schell ever being confused about anything. The revelation disturbed me, and Antony must have seen this in my expression.

"Don't worry, we'll think of something," he said, dropping the spent butt into the champagne glass. He stood up. "I'm hitting the sack." He pointed to the glass with the butt in it. "Do me a favor and get rid a this crap so I don't get in trouble."

"Okay," I whispered, still deep in thought.

Antony walked around behind me and put his palm on top of

my head, his long fingers encompassing my crown like a normal size hand holding an apple. He shook me gently back and forth. "Schell's gonna be fine," he said. "You're a good kid, Diego. You're a helluva swami."

He let go and lumbered toward the door, a small swarm of pine whites following in his wake.

"Good night, Antony," I said.

"Sleep tight, babe," he called back and then slipped out of the room as quickly as he could to keep the butterflies in.

I sat quietly, surveying the veritable jungle of plants and potted trees surrounding the table and chairs. The blossoms were as varied in color and shape as the insects. Up above, I could see the stars through the glass skylight. In his room, Schell had exchanged the platter on his Victrola for some equally melancholic piece, and the serenity of the scene made me ponder this turning point in my life. I'm sure the moment comes to most earlier, but few have had a "father" as extraordinary as mine. In my conversation with Antony, it had struck me for the first time that Schell was merely mortal. The thought of him troubled, confused, made the world seem instantly more sinister.

THE EXTENT OF SUSCEPTIBILITY

The next day, Schell and I took off in the Cord to stake out a new mark. There was a very wealthy gentleman over in Oyster Bay whose bank account required lightening. It was our practice to meet with perspective patrons first before performing a séance in order to case the room where the event would take place and judge what effects would be possible. It was also an opportunity to pick up clues that we could spin into prescient revelations. The boss focused on artwork, the type of furniture, jewelry, repetitions of words and phrases the mark might use, hand gestures, pets. Not an errant nose hair escaped his attention, and he'd extract from these crumbs of information secrets of the bereaved as if he were Conan Doyle's detective.

The thing he most concentrated on, though, was the apparent degree of the mark's grief, for as he always reminded me, "The depth of loss is directly equivalent to the extent of susceptibility." In other words, the more one longed for contact from the other side, the more readily one would embrace the illusion. Occasionally, we would run into a snake, some self-professed debunker, whose intent was merely to out us as frauds, but Schell could spot this within the first five minutes of an interview.

"Watch the nose, Diego," he would say. "The nostrils flare

slightly when one is lying. The pupils dilate an iota. In a thinner person, you can detect treachery by the pulse in the neck." For a man who trafficked in the spiritual, he was ever focused on the physical.

"And how are your studies going?" Schell asked me as we sped along.

"I'm reading Darwin, *The Origin of Species*," I said.

"My hero," he said, laughing. "What do you make of it?"

"We're apes," I said, adjusting my turban.

"Too true," he said.

"God's a fart in a windstorm. It's only Nature that rigs the deck."

"It isn't a perfect being that's brought all of this about," he said, lifting his right hand off the wheel and gracefully describing a circle in the air. "It's all chance and tiny mistakes that give an advantage, which are compounded over time. Think of the intricate, checkered patterning of the spanish festoon [a butterfly we'd had a specimen of some time back]; all a result of some infinitesimal, advantageous mistake in the makeup of a single caterpillar."

"Mistakes are at the heart of everything," I said.

He nodded. "That's the beauty."

"But you never make mistakes," I said.

"When it comes to work, I try not to. But, believe me, I've made mistakes—great yawning gaffes."

"Such as?"

He was silent for a time. "I let my past dictate my future," he said.

"I can't think of you employed in any other career," I said.

"Perhaps," he said, "but I can certainly conceive of *you* doing something else. You don't want to remain Ondoo for the rest of your days now do you? This repatriation business will blow over eventually. The economy will rebound. By the time you're nineteen, I'd like to see you in college."

"As far as my records are concerned, I don't exist. I have no past.

I'm illegal." My education, although superior to any that could be obtained at a public school, was all garnered through a series of quality tutors that Schell had paid a small fortune for.

"You leave the records to me," he said. "Arrangements can be made."

"What if I want to stay in the séance business with you and Antony?"

He shook his head but said nothing. We drove on for a few more minutes, and then he turned off the road onto a private drive. The path wound, eel-like, for almost a mile before coming to a guarded gate. A man in a uniform approached the car. Schell rolled down the window and gave his name. "We're here to see Mr. Parks," he said. The guard nodded, and we continued on toward an enormous house that had turrets like a castle.

We parked in the circular drive, and before exiting the car, Schell touched my shoulder and said, "Time to be mystical." We walked slowly, single file, to the entrance. As we ascended a long flight of marble steps, the front door opened and a man in a butler's uniform greeted us.

I'd grown used to the opulence of the residences we frequented on our jobs, but, as they went, the Parks estate was impressive. Antony and I had done the legwork on him and found he'd had money left to him by his father, who'd invested in railroads and trucking and increased it during the Great War by selling munitions to both sides. Parks's wife had died recently at a sanatorium from TB.

We met the man, himself—portly, with thinning sandy hair—in a parlor at the rear of the mansion. The large window that took up much of the back wall offered, at a distance, a view of the Long Island Sound. He sat, dressed in a white suit, in an overstuffed chair that resembled a throne, smoking a cigarette attached to an exceedingly long holder. I doubt he was much older than Schell, somewhere in his forties.

"Mr. Schell," he said upon seeing us, and rose to shake hands with the boss. He turned to me and nodded but didn't offer his hand.

"This," said Schell, waving at me, "is my assistant, Ondoo, a native of India. He has a remarkable facility with the mystical. Since working with him, I've found that the channels through which the departed travel from the other side are clearer in his presence."

Parks nodded and took his seat.

"There are spirits present now," I said as I sat in one of the chairs facing him.

"Preliminary ethereal sensations have led me to believe you seek contact with a woman who has passed over," said Schell.

Parks's eyes widened, and he gave a smile devoid of joy. "Remarkable," he said.

"You must miss her very much," said Schell.

Parks stubbed out his cigarette in a large, sterling silver ashtray in the shape of a sleeping cat. He nodded, and tears came instantly to his eyes. "Yes," he said, his voice having shrunk to a peep.

"Your wife . . . ," Schell said, but at the same moment, Parks said, "My mother . . ."

Before Parks could register the slip, Schell continued, "As I was saying, your wife, of course, is sorely missed, but I knew it must be your mother to whom you wish to speak."

"I won't lie, Mr. Schell," he said. "You're right again. I miss my mother. When she was alive, I would sit with her for an hour every day and confer with her on business, the news, the drama of the household. Though she's been gone for ten years, I still find myself thinking, after making some astounding transaction, 'I can't wait to tell Mother.'"

"I understand," said Schell.

"The mother is the milk of the universe," I added, wondering what kind of relationship he'd had with his wife.

"Perhaps pathetic in a man of my age," he said. "But I can't help my feelings." He broke down at this point, lowering his head and lifting a hand to cover his face.

I looked over at Schell, who shifted his gaze to direct mine to the wall. There were three paintings in the room—one was a Madonna and child, one was of a child standing alone by the seashore, and the last was of a train. Beyond this, I noticed that the room was painted and decorated in primary colors.

My analysis of Parks's surroundings was leading me to a psychological revelation, but just then a young woman, no older than me, walked into the room. She was carrying a tray holding a pitcher of lemonade and three glasses with ice. "Will you have the drinks now, Mr. Parks?" she asked.

He dried his eyes. "Yes, Isabel," he said.

I looked at her again and somehow knew instantly that she was Mexican. At the same moment, she took me in, and in the subtle heave of her chest and signs of a suppressed smile at the corners of her lips, I knew she had made me. I looked at Schell, and he at me. He ran his index finger along the thin line of his mustache, our signal that I should remain calm.

Isabel poured Parks a glass of lemonade and handed it to him. Then she did the same for Schell. When she handed me mine, she nonchalantly turned her back to her employer, leaned in close to me and whispered, "Me encanta tu sombrero," glancing at my turban. I wanted to smile at her because she was pretty with a long woven braid of black hair and large brown eyes. At the same time I wanted to cringe in embarrassment. Instead I held fast to my Oriental role and never flinched. As she backed away, she winked at me.

IMAGINE THAT

I
magine that," said Schell as we passed the guard at the gate
and traveled back down the winding driveway, "a captain of
industry, a financial powerhouse, and what he wants most in
life is his mother. I'd be touched if I went in for such things, but on
a purely analytical level, it's instructive. Two points: there's little
comfort in wealth, and one's childhood tags along through life like
a shadow." He gazed out the windshield as if trying to reconcile
these ideas.

"But we're not going to take the job," I said.

"Certainly we are," he said. "We'll do a world of good for Mr.
Parks."

"But the girl, Isabel, made me in a second," I said. "She whispered to me, 'I love your sombrero.'"

"I think she liked you," said Schell and smiled.

"She'll rat me out to Parks."

He shook his head. "No she won't."

"Why not?"

"She's obviously a bright girl. You could see it in her eyes. And
the phrase she spoke to you indicates wit, which indicates intelligence. She's too smart to interfere with her employer's business. I
daresay she either finds him pathetic—his word—or she feels bad

for him. Parks, for his part, wouldn't be able to tell the difference between a Hindu wise man and a Hottentot. I'm afraid, for him, you are a permanent resident of the kingdom, Other, phylum, Rabble. The fact that you might be useful in gaining him what he wants is, in his mind, your sole purpose in life. I'm sure he feels the same about the young lady. No, Parks is oblivious on this score."

"Whatever you say," I said, and as Schell turned out onto the road and gunned the engine, I recalled a few years earlier, when I was in the process of becoming Ondoo. We had taken the train to New York City to visit the lepidoptera display at the Museum of Natural History. Along our route, from the train station uptown, Schell had regaled me, apropos of nothing, at least it seemed so then, with his opinions concerning bigotry.

"I hold no preconceived prejudice against anyone," he'd said, "because to do so is utter folly for someone in my line of work. It's only ignorance that causes individuals to label an entire race as either good or bad. These are generalities so broad as to be both worthless and dangerous. I deal only in specifics. God, as they say, is in the details. I must focus on the unique traits of the individual in order to tailor an illusion that will ultimately enchant. To see others in this manner is to never give in to labeling. To fail to do this is the equivalent of putting on a blindfold. Do you understand? The devil is in the details."

I understood well enough, and although, thanks to the reading I'd done the terms he used were not foreign to me, even at the age of fifteen it struck me as troubling that he'd never once mentioned the immorality of it. Schell never seemed to operate out of a sense of morality but instead took his cues solely from what worked and what didn't. In his view, prejudice wasn't evil, it was merely bad business.

I asked him what he had in mind for Parks.

"Parks has never left the nursery, one might say, so I think we should keep things light. I'm considering levitations, some butterfly effects, and to steal your idea from last night, I thought we could have Antony pose as his mother."

"He'll have to go about on his knees," I said, laughing.

"Precisely," said Schell, smiling at the thought of it. "And as the hoary old Mrs. Parks, what should she say to her son? Think hard now, how should she address him? What does he want to hear from her?"

I thought for a moment and said, "A good scolding."

Schell beeped the horn. "You're getting frighteningly expert at this," he said.

"Did you get a good look at the old lady's photograph?" I asked.

"Her image is emblazoned on my memory. Al Capone with rouge and a wig, minus the cigar," he said.

"I think Ma Parks should suggest a raise for Isabel."

Schell nodded. "Antony will have to start practicing his falsetto."

When we arrived home, we found the future Ma Parks sitting at the kitchen table. He was wearing a sleeveless undershirt, his mountainous tattooed biceps on display. Upon hearing us, he looked up, and it was evident that he'd been crying.

"I hate to tell you guys this," he said, "but I got a call a little while ago from Sally Coots. He wanted to let us know that Morty bought the farm. Blew a fuse. They found him in his apartment."

I watched the air go out of Schell as it went out of me. He took off his homburg, laid it on the table, pulled out a chair, and sat down. I did the same with my turban, and took the other seat. He simply stared, but the tears came easily to my eyes. We all sat there in silence for a long time, as if about to begin a séance.

Eventually Antony spoke. "Morty was a fucking ace."

"A gentleman and a pro," said Schell. "Best rope trick I ever saw. This truly marks the passing of an era."

I dried my eyes. "Who's got Wilma?" I asked.

"Sally said that the snake was dead too, must've died from a broken heart when Mort went. They were two peas in a pod. Sally said

Mort had told him a while ago that if anything happened to him, he wanted you should get Wilma since you were his prodigy."

Antony obviously meant *protégé* and in this he was correct. I had learned everything I knew about being a swami from Morton Lester.

In 1929, when the economy was really starting to slip and things got uglier than usual for illegals in the United States, citizens perceiving them as stealing scarce jobs, Schell and Antony were worried they might lose me. By 1930, Mexicans were being rounded up by law officers and "repatriated" across the border. Schell considered adopting me, but to do so would have made it necessary to reveal my illegal status. The nasty tenor of the times made him uneasy with this move, so it was decided that another way had to be found.

Schell had told me that one afternoon he was in the Bugatorium, reading a treatise from 1861 he had recently acquired by a famous British naturalist, Henry Walter Bates. In it, Bates discusses the ability of certain Amazon species of butterfly to practice mimicry. According to him, in some cases, butterflies, specifically the yellow or orange *Dismorphia*, which predators find particularly tasty, are able to change their outward appearance to mimic the appearance of less tasty brethren, most notably, *Heliconia*.

It was while Schell was in the midst of reviewing this essay that a brainstorm struck, and he hit upon the idea of changing my nationality. By that time, I'd been at him for a while to find me a role in his business, and so he conceived of a persona for me, that of a mystical assistant, whose very presence elevated spiritual possibility.

As he'd put it at the time, "We can't change your complexion, so we'll shift your point of origin. From this day forward, you'll be a Hindu."

"But I know nothing of what a Hindu is or does," I said.

"Yes," he admitted, "but neither does anyone else. They'll maybe think of Gunga Din, or perhaps a brown man atop the back of an elephant, or, if you can carry it off, a turbaned swami whose holy presence negates the border between life and death."

"People will be fooled?" I asked.

"Diego, there was once a very famous Chinese magician whose name was Chung Ling Soo. He was world renowned. Part of his act was a trick called Defying the Bullets. Two bullets, marked by audience members, were loaded into rifles. Two marksmen fired across the stage at Soo. Night after night, he would catch those bullets on a china plate. One night, after having performed the trick for eighteen years, one of the guns malfunctioned, and a bullet was actually fired. It passed through his body, and he fell to the stage mortally wounded. When he was rushed to the hospital, it was discovered that he wasn't Chinese at all, but a fellow by the name of William E. Robinson. No one had ever suspected this, for Soo often spoke Chinese. Or was it Chinese? For all those years, he might have been mouthing gibberish. But he had the Oriental costume, beautiful stage settings, the right makeup."

I never really considered what it would take for me to become a swami, and to be honest, I didn't care, as I was hot to participate in the séances. But I'd had to admit to Schell, "I don't know where to begin."

"Leave that to me," he'd said and went straight to his office and made a phone call. Early the next day, Antony and I took the train from Port Washington into Jamaica, and from there boarded a train for Coney Island. We arrived at the gate to the Nickel Empire by the sea at midmorning. I'd never been there before, but Antony had. Upon taking a look around, he proclaimed, "This place is looking shabby. I remember the old days here. What a blast, the Drop and Dip, the Red Devil, the Ben Hur Race, Hula Hula Land, and dinner at Stubenbord's. Jeez Louise, this place is a dump now."

We walked along The Bowery until we came to Sam Wagner's World Circus Side Show. Antony gave me two dimes and told me to go in and find Chandra. "He knows you're coming," said Antony.

"Aren't you coming in?" I asked.

"I'd come with you, kid, but I'm afraid of seeing those pinheads they've got in there." He shivered slightly. "They give me the yips. I'll be over banging the high strikers when you're done."

I found Chandra, Prince of Swamis, after having spent a little time gaping at Laurello, the man with the revolving head, and Pipo and Zipo, pinheads extraordinaire. Chandra was a small, severe-looking Hindu fellow, sitting cross-legged on a platform before a velvet curtain. He wore a turban and a kind of diaper and was playing a long flutelike instrument with a bulge at the end. As he blew on that pipe, the odd music caused an enormous, hooded cobra to rise straight up out of a wicker basket that sat a few feet in front of him.

There were no customers around, so I stepped up, giving the snake a wide berth and said, "Excuse me, Mr. Chandra, I've been sent by Thomas Schell to see you."

He removed the flute slowly from his lips, but didn't turn his head to take me in. Instead, his eyes merely shifted while he remained facing the snake. He laid down the flute and rose in one fluid motion. As he stood, the snake descended back into the basket.

"Follow me," he said with a distinct Indian accent, parting the curtain and leading me down a hall to a large dressing room. Once we were inside, he turned and looked me straight in the eyes with a penetrating stare that made me uneasy. He pursed his lips and breathed out, and as the air left him he changed. Before he inhaled again, it became obvious to me, as it hadn't been at all before, that he was definitely not Indian but a white man with some kind of dark makeup applied to his skin. Suddenly, he smiled.

"So," he said, "how's those two knuckleheads you live with?"

In my surprise, all I could do was nod.

"Tommy wants me to make you a swami? No sweat, kid, we got it covered."

ACE OF HEARTS

The next evening, Antony, Schell, and I drove to Flatbush for the wake. Upon entering the viewing parlor at the funeral home, shouts of "Tommy" and "Henry" went up. In my time with Morty, I'd gotten the idea that Schell was something of a celebrity among the show folk at Coney and with magicians and con artists from around the city. A lot of the old-timers still called Antony "Henry," which was his real name, Henry Bruhl. Antony Cleopatra had been his stage name, taken more than twenty years earlier from a Broadway marquee announcing a play about the famous ancient lovers. He didn't care what they called him but smiled and hugged them all anyway. I was introduced as the kid, or Diego, or Ondoo, my perceived identity shifting madly from one to the other.

I knew some of the crowd—Sal Coots, a magician who went by the moniker Saldonica the Wizard; the dog man, Hal Izzle, who had been born with a rare disease, the effects of which had left him hairy from head to foot; Marge Templeton, the fat lady; Peewee Dunnit, a two-bit con man who ran shell games and card scams all over the five boroughs; Miss Belinda, a female magician whose act involved twenty pigeons; and Jack Bunting, the legless spider boy, who walked on his hands and could bite a silver dollar in half. There were others, too: Captain Pierce, the retired, doddering knife thrower, and Hap Jackland, part-time geek, part-time traveling shoe salesman.

The place was packed. Morty was laid out in a coffin amid bouquets and floral arrangements at the front of the room, but the mood was less than somber. The constant rolling sound of conversation was occasionally interrupted by outbursts of raucous laughter. Every now and then, one of the mourners would wander up to the coffin, spend a few moments, and then drift away, drying his eyes.

After the initial introductions, Schell whispered to me, "First things first," and nodded toward the coffin. We approached it together, and as we drew near, I felt a tightening in my stomach. I had seen death before, when I was younger, living with my brother on the streets. I found the prospect of its finality frightening, and no manner of study, no intellectual ideal, could offset that response. Schell must have sensed the difficulty I had standing there so close to it, and he put his arm lightly around my shoulders.

Morty was frowning as he never had in life. Even in the guise of Chandra, when a serious demeanor was an integral part of his role, he worked to never let that solemnity slip into negativity. As he once told me, "Look, kid, nobody's paying to come here and see me sniff shit for a dime. A swami isn't usually gonna be cutting up, telling jokes, but you gotta be careful that your look never slides into the sad or the angry, 'cause then your audience is gonna think you're judging them. You're supposed to be a metaphysical conundrum, not God almighty, get it?"

He was dressed in a brown suit and was wearing his eyeglasses. His sparse hair was neatly combed over his balding head. Whenever I'd seen him without the turban, that hair was in a twist or a whirl, but never combed. I shook my head to see how death puts its own disguise on a person. Coiled up next to the pillow on which his head rested was Wilma, his close companion and best friend. Who would have thought that a man and a snake could be so close, but they were. The snake had even answered to verbal commands. Morty told me that a lot of times all he had to do was think something and Wilma would do it. The cobra carried the name of a girl who'd once broken his heart.

Schell took his arm from around my shoulders and reached into the breast pocket of his jacket, retrieving a playing card. From his pocket to the coffin, he rolled it from finger to finger, turning it over and over, and I saw that it was the ace of hearts. Just before he laid it facedown on the satin, he snapped it, and said, "Okay, Morty." He forced a smile, although I could see sadness on his face (Schell never cried), and then turned away.

I stood there uneasily, unable to reach that place in my mind where I could hold a mental discussion with the dead. Behind me the conversation swelled and ebbed, and at one point I heard someone say, "How's the kid doing?" and Antony answered, "I swear to Christ, the kid's a damn genius." From another quarter, I heard someone say, "I'm developing a trick where I pull a pig out of a hat. A big pig. Anybody can pull a rabbit out, I'm pulling a pig as big as a dachshund." In answer, I heard Sally say, "You couldn't pull your dick out of your pants." There was a burst of laughter, and then the conversation turned somber as it moved onto the topic of Coney and how it was failing. "Morty's in better shape than that joint," said Peewee. Someone recounted the story of Electro's demise. "Dreadful," said Marge. "I was there. His eyeballs caught fire and smoke came out of his ears." "Sounds like my ex," said the dog man, and then he howled.

I was about to turn back to the group, when in the back of my mind I felt the stirrings of a memory. Concentrating on it, it slowly blossomed into a full-blown recollection. It was from the last day of my weeks of instruction with Morty. We sat at the counter at Nathan's, eating hot dogs. It was midsummer, overcast, in the middle of the week. The crowds had stayed away in droves, and the park was almost deserted. There was a breeze rolling in off the ocean, and rain was imminent. Morty, still dressed in his swami getup, turban and diaper, fingered a pile of sauerkraut to his mouth and wiped his hands on a napkin.

"I gave you the books, right?" he asked. He'd lent me his Hindu texts, translations of holy books I was to scour for incomprehensible phrases that would dazzle Western minds.

I nodded.

"You got the turban?"

I nodded.

"You're working on the voice? Let me hear something," he said.

"May Shiva dance like a flame in your heart," I said, in the rigid-tongued, singsong method that he'd taught me.

He smiled. "You're a swami's swami."

I laughed.

"Okay, kid, here's the last thing I'm gonna tell you. Maybe it's the most important." He reached over and gave me a gentle slap on the cheek, something he did often when teaching me. At first I'd been angry at these intrusions on my personal space, but over time they'd become for me like pats on the back. "I hope all of this nonsense helps you out, but you've gotta promise me one thing. Never forget who you really are. What we're doing here is actually an abomination. We're not swamis, we're the swamis of peoples' imaginations, swami knockoffs out for a buck. For us, the turban's a job, you see? Always remember that." He laid three quarters on the counter and hopped off his stool. I stood up next to him.

"Thanks for everything," I told him.

He reached up and swatted me again across the cheek, but this time harder than usual, so that it stung. "Adios, Diego," he said. As he walked away there was a crack of thunder, and it instantly started to pour. I glanced up at the sky, and when I looked back, he'd vanished.

"Thanks, Morty," I whispered to the corpse and then leaned over and lightly petted Wilma's hood. I turned away from the coffin and went to sit with a dozen people discussing some intricate con Schell had worked when he was younger. It involved a hansom cab, a cop, and a red balloon filled with helium, but I wasn't able to piece it together. Every once in a while, one of them would call back to Schell, who sat by himself in the last row of chairs, "What was the take on that little mission, three grand?" or, "The bull was McLaren, wasn't it?" and I'd see him force a smile and nod. In another small group, Antony was regaling three women with his exploits in the traveling carnival trade, specifically his act in which he stopped a cannonball with his gut.

I slipped away and went to join Schell. Neither of us spoke for a few minutes. Finally, I asked him how long he'd known Morty.

"Long time," he said. "When I was a kid and my father would be gone for days on end, Morty let me come and stay at his place. I'd sleep on his couch, and he'd have Wilma do tricks for me. Sometimes he'd read me a book."

"He was good," I said.

"They're all good," he said, nodding at the assembled mourners.

Time passed and people started heading out. Antony approached and leaned over us. "Boss," he said. "Do you mind driving home? I think I'm gonna stick around and spend some time with Vonda over there."

"Who's Vonda?" asked Schell.

"You know," Antony said, pointing backward with his thumb, "the Rubber Lady. We're gonna go and get a few cocktails."

"The Rubber Lady?" asked Schell.

"Hey, she's got a friend," said Antony. "You should join us. We can put the kid on a train, and he can catch a cab from the station."

"Thanks, but I think I'll pass," said Schell.

Antony leaned even closer to Schell and I heard him whisper, "I hear she's a sword swallower."

Schell begged off, and soon after, he and I said our good-byes and left. On the long drive home, he said nothing. Later that night, as I lay in bed nodding off to sleep, I heard the strains of melancholic music drifting down the hall from Schell's room.

I was awakened the next morning by the sound of Antony's voice, yelling, "Come off it," and realized Schell must have just informed him that he would be playing Ma Parks. I got dressed and went out to the kitchen.

"This was your doing, you little piss nob," said Antony as I entered the kitchen.

"What?" I said but couldn't hold a straight face.

"Old lady Parks," he said.

"Typecasting," said Schell, who looked as if he hadn't slept all night.

"I heard you yesterday, Antony," I said. "You said I was a genius."

"I take it back," he said and got up to get himself a cup of coffee.

"How was the Rubber Lady?" asked Schell.

Antony poured cream and stirred. "My little pretzel? I told her about how I used to let cars run over my head, and she was swept away with me."

"A true romantic," said Schell.

"I spent three hours waiting for the first train out here this morning. Didn't catch a wink. I'm gonna hit it for a while."

"I'll call you at one," said Schell. "We have to go to the Salvation Army and see if we can find a nice dress for you."

"You two are just jealous," he said, leaving the kitchen.

"I have a new makeup for you to try," said Schell. "It glows in the dark."

From down the hall, we heard, "I *hate* being dead people."

MANY DOORS ARE OPENED

P athetic" might just have been an apt description of Parks's existence, for the night of the séance, when we arrived, he informed us that he could find no one among his acquaintances or family who would participate in it with him. It was to be only Schell and Parks and myself. This then, as it looked from the outset, promised to be the equivalent of shooting fish in a barrel. All the better, as I was somewhat distracted, hoping for another glimpse of Isabel, whom I hadn't been able to get off my mind since we'd been there a week earlier.

We met the tycoon in the same room his butler had led us to on our initial visit. After the normal pleasantries, Schell described the rules of engagement for calling forth the dead: breathe deeply and regularly so as not to hyperventilate; do not shout (it might scare the spirits away); keep your distance from any visual or physical manifestation that might coalesce (to make contact with it could possibly be fatal); be solicitous of the dead (humor them); do not leave your seat unless otherwise instructed. Parks nodded eagerly, obviously anxious to get through the preliminaries and on with it. His voice had gone up an octave or two, and he swung his legs back and forth while sitting in his throne.

We moved to the room that Schell and I had reconnoitered on

our last visit, a small drawing room on the eastern side of the mansion. It was at ground level and had a pair of wide glass doors that gave a view of a landscaped terrace with faux Greek statuary and a series of waist-high hedges. The room itself was comfortable, not quite as large as we liked but with a nice round wooden table and rafters over which we could toss a line in order to levitate an object.

Before we began, as Schell lit the candle at the center of the table, Parks made a request. "I don't know if this is possible or warranted," he said, "but, please, Mr. Schell, if my wife tries to . . . come through, please do everything in your power to prevent it."

"I understand," said Schell. "Her death is too close to you right now."

"Something like that," said Parks.

Schell nodded to me, an indication that I should turn off the lights. This I did while he assumed the mediumistic state. When he went under, so to speak, it was a sight to behold. His entire body trembled, eventually giving way to what appeared to be a kind of living rigor mortis. The eyes turned upward so that the pupils were hidden beneath lowered lids, and his mouth opened wide in a grimace. Parks was entranced by the performance, giving me the opportunity to toss a length of near-invisible thread, a small washer attached to the end to give it weight, up over a rafter. Just as it cleared the beam and began its descent, I took my seat and let loose a string of incomprehensible gibberish. Parks's attention now swung to me, and as it did, Schell caught the end of the line and pulled it down next to him, where it couldn't be detected in the dim candlelight. When Parks turned back to look at Schell, he was again wrapped in his rictus of spirituality.

Before long, there came from out of the darkness a low murmuring, the candle flickered as if caught in a breeze, and sounds of weeping filled the air. Schell, far more expert at projecting his voice than I, covered the murmuring, and I was responsible for the weeping. Parks looked everywhere, up and down, wide-eyed. When I rapped my toe against the bottom of the table, he nearly jumped out of his seat.

Schell lifted his arms in the air and said in a low, croaking voice, filled with urgency, "The gates to the other side open," and a dozen pine whites suddenly appeared between his hands. They swarmed in a chaos of pale, fluttering wings above the table and then made for Parks, who'd already been marked with sugar water. The millionaire panicked and began swatting the air in front of him. Schell then had a chance to slip from beneath his jacket and attach to the end of the line a toy bear we'd picked up at the Salvation Army.

"Georgie, Georgie," came a voice from above. "It's me, your mother."

"Mother?" said Parks. "I can hear you." He raked his fingers through his hair, and within seconds his eyes glistened with tears. "Mother," he called, looking around the room feverishly.

As Parks looked behind him, Schell blew a few grains of flash powder into the candle flame and there was a tiny, bright explosion in the middle of the table. Parks covered his eyes and when he looked again, the bear hovered in the air five feet above our heads.

"I've brought your bear, darling," said the ghostly female voice.

Parks began to stand, as if to grab for the toy, but I cautioned him, "Remain seated, sir. To touch this apparition could mean your life."

He sat back down, but his hands remained thrust upward, the perfect image of a child begging to be carried.

"George, I've been watching you."

"Yes, Mother," he said.

"You've not been on your best behavior."

"I have, Mother. I have."

"No you haven't. If you lie to me I'll go away."

"I'm sorry," cried Parks, "please don't leave."

"Caroline is here with me, George."

Parks groaned.

"She said you were unkind to her."

"I wasn't," he said.

"Good-bye," said the voice.

"All right, yes, I didn't like her. She was too . . . forceful. I'm sorry."

"That's better, dear. To make up for it, I want you to be kinder to others. Treat the young woman Isabel nicely. She works so hard."

"I'll raise her salary," said Parks.

"That's an excellent start. Be kinder to everyone, George. That way Death will treat *you* kindly when it's time for you to make the voyage."

"Yes," he said, his voice and body trembling.

"I'm on the terrace, dear. Come to the glass and I will let you see me, but you mustn't open the doors."

Parks looked over at me. I nodded. He got out of his chair, and Schell and I also stood. We moved toward the glass doors, I in front of Parks, and Schell bringing up the rear.

"Behold, sir, your mother's ectoplasmic form," I said.

He stepped up next to me and pressed his face against the glass. Outside the wind was blowing through the giant oaks that bordered the property. There was a half moon that night, its pale light shining through a very light mist. Standing behind one of the hedges, so that she was visible from the waist up, was the glowing form of Ma Parks, a good deal larger in death than life. She wore a wide-brimmed hat as she did in three of the photos in Parks's parlor, and stared directly at us. Through the glass, we could hear her repeating the name "Georgie."

Parks lost control and started fumbling with the knobs on the doors. I put my hand upon his shoulder and cautioned him not to open them. He paid no attention to me, and I tried to restrain him long enough so that Schell could get a hand on him. But Schell just stood there, staring at the glass, a strange look on his face, completely immobile. Then Parks rammed me with his elbow and sent me tripping backward onto my rear end.

From where I lay on the floor, I expected to see Schell jump to action, but he didn't. Parks got the doors open and slipped out onto the terrace. He ran toward the apparition, screaming, "Mother!"

I scrambled to my feet just in time to see him reach the hedge behind which the ghost stood. Schell finally came to and lunged forward out the door after him. As Parks reached out for the object of his affection, his mother's spirit feinted to the side and threw a right cross. The punch caught him on the jaw and dropped him, unconscious, onto the grass.

I reached the scene in time to see the ghost of Ma Parks, now grown to something well over six feet tall, lumbering across the perfectly manicured lawn toward the circular driveway at the front of the house.

"Help me lift him," said Schell.

He took the arms and I the legs. There were a hundred questions I had concerning what had just happened, but I knew to keep my mouth shut, not sure as to how deeply Parks was under. We managed to get him inside and lay him on a divan in the drawing room. As Schell tried to gently revive him, I latched the glass doors and wound up the line we had used for the levitation. I left the bear at his spot on the table, a sort of party favor to make up for the séance having ended with him getting slugged. When I was finished with these small tasks, Schell instructed me to turn the lights on and blow out the candle.

"He's coming around," Schell whispered, crouching next to the divan.

I stood at a short distance and watched as Parks surfaced, calling for his mother.

"Lie still," Schell said to him. "You're all right. You've had a physical encounter with the void. Breathe deeply."

Parks's eyes were wild, and he was agitated to the extreme. He flung his legs over the side of the divan and sat up, rubbing his jaw.

"I warned you not to make contact with the materialized forms of the dead," said Schell, "and now you see why."

"The veil must remain intact," I said.

Parks calmed down and winced as he touched his chin. "I'm okay," he said. "I apologize for getting carried away." He couldn't look directly at either of us.

"Window," he said, addressing me. "There's whiskey and a tumbler in that small bar in the corner. Please pour me a drink."

"Ondoo, your excellency," I said as I moved to the task.

Schell stood and backed away from our patron.

"My mother hasn't changed in death," said Parks. "She still packs a wallop."

"One of the most remarkable visitations I've ever witnessed," said Schell.

I brought Parks his drink, and he dashed it off in three gulps. He then handed me the glass and stood unsteadily. It took a few seconds for him to get his bearings, but then he saw the toy bear lying on the table. He rushed to it, almost losing his balance in the process. "Look here," he said, "she's left it behind for me." He took it up and held it cradled in his arms like an infant. "You know, Schell, I had absolutely no recollection of this bear until I saw it hovering in the air tonight. Then it all came back to me."

"Yes, Mr. Parks," said Schell, "this is often the way. Many doors are opened when the dead pay a visit."

DUBIOUS RIGMAROLE

A mile down the road from the entrance to the drive that led into the Parks estate, Antony pulled off the blanket that had concealed him and sat upright in the back seat of the Cord.

"Sorry I had to clip Georgie," he said, removing the powdered wig from his glowing head.

"It was probably for the best," said Schell, the first utterance he'd made since we'd gotten in the car. I could tell before we left the mansion that something was wrong with him. His not having reacted when Parks opened the terrace doors was unthinkable. I was reminded of my statement to him a few days earlier that he never made mistakes and now felt badly, as if I'd jinxed him—a concept Schell himself would scoff at.

"Parks wants us back as soon as possible," I told Antony to assuage his guilt.

"There's something not Jake about that guy."

"That's an understatement," I said.

Schell spoke no more for the entire ride home, and Antony and I both sensed it was better to leave the silence alone. When we arrived at the house, the boss said nothing but left us in the living room and went down the hall to the Bugatorium.

"Is he pissed off at me?" asked Antony.

"No," I said. "I think he's upset with himself."

"What happened in there?" he asked. "All I saw was Parks come through those doors like gangbusters."

"Once he saw you done up like the old lady, he knocked me over and was gone."

"Where was Schell?" he asked.

"Standing right there behind him, but it was like he couldn't move."

"That's not right." He shook his head. "I'm gonna get a bath and get this crap off me," he said, referring to the phosphorescent makeup we'd painted on his face, neck, and arms.

Normally, I'd have wisecracked about his dress, but everything was off-kilter. Antony retired to his room, and I went in search of Schell.

I found him in the Bugatorium, sitting at the table amid his plants and beloved butterflies, a bridge deck in his hand and a large *Taygetis echo* hovering above his head like some dark thought. He was repeatedly doing one-handed cuts with the deck. I sat across from him, knowing full well that he would not speak for a long time. I'd seen him like this before. He fanned the cards, closed the fan, and then subtly crimped one. That card, the jack of spades, kept reappearing in all the tricks he ran through. The graceful flourishing of his hands, and the popping, flipping, and sailing of the cards was hypnotic.

Just when I thought he might be winding down, another deck appeared as if out of thin air in his free hand, and he now worked two decks with the facility that any normal sharp might only one. He was completely lost to his thoughts, and I knew I might as well go to bed. Sleep didn't come easily that night, for it was a certainty that something was very wrong.

I was just dozing off when I heard a knock on my door. The door opened, letting in a sliver of light. From the size of the silhouette, I knew it was Antony. He stepped inside and closed the door behind him, bringing the darkness back.

"I really botched it this time," he said.

"What?" I asked.

"When I was running for the car, the old lady's hat musta flown off my head. I can't find it anywhere. Can you imagine?"

"I wouldn't worry about it," I said. "Parks doesn't seem to be that with it. Even if he finds it, he'll think it's like the bear; a gift from his mother."

"I hope so," said Antony. "Hey, how's the boss?"

"He's in the bug room doing his card thing. He'll probably be at it all night."

The next morning, Antony and I had already eaten breakfast and washed the dishes by the time Schell appeared. He poured himself a cup of coffee and joined us at the table.

"Get much sleep?" asked Antony.

Schell shook his head.

"I guess we really mucked it up yesterday, huh?" asked the strongman.

"On the contrary," said Schell, "I think we improvised like true pros. Your downing Parks was actually a stroke of genius. Diego and I set it right with him, and all's well that ends well. Don't worry, you'll not get out of reprising your role as his mother."

"Christ," said Antony.

"Why were you so silent last night?" I asked.

Schell took a sip of his coffee and then reached across the table to steal one of Antony's cigarettes. It was a rare happenstance when the boss smoked and usually signaled something was awry. He lifted the lighter, used it, and returned it to the table. After taking a long drag, he seemed to compose himself before answering. "You two have to be honest with me," he said.

Antony and I both nodded.

"Were you playing a game with me last night?"

"What do you mean?" asked Antony.

"Don't get defensive," said Schell. "I simply need to discount that possibility. Yes or no: were you two up to some scam last night?"

"No," I said, and Antony said, "Never on a job, Boss."

"As I thought," said Schell.

"Why do you ask?" I said.

"Because I saw something last night I can't explain," said Schell. "I've gone over it and over it in my mind, but there's just no explanation, unless of course Parks was playing us, which I hardly would believe possible."

There was a silence during which Schell took another drag of the cigarette.

"Well," said Antony, "are you gonna tell us or do we have to guess?"

"After Diego and I ran the levitation with the bear, and Mrs. Parks stopped by to gently tongue-lash her son a bit," said Schell, "we got up and moved toward the glass doors to watch your command performance amid the hedges. Diego was to the front and left of Parks as we approached, and I was behind and to the right. As we came up to the doors, I distinctly saw, on the right-hand panel of glass, the image of a child. It was as if she was *inside* the glass. About six or seven, somewhere around that age, curly, chestnut hair, large eyes, wearing a simple dress with a flower pattern." He stubbed out the cigarette and rubbed his forehead with his opposite hand.

"What was she doing?" asked Antony.

"Just standing there, looking at me," said Schell, a vacant look in his eyes.

"Eerie," I said.

"She remained there until Parks finally flung open the doors and took off after Antony. How do I explain that?" he asked.

"Now I know why you didn't react," I said.

"It's really no excuse," said Schell, shaking his head. "I should have stayed with the job at hand, no matter what."

"So what do you think it was?" asked Antony.

Schell shrugged.

"Maybe with all of our séance business we actually called over a ghost," I said.

"It's almost too easy to believe that," said Schell, "but I don't buy it. There are no such things as ghosts. Houdini may have been someone who could have made life very difficult for us if he'd ever caught wind of our operation. But I have to say I had the utmost respect for him, because he was right: the spiritualist phenomenon is all sleight of hand, relying one hundred percent upon gullibility. I dare say it doesn't end there, but you can throw in religion, romantic love, and luck as well. No, this was something else."

I was timid about bringing it up, but I offered, "Maybe your mind played a trick on you."

Schell turned, and I thought at first he was going to rebuke my suggestion, but instead he said, "I've considered that. It seems the only thing possible."

"Look," said Antony, "we've done a dozen jobs in the last two months. That's an awful lot."

"True," said Schell.

"Hows about a vacation?" said Antony.

"Not a bad idea," said Schell, "but it seems rather criminal to take a vacation in the midst of a depression."

I threw caution to the wind and said, "By depression, you mean the economic crisis or your own?"

Antony winced and said, "Oo-faa."

"Crisis, me?" said Schell, wearing an expression of incredulity.

"Boss," said Antony, "I wouldn't have brought it up, but now that the kid's mentioned it . . . He's right, you've been dogging around here like some kind of ghost yourself lately."

Schell reached over to pat me on the shoulder. "I confess," he said, turning his gaze toward the table. "I know what you're saying. Things have been very . . . how shall I put it? . . . sodden for me lately. I can explain it less than my seeing the image of that girl."

"How about we go to the city, like in the old days, get a couple of rooms at the Waldorf, catch a show, meet some ladies, grab a rasher of cocktails? The kid can stay here and keep an eye on the butterflies."

"Hey," I said, "how come I have to stay home?"

"There could be some dubious rigmarole," said Antony.

"Let me think about it," said Schell.

INNOCENT

In the days that followed, I made it my mission to get to the
bottom of Schell's predicament. This, of course, was easier
said than done. Wandering around like a somnambulist, he
skipped meals, slept late, and forsook his usual work of perfecting
new seance techniques. The classical dirges never stopped flowing
from his Victrola. More than once I found empty wine bottles in
the kitchen garbage. Whatever time he did spend employed in
some conscious task was spent in the Bugatorium, away from
Antony and me.

I knew I couldn't get him to discuss his feelings (I'd have had
more success with Wilma the snake were she still alive), and whenever through the years I'd tried to get him to talk about his past, he'd
always slyly change the subject. Instead, I decided to pump Antony
for information, thinking that the key to the trouble lay somewhere
back in the caterpillar stage of Schell's life. It made sense to me that
the grim aspect that had recently emerged and spread its dark wings
had its origin sometime in those early years before I knew him.
Otherwise, I was sure I'd have understood. I didn't agree with
Antony's assessment that it had to do with the "*unhonestness*" of our
present occupation. I'd read Freud just the previous year and rather
believed the issue was something more fundamental.

On the third day following our engagement with Parks, I asked Antony to take a walk with me. Schell was holed up with his butterflies. We left the house through the back door and struck out on the path that led through thick woods to a cliff overlooking the sound. I carried a notebook and pencil with me. He was amused by my earnest nature, but I didn't care.

"Who are you, Walter Winchell?" he asked.

I cut him a look, and he knew from then on I meant business.

We came to the end of the trail—an awe-inspiring vista of the sound framed by two huge oak trees, their gnarled roots growing out of the cliff-side into thin air. He sat down on a fallen log and lit a cigarette. I took up a position on a flat rock some few feet across from him. It was a clear, windy day. Branches swayed and leaves fell around us.

It had struck me at the wake, when Schell had told me a snatch of how Morty had taken him in from time to time when he was a kid, that I had never heard the story of his early years.

"I'll tell you what I know," said Antony, "but I'm not saying it's the truth. Schell's a strange cat. The man has secrets."

I nodded.

"Okay," he said, "here goes. What I know is he was born in Brooklyn, I think. His mother died when he was a babe—two, three maybe. Only kid. His old man was a piece a work, a gambler. I'm not just talking like a poker game here and there, I mean a real gambler, a shark and a sharp. A legend with the cards. You see the stuff that Schell does with a deck? Child's play compared to what his old man could do. I never saw it, but it was said he knew how to throw a single card with such force and accuracy, it could paralyze a man.

"I'd heard his name before I even met Schell. Magus Jack was what they called him. He did some sleight-of-hand stuff too, worked a smooth con from time to time, would bet on just ab anything, knew everyone from Legs Diamond to Jimr when they were all on the way up.

"So he had this kid. He took good care of the kid. Everything was slicker than snot on a doorknob until he got involved in one particular con. I don't know, I think him and a couple of other guys were trying to blackmail this businessman. They set him up with a young down-and-out actress that they hired. The usual—caught him up in a compromising situation and then threatened to have the tart spill to the guy's wife. It was low stuff, not the kind of thing that Magus Jack usually got involved with. Stupid. I don't remember the details, but it ended with this milquetoast businessman going on a rampage and shooting the young actress, the wife, and himself to finish it off. A fucking bloodbath. Now, almost nobody knew Magus Jack was behind it, but he did. He was offstage, so to speak.

"Anyway, after that disastrous con, Magus Jack started to slip into the bottle, if you know what I mean. The kid was older now, maybe around eight, and the old man would take off and leave him in the apartment for a couple a days at a time. Whenever Jack would return, he'd make amends by spending time with the kid, but instead of going to a ball game or something normal, what he did was teach the kid how to work the cards. Instead of taking the kid to church on Sunday, he'd take him out to the park and show him how to con people.

"By the time he was twelve, Tommy was basically on his own, running the streets, involved in all kinds a cons and games and shenanigans. That's around the time that he met Morty. I think he tried to scam him on the street one day with a three-card monte or something, and Morty just took him apart. But Mort saw potential in the kid and took him under his wing somewhat. The old man came home less and less and the kid was left more and more on his own until he was paying for the apartment himself and living there like it was his own place when he was fifteen.

"I know he's not really your old man, but he might as well be. He's got a brain like you do, you know, for book study, and it was Morty turned him on to books. Mort was a kind of scholar, I guess you could say. Schell taught himself everything he knows. I think he only got up to about the first year in high school and then bagged it. But when he was seventeen, around there, he got himself hooked into some deep trouble. I don't know what it was, but the cops had the nippers on him, and he was drug before a judge. The judge gave him a choice: join the service or go to jail. So, the army not being good enough for him, he joined the marines and went to war.

"He wound up in France and saw the real shit. I know for a fact he was at this famous battle at a place called the Balleau Wood. I met a guy who knew him then, was there with him. The Germans were held up in this wood, and the good guys didn't know how much firepower they had. They could've just shelled the whole thing to splinters but they didn't. Tommy's regiment, division, whatever it was, was made to charge the wood across a wheat field. The Huns just tore them to ribbons with machine guns. I heard it was the worst beating we took in the war.

"Schell survived and came back home to find that his old man was killed, rubbed out by some shady characters he got involved in a card game with. Magus Jack was a has-been by then, squeezed through the end of a whiskey bottle. He got sloppy and took these mooks' dough too fast. They caught him crimping cards, put a bullet in his head, and threw him in the East River. I'll say no more about this but that Schell later caught up with them and settled the score.

"Afterward, he figured for a while he needed a bodyguard. Hal, you know, the dog man, sent him to me. I was looking to get out of the strongman trade. You can only have so many cars run over your head before it gets *tiresome*. I couldn't bring myself to bend another iron bar with my teeth, but I didn't mind busting heads if I had to. That's easy, almost a pleasure sometimes. So me and Schell hooked up, became partners sort of and worked together ever since. How's that?"

I looked down at my notebook and realized I hadn't written a word. Antony's recounting of Schell's life had been as complete as I could ask for, but nothing in it, although it was turbulent, led me to see why he'd envision a little girl on the pane of a glass door.

"Thanks," I said.

"What's your diagnosis?" he said.

I shook my head, "I'm more confused than before," I told him.

He smiled and lit another cigarette.

"What about the butterflies?" I asked.

"Who the fuck knows?" he said. "The guy likes butterflies."

"There's got to be a reason," I said.

"Yeah," said Antony, getting up. "'Cause he does. Come on, kid, I gotta get back and start dinner. I'm making stew tonight. No comments, please."

"I'm glad to find out about him. I never knew that stuff, but I thought it would tell me something about why he's down now."

"Look, Diego," he said, putting a hand on my shoulder as we walked along. "This ain't fucking geometry. It makes sense that when he goes loopy he sees a kid. He had no childhood. That's why he took you in. Why's a guy without a wife, a con man no less, take in a Mexican kid off the street? He's making up for what his old man didn't do. Makes sense, right?"

"It does, actually," I said.

"When you see things, when your eyes play tricks on you, what you see is what you want. Maybe Parks is a screwball, but in a way Schell wants his mother too. Or at least he wants his childhood, get it? He grew up hard and doesn't believe in anything but the con, or so he says. He's taken people six ways to Sunday for years. So he sees a little girl. What's a little girl?"

"What?" I asked.

"Innocent," he said.

"Antony," I said, "you should move to Vienna and hang a shingle."

"Hang my ass," he said.

EXCEEDINGLY STRANGE

There's a certain species of parasitic wasp that attaches itself to the hind wings of female butterflies. When those females lay eggs, the minuscule moochers disengage and drop onto the nascent clutch to feed. The North Shore of Long Island, with its mansions and fabulously wealthy citizens, the Vanderbilts, the Coes, the Guggenheims, was like some beautiful butterfly, floating just above the hard scrabble life of most Americans after the crash in '29. We, of course, were the parasitic wasps, thriving upon the golden grief of our betters.

As Schell had explained, "To our benefit, death isn't affected by an economic failure, and it never takes a holiday. In addition, a bereaved rich man is easier to con than a poor one in the same condition. A poor man, straightaway, understands death to be inevitable, but it takes a rich man some time to see that the end can't be circumvented with the application of enough collateral."

I considered this equation as I watched, from the train window, the passing signs that held the names of those towns comprising that stronghold where the rich hid out against a spreading plague of poverty. There had even been news recently of foreclosures among some of the elite families, but there was still plenty of affluence to sustain three enterprising parasites the likes of Schell, Antony, and myself.

It might have been true that Death never took a holiday, but we were. To his credit, Antony had been persistent with his suggestions of a week off in the city. Schell vacillated, unable to make a commitment. He was obviously weary from whatever emotional or intellectual issue he'd been obsessing over for the past few months. The death of Morty had hit him hard. Still, he'd continued to take calls from new marks for séances and used the list of prospective patrons as his main defense against getting away.

"What's the rush?" Antony had asked. "It's not like the dead are going anywhere in the next week."

Schell almost lost his temper one morning in the face of the constant barrage and then threw his hands up and agreed to two days in New York. Antony knew to take what he could get, and even said okay when Schell insisted that I be allowed to come along. The butterflies would survive on their own for forty-eight hours. Once it had been decided we were going, we had to move quickly before he changed his mind. I'd dressed in my Indian traveling garb—high-collared shirt, mystical medallion of the many-armed Shiva, baggy pantaloons, and sandals. I gave the turban a rest.

Schell sat next to me on the aisle, dozing, and Antony took up his own seat directly facing us, reading an old newspaper someone had left behind on an earlier journey.

With a sudden start, Schell roused and sat forward, as if waking from a nightmare. He shook his head and then slowly eased back into the seat, rubbing his eyes. "What else is in there?" he asked Antony. "I haven't bothered with a newspaper in days."

Antony kept scanning whatever it was that had his attention and at the same time said, "Looks like we're headed for a Yankees/Cubs series. Otherwise, the usual bullshit." Then he looked up and said, "Let's go see the Marx Brothers' new one while we're in town."

"What's the name of it?" I asked.

"*Horse Feathers*," said Antony.

"Sounds enlightening," said Schell.

"I know, Boss, you're holding out for Marlene Dietrich."

Schell gave a weak smile.

"I want to go see *Doctor Jekyll and Mr. Hyde*," I said.

"Fredric March downs the giggle juice and turns into me," said Antony. "Forget that."

Schell turned to me. "Did you cancel your tutoring appointments?" he asked.

I nodded. "All but Mrs. Hendrickson, she doesn't have a phone."

"That should be good for a half hour of admonition next week," he said.

"Mrs. Hyde," said Antony and grimaced. He turned the paper over, folded it, and went back to his reading.

I was about to fill Schell in on the work she'd been having me do, Chaucer in Middle English, when he lunged forward and snatched the paper out of Antony's hands and brought it up close to his face.

"What gives, Boss?" said Antony.

Schell shook his head and held one hand up to silence us. It was obvious he was heatedly reading some article. Antony looked at me with a quizzical expression. All I could do was shrug.

Eventually Schell turned the paper around and held it out to show us. He pointed at a photograph on the side of the page he'd been reading. He was as pale as when he'd go under in his medium trance, and his hand trembled slightly.

"There she is," he said.

It was a bright day, and the light coming in the train window obscured my view with its glare. Both Antony and I leaned forward, almost touching heads.

"The girl," said Schell, tapping his finger against the paper. "The girl in the glass."

I only caught a brief glimpse of the child he'd described seeing at Parks's place—the dark, curly hair, the floral design of the dress—before he turned the paper around again and began reading aloud to us in an urgent whisper.

"The serene North Shore borough of Wellman's Cove has been devastated by the recent disappearance of seven-year-old Charlotte Barnes, daughter of that town's most distinguished couple, Mr. and Mrs. Harold Barnes.

"On Wednesday, September twenty-first, the child was last seen some time after one P.M. in the afternoon, playing in the garden of the family estate. She did not respond when called in for dinner at four P.M. It was soon determined that she was missing. Local police were called and the grounds and house were thoroughly searched to no avail. On the following day, a party of concerned citizens continued to comb the nearby woods and shoreline for signs of young Charlotte.

"At the time of her disappearance, she was wearing a yellow dress, black shoes, white socks and had gold clips in her hair. She is approximately four foot tall with brown hair in pigtails, green eyes, and a missing front tooth. Should you see a child fitting this description, please contact your local authorities.

"Harold Barnes, well-known shipping magnate, is offering a sizable reward for information concerning his daughter's whereabouts. He could not be reached for further comment. The community's hope is that the child has wandered off and will soon be found and reunited with her family."

Schell finished reading, sat back, and stared straight on.

"How?" I asked.

Antony reached over and slipped the paper out of Schell's hand. He turned it and looked at the photograph.

"Exceedingly strange," said Schell.

"Does this mean the kid's dead?" asked Antony.

"How old is that paper?" asked Schell, suddenly becoming animated.

Antony unfolded it and flipped to the front page. "Four days old," he said.

"We were at Parks' place five days ago," I said.

"Yes," said Schell, "the twenty-second."

"A ghost?" asked Antony.

"I'm not certain of anything," said Schell. "But I mean to find out. What's the next stop?"

"Jamaica," I said.

"I hate to disappoint you fellows, but I'm getting off there and turning back. You two can go on to New York without me."

"Come on, Boss," said Antony. "You need a rest."

"No, no, no," said Schell. "I'm heading back. I have to make an appointment to see Mr. Barnes."

"You're not going to take this poor bastard now, with his daughter missing," said Antony.

"On the contrary," said Schell. "I'm going to try to find her."

"I'm in," I said.

"Free of charge," said Schell.

"Three words I never thought I'd hear you say," said Antony.

"I've got to get to the bottom of this," said Schell.

"Okay," said Antony, "what the hell."

We got off at Jamaica and toted our luggage over to the eastbound track. While we waited for the next train, Schell paced impatiently up and down the platform. Antony and I sat on a bench. When Schell was some distance from us, the big man leaned toward me and said, "So much for our head shrinking, kid."

I didn't answer as my mind was caught up in the notion that Schell's occult experience offered possible proof of an afterlife. The fact that there might actually be another side from which the dead might travel, and that we had played so fast and loose with it, didn't bode well for our eternal souls. Antony's thoughts must have been running along the same path, because when I asked him for a cigarette, he actually gave me one and lit it.

THE CHEATERS

Harold Barnes wasn't an easy man to get to see, even if you wanted to offer your services "free of charge." Schell had called the estate but got no further than a secretary, who had curtly informed him that Mr. Barnes was not available for comment or interview. He admonished himself afterward for not thinking through the situation. "The press is most likely hounding the family at every turn. I let my eagerness get the better of me," he admitted. "From now on, I have to treat our efforts as a con, even though delusion's not the goal here."

Antony and I were dispatched on a research mission. We drove into Jamaica to the offices of the *Republican Long Island Farmer*, where Peewee Dunnit's sister, Kate, worked as a clerk in the file room. Antony slipped her twenty dollars, and she slipped him the newspaper's dossier on Barnes. Usually when we tapped her for a file, she'd let us have it for a day or two, but with the millionaire's daughter missing, it was in hot demand by their own reporters. We could have one hour with it before it had to be returned.

We staked out a table in a diner around the corner from the paper, ordered coffee, and set about consuming and recording as much pertinent information as possible. It was a thick file, as Barnes was well-known; even if we had all day with their file, it would be difficult to decide which pieces of information were relevant to our investigation. What we might consider inconsequential, Schell could possibly snatch up and spin into gold. We had to work fast, with a scattershot method, and merely hope for the best.

For eye work this important, Antony wore what he referred to as his "cheaters," a pair of black, horn-rimmed glasses that he'd swiped, years earlier, from someone obviously on the verge of blindness. The scratched lenses did nothing more than magnify things ten times—not the least his own eyes. Whenever we'd chance to look up from our work at the same time, I'd get a start from the sight of those two huge peepers, big as pansies, staring at me. With me in my turban and him looking like a three-hundred-pound, six-foot-four owl, no one bothered us while we worked.

We rifled madly through the stack of clipped articles, typed sheets, photographs, jotting down snippets of information. The minute hand on the big clock above the grill moved like a thoroughbred on the back turn as I noted information about Barnes's shipping business, his political affiliations, the movie stars who'd visited his home, the charitable contributions he'd made. From what I'd uncovered, he seemed like a typical member of the American aristocracy, yet somewhat more staid than his Gold Coast compatriots.

Only five minutes before we had to return the dossier to Kate, Antony looked up, fixed me with that gigantic stare, and said, "We got him."

"How?" I asked.

"I'll tell you in the car," he said.

We shuffled the loose pages together in as close to the order as we'd found them, and I lifted the stack and banged it twice to even it out. Antony took fifty cents from his pocket and threw it on the table. Whipping off his cheaters and stowing them in his inside jacket pocket, he said, "Let's blow."

I had to wait until he'd emerged from the newspaper building to get the dope on his catch. He returned to the car with a big smile on his face. As he got in behind the wheel he said, "I told Kate we might want another twenty-dollar peek at that file."

He started up the Cord, and we pulled away.

"What did you find?" I asked.

"Kid, I'm good," he said. "Nothing escapes the gaze of the cheaters."

"Okay, you're good," I said.

"Guess who stayed with Barnes when he visited the U.S.?" he asked.

"I give up."

"None other than A. Conan Doyle."

"The author?"

"Yeah."

"So what?"

"The guy's a first-class spook booster, a true believer. Faeries, ghosts, spirits, séances, psychics, you name it, he'll believe it. You could serve him the holes in doughnuts. I found an article about Conan Doyle's stay with Barnes, which noted that they share an interest in spiritualism. Barnes is a mark."

"That's good to know, but how's it get us in to see him?" I asked.

"This is the kicker. Another article from a few years ago mentions Barnes and his fellow Harvard alumnus and close friend . . . guess who?"

"Parks," I said.

"Hey . . ." he said and turned so quickly to look at me, the car swerved momentarily into the oncoming lane.

"Watch the road," I told him.

"How'd you know?" he asked, steering back into our lane.

"I saw a diploma from Harvard on Parks's wall when we were there the first time. I just guessed."

"You're becoming more like the boss every day," he said. He shook his head and then added, "So we get Schell to talk to Parks, who gets on the blower to Barnes and puts in a good word for us. Bingo."

"That might actually work," I said. "Nice fishing."

"Nothing escapes," said Antony. "Nothing."

Even though Schell wished we'd had more time to gather basic information, he was pleased with our work and agreed that Antony's plan was sound. I listened in as he put the call through to Parks. Witnessing Schell get his way with words was like watching a knife thrower split a hair at twenty yards. He peppered his spiel with mentions of Parks's mother and how much she'd no doubt appreciate seeing us help poor Barnes. By the time Schell was done, Parks would have called the emperor of China on our behalf.

Then we waited. A day passed, and we checked the papers to see if there had been any break in the case. The search parties continued, the police were still on the job, but the girl had not surfaced, dead or alive. Schell pored over the meager information we'd brought him, and to see what he could turn up, he put in some calls to friends of his who traveled in high society. He was curious to find out if our subject had any shady dealings and if his marriage was sound. From all accounts, Barnes, though filthy rich, seemed to be a straight shooter

On the afternoon of the second day, Schell and Antony were out getting the local papers and I'd just sent Mrs. Hendrickson on her way after a brutal session focusing on my Middle English pronunciations, when the phone rang. I ran through the kitchen to the office and grabbed it on the fifth ring.

"Hello," I said, out of breath.

There was silence, and I thought for a moment that I'd been too late. Then a soft voice said, "Hola." A pause followed. "Do you know who this is?"

There was a vague fluttering in my chest. "Yes," I said.

"You left something behind when you were here last," she said.

"A sombrero?" I asked.

"Sí."

"Have you shown it to anyone else?" I asked.

"Solamente los fantasmas," she said.

I forced a laugh.

"Si lo quieres, ven esta noche. Eleven o'clock on the beach behind the mansion."

"What'll happen if I don't show?" I asked, but she'd already hung up.

THAT'S WHAT HAPPENS AT NIGHT

At ten o'clock that night, Antony went down the hall to the Bugatorium, knocked on the door, and called, "Boss, me and the kid are going out for a drive. I gotta get some smokes. Do you want to go?"

We were hoping he'd stay put, because all Schell would have needed was one look at us to tell we were up to something. Luckily, he called out, as I had surmised he would, "No, I'd better not in case Barnes tries to contact us."

I wasn't happy about hiding our venture from Schell, but Antony was dead set on him not finding out about the hat. "Schell doesn't look kindly on screwups," was how he'd put it to me.

"He screwed up himself that night," I said.

"You don't get it, kid," he said. "I'll take you over there. You get the hat from the girl and we'll be back here before anybody knows what's up."

I went along with it, hating to see the big man in a quandary.

Antony knew of a spot along the North Shore, close to the Parks place, where there was a municipal stairway that led down from the cliffs to the beach. All of the estates had their own private access, usually protected by locked gates. The cliffs were an excellent security feature, and since most of the real estate along the sound was privately owned, it was tough finding a way onto the beach unless you wanted to hoof it in from one of the more eastern towns.

At about ten-thirty, he pulled over at the side of a road bordered by woods. Through the dark I could just make out the head of a trail leading in among the trees toward the sound.

"Once you hit the beach, head west. Parks's place is about three-quarters of a mile down the beach," he said. "And for Christ sake, be careful on those steps."

"You're going to wait for me, right?" I asked.

"I'm gonna drive up to Wintchell's speak, have a beer, get a couple of packs, and be back in forty minutes. If I'm sitting here all that time and a cop comes along, they're gonna want to know what I'm doing. So move your ass as fast as you can. Don't make me wait."

"It's dark out there," I said.

"Yeah, that's what happens at night. Don't worry, the moon's out tonight. Once you get past the trees, it won't be so bad."

I sighed, shook my head, and got out of the car.

"Good luck," he said as I swung the door shut. Then the Cord pulled away and was gone.

Although the late September days had been warm, this night was windy and cool, a strong breeze blowing in from the east. Laced in with the distinctive aroma of the sound was that of true autumn. I'd chosen to leave all of my Ondoo regalia at home and dress in normal street clothes, the easier to move in, and so as not to draw the derision of Isabel. It was her image in my mind that kept me forging on through the pitch-black woods. Acorns dropped and small animals scurried through the brambles. If there were such things as ghosts, this lonely tract of trees would have been a perfect place to meet one. I crept along, spooked by every little snap and pop.

Antony was right, as I approached the edge of the cliff, I could see moonlight shining amid the branches of the pines and oaks. When I finally broke free of the woods and stood at the head of the stairway, leading down to the beach, I had a view of a milky white, full moon off to the east, a beacon reflected in the choppy waters of the sound. I took the rickety wooden stairs, holding tight to the handrail and braving the threat of splinters. The descent was steep, occasionally broken by a series of landings after each of which the steps changed direction in a zigzag course.

Once I finally reached the beach, I breathed a sigh of relief but realized, as I looked back up the rickety stairs, what a struggle the return ascent would be. The wind was really whipping down there next to the water. I looked around to find a landmark to fix the spot in my mind. If clouds should roll in it would be easy to miss the stairs. I saw, fifty paces or so off to the east, the rusting remains of an old buoy, tipped at an angle and half-buried in sand. I made a mental note that if I passed it, I would know that I'd gone too far. I turned west and started to walk.

The wide beach was littered with stones and broken shells, causing each footfall to sound as if I were traipsing along a gravel path. I turned my thoughts to Isabel and wondered why she'd asked me to meet her. My speculations ranged from blackmail to the possibility that Schell was right and she liked me. I rather hoped for the latter, as I had brought no money, and even though I'd only met her once, I found I couldn't forget her.

I'd paced off what I'd thought to be a little less than a mile and then turned and surveyed the area. The beach was wider now, and there were a number of larger rocks and boulders at the base of the cliffs. The moon still shone, although it appeared smaller and was rising quickly. Clouds were now intermittently skirting by, obscuring it for a minute or two at a time. Its light showed me the way to the base of a set of steps. I had no idea whether they led up to the Parks estate or if I'd overshot or underestimated my destination. On closer inspection, I found that the gate that barred entrance to them was swinging free, an open padlock dangling from the hasp.

I felt a tingling at the back of my neck as I slowly turned, peering through the shadows. In that second I wondered how I'd let Antony talk me into this foolishness. My anticipation finally got the better of me, and I called out in a whisper, "Hello? Isabel?" No sooner had I spoken than a pebble hit the rocks at my feet. I spun around, but saw no one.

Then, from very close by, I heard, "Psst, Señor Swami, over here."

I was relieved to hear her voice, but when I looked in that direction, I saw only a clutch of boulders.

"Psst," she repeated, and I turned my gaze upward to find her sitting atop the tallest one, wearing the hat.

I walked over to stand beneath her. "Hola," I said.

"Sube," she told me and pointed to a smaller boulder that led to a larger one, and then to her.

I climbed the rocks, almost slipping on my last big upward step, and this drew a laugh from her.

"Nice running into you here," I said as I sat down, cross-legged.

"¿Has traído los fantasmas?" she asked.

"The ghosts were too afraid to follow me tonight. They heard I was coming to see you."

She smiled as she removed the hat and handed it to me. Her hair, now unbraided, blew wild in the wind, and I couldn't stop staring long enough to take the hat from her. She reached over and placed it on my head.

"It looks better on you than on el gigante," she said.

"Antony? You saw him?"

"From the upstairs window. I watched the whole thing."

"I have one question," I said. "Why are you helping us?"

"Not us," she said. "*You.* We Hindus have to stick together."

"You were never convinced, even for a second, by my turban?"

She shook her head.

"When did you come north?" I asked.

"In twenty-four," she said. "I was eight."

"The big year," I said. "Me too, but I was nine."

"We got on a bus in Ciudad Juárez," she said, "and it took us to California. My parents went to work in Parks's orchard out there. I was sent to the mansion to work in the kitchen. My mother died of typhoid. My father was eventually repatriated. I was lucky, I suppose. When Parks moved here from California, I was brought along."

The moonlight illuminated her face, and I could see the sadness in it. "¿Y tú?" she asked.

"We lived in Mexico City, and my family survived the worst of the struggle—the shelling, Zapata's siege of the city, all of it. Just when it seemed that things were looking up, my father was caught in an exchange of gunfire between Zapatistas and Carranza's soldiers. He was on his way to the market."

"How old were you?" she asked.

"Four. Later, when the border opened in twenty-four, my mother took me and my older brother, Hernando, and we fled."

"You pick crops?" asked Isabel.

"No," I said. "My mother wanted to go east, to New York."

"¿Por qué aquí?"

"She heard farm labor was bad, that factory work was better. We got a small apartment in a building on the East Side, no heat, and we had to boil the water that came from the pipes. We were only there for a month before she didn't return from work one day. No one knew what happened to her. She just never came back."

"You must have been scared," she said.

"My brother and I were evicted and roamed the streets, eating out of garbage pails and scrounging leftovers from the back doors of restaurants, begging change."

She put her hand out and lightly touched the side of my face. "And the handsome man with the mustache?"

"He found me in the street, unconscious," I told her. "I'd been separated from Hernando, and I couldn't survive without him. I passed out in the gutter one night, and Schell just happened to be in the city on a job. He took me home and raised me."

"Un milagro," she said.

I nodded, clearing my eyes. It had been so long since I'd allowed myself to think about the past. All of the considerable effort put toward my studies had been an attempt to erase it. Sitting close to Isabel made the early days return, vivid and full of life, as if my memory was a room full of butterflies.

LIKE A GHOST

Your English is perfect," she said.

"Better than my swami?"

She laughed. "Me da problemas."

"You do well," I said. "I had private tutors. They came five days a week. Schell told me if I wanted to succeed here, I needed to get so good at the language that I could convince people that night was day."

"And that's your life now," she said.

I nodded, lifting the hat off my head.

"What's your name?" she asked.

I told her.

"Siéntate a mi lado, and we'll watch the water," she said, patting the air beside her.

I moved closer to her and turned to look out over the sound. Her hair lightly whipped across my face, carrying the vague scent of some spice. Leaning back, arms behind me and fingers braced against the rock surface, our shoulders touching, I was in a daze. My head swam, I felt weak and there was a nervous energy in my chest. We sat for some time in silence, and then she leaned against me.

"Parks is sending me back to Mexico in the spring," she said.

"The only reason he's waiting is that he doesn't want to train someone new during the holidays."

"Why?" I asked, sitting forward and slipping my arm lightly around her shoulders.

"His friends have told him it's not right to have a Mexican working for him. You know, La Depresión, the repatriation . . ."

I wanted to say something to comfort her, but all I could offer was silence and a firmer grip.

"It's fine," she said. "I want to go back and find my father."

"In twenty-four they invited us to come, because they needed us. Now we're vermin."

"Un país desconocido," she said and shook her head.

We sat very still then, watching the water and the moonlight upon it. Eventually I remembered Antony and the promise I'd made to be back within an hour. Saying nothing, I turned, kissed Isabel on the cheek and got up. She took hold of my shirt before I could rise, though, and pulled me close to her, kissing me quickly on the lips. In that moment, I realized I had fallen in love.

When I stood, I nearly toppled off the boulder and had to scrabble for a moment to right myself. She laughed. "I want to stay, but I can't," I told her.

"I'll call you," she said.

"I'll come," I promised as I stepped down onto the beach. Filled with a new kind of energy, I sprinted for a distance. Then missing her already, I turned for one more glimpse. I scanned the dark beach but didn't see her. Finally, I caught sight of her white dress, glowing in the moonlight as she ascended, like a ghost, the long flight of steps. I waved to her with the hat, but she couldn't see me.

I began to walk quickly, hoping I hadn't kept Antony waiting too long. A bank of clouds moved in, obscuring the light of the moon. My thoughts were still with Isabel, and memories of our street in Mexico City mingled with my image of her. I trudged along, awake but dreaming, until I heard a voice.

I started and looked toward the water's edge. There, I saw a cigarette ash go red hot for an instant, and I realized I was not alone on the beach. I stopped walking and listened. There were four or five shadows moving, gathered around the larger shadow of what appeared to be a boat pulled up on the shore. The sound of voices came more clearly to me now. I stayed very still, hoping they hadn't seen me.

Who they were, I had no idea, but I was certain I didn't want to be discovered. In a moment, my elation over having kissed Isabel gave way to fear. I thought if I stepped carefully, making as little noise on the rocks as possible, I could get past them without their noticing me. After no more than ten steps, though, the moonlight found a break in the cloud cover and bathed the beach in its glow. I panicked and began to run, and the moment they heard my shoes on the stones, I heard one of them whisper, "Over there, get him."

I broke into a full sprint, and above the sound of my own pounding heart, heavy breathing, and footfalls, I heard my pursuers close behind me. There was no time to turn and see who was following, but from the sound of it, I surmised there were at least two of them, maybe three. Now that I had been spotted, I hoped the moon would continue to shine, as I could not spare an instant trying to locate the stairway leading to my rendezvous with Antony.

I ran like a rabbit, spurred on by fear, for at least five full minutes before I began to weaken. My legs cramped, there was a pain in my side, and I gasped for air, but I pushed on as they closed the gap afforded by my head start. Then I saw ahead, along the shore, the outline of the white buoy I had noted earlier. With a quick cut, I turned in toward the cliffs, searching frantically for the stairway.

For a few moments, I ran with no destination in sight, merely guided by faith that I would find my escape route. Another cloud covered the moon, and the beach was again plunged in darkness. Almost at the last moment, I saw the steps running up the cliff face and made for them. One of the pursuers had broken away from the others and was so close I could hear him panting behind me.

I reached the stairs and took the first ten steps in three inspired bounds. I lingered on the tenth step, and when I heard the wood of the stairs creak behind me, I turned, sat, and lifted my legs, drawing them in toward my chest. He was a big man with wide shoulders, a knitted cap on his bald head, and grasping hands that appeared huge as they lunged for me out of the dark. That was all I saw of him, though, because when I released my legs, the soles of my shoes hit him square in the face, and he tumbled backward and away. I didn't wait to see where he landed but immediately rose and continued upward.

In the meantime, another of them had gained on me and was already on the steps. The exertion of stopping the lead fellow had sapped my strength, and with every step in the ascent, I lost a measure of speed. I was literally gasping now, and I thought my heart would explode. There was no choice, I had to stop, if only for a moment to catch my breath. In doing so, I looked down and saw the second man just a dozen steps below me. Luckily, he was also winded and had paused briefly.

During that respite I looked up and saw that I had only twenty steps to go. I knew I could make it. One more deep breath, and I plunged forward. I saw the trees of the woods above me, saw the final step of the stairway, and felt a new burst of energy. That's when I slipped, lost my footing, and fell forward, banging my shins and elbows on the hard wood. My stumble gave the man behind me just enough time to catch up.

Yes, I made it to the top and onto the forest path before he caught me, but I wasn't too far in among the trees before I was hit from behind. He lunged and managed to wrap his arms around my ankles. The hat I'd carried through all of it flew out of my grasp, and the impact of the fall jarred me. Still I squirmed like an animal to escape his hold. Managing to roll over and free one of my legs, I began kicking him as hard and fast as I could.

"I'll kill you, you son of a bitch," he groaned.

On the last wild kick, my shoe flew off and hit him in the face, and that was the moment of distraction I needed to free my other leg and scrabble to my feet. I was off again, hobbling over sharp sticks and stones littering the path. Then a gunshot sounded from a few feet behind me and I froze. When the echo of the explosion died away I heard him say, "Move an inch and I'll drop you."

I turned to face him, bent in half, trying to catch my breath. He was only a silhouette, but most definitely a silhouette with a gun. Resting a hand against a tree at the side of the path, he too was panting. "Over here, Bill," he called out, apparently signaling his position to his friend somewhere behind him.

He lifted his gun arm and said the word "What . . . ," but that was all he said. A shadowy figure darted out from behind the tree he leaned against. There was a heavy thud whose center was a quiet crunch of bone, and my captor went down fast without so much as a peep. The large shadow moved toward me.

"Let's get out of here, kid," it said.

"There's another one coming," I told Antony.

"No there isn't," he said.

DANCING IN THE DARK

Bootleggers," he said as we took the road back to the house. He drove with the window open, flicking ashes into the night.

"What?" I asked.

"They're running booze in from Canada," he said. "Probably some lousy grain they mix with juniper berries and perfume."

"I think they wanted to kill me."

"I doubt it," said Antony. "They don't need bodies. They wanted to know who you were. If they thought you were a fed, then they might kill you."

"Thanks," I said.

"Hey, where's the hat?"

"Back on the trail. I dropped it when the guy jumped me."

"Well, at least Parks won't find it now. So, you saw the girl?"

"Yeah," I said, and there must have been something in the way I said it because Antony hummed and mumbled "Dancing in the Dark" the rest of the way home.

Schell was waiting for us in the living room when we came in. He eyed me up and down once, focusing on the dirt stains on my pants and shirt, my torn collar, my missing shoe. He didn't ask any questions but merely raised his right eyebrow.

I knew he was expecting an answer, and I was more than willing to tell him what had happened, but Antony had sworn me to secrecy. Stammering, "I've got to get changed," I quickly left the room and went down the hall, leaving it for the big man to sort out. Stopping short of my bedroom, I waited to hear the excuse he'd concoct.

"I thought you were going for cigarettes," said Schell.

"Well, Boss," said Antony, and there was a long pause in which I could almost hear the gears in that enormous head slowly turning. "I did get cigarettes, but the kid asked me to drop him off for an hour so he could meet up with that girl he'd met at the Parks place a couple weeks ago."

"What was it, a bare knuckle match?" asked Schell.

"You know," said Antony. "First date."

"It's against policy to socialize with the clients," said Schell.

"Boss, she's Mexican. I thought it'd be good for him."

"Why didn't he just tell me?"

"You're his old man. No kid tells their old man that kind of crap."

Some time passed, and then Schell added, "She must be a tough customer."

"What could be better?" said Antony.

Schell must have known I was eavesdropping from the hallway because he called for me to come into the living room. I hobbled in, one shoe still on my right foot. He pointed for me to take a seat in the chair opposite his. Antony was sitting on the couch, his elbows on his knees, his hands folded.

Schell leaned forward and rested his wineglass on the coffee table. "Gentlemen, we're in business," he said. I thought a lecture would follow, but instead he told us that Barnes had called and was eager to meet us.

"When?" I asked.

"Tomorrow morning. Ten sharp. I think we should appear in

force. So Antony, you'll wear the chauffeur rig. Diego, you'll be in swami mode, but let me do all the talking on this venture."

"Have the police come up with anything?" I asked.

"As far as he said, nothing," said Schell. "Tomorrow, after he meets us, if he's convinced, he promised to fill us in on the details."

"I hate to say it," said Antony, "but the girl's probably dead."

"Why?" I asked.

"Unless Barnes tells us otherwise tomorrow, it's been too long a time without a ransom demand," said Schell. "If someone kidnapped her, there'd be a reason, and usually that's money, especially with a mark like Barnes."

"There could be another reason," I said, not wanting to think of the girl having been murdered.

"Slim," said Antony.

"And," said Schell, "the chances are it was someone who knows her. That's just the odds. So keep your eyes peeled when we get over there tomorrow. Watch the help, the wife, everybody's a suspect. Even Barnes himself."

"We'll figure it out," said Antony.

"I don't take kindly to being a patsy for the spirit world," said Schell. "The girl in the glass, when she looked at me, it was almost as if she was daring me to figure her out."

Antony stood up and announced that he was turning in. As he left the living room, walking behind Schell's chair, he turned his head and winked at me, a smile on his face. He'd sold me down the river to hide the fact that we'd gone out to get the hat, and I was somewhat upset with the story he'd told, but I had to hand it to him, he wasn't a bad con man.

I also stood up then, but the moment my rear end left the seat, Schell said, "Sit down." I did.

"You went to see Isabel tonight?" he asked.

"Yeah."

"Does Parks know?"

"No, we met on the beach."

Schell sat quietly, as if weighing this information. When he finally spoke, his tone led me to believe he was overriding his better judgment. "Do what you have to do, but make sure he never hears of it."

"I understand."

"One mistake and we could be out of business," he said.

I nodded and then stood up to leave. As I passed by him, he reached out and grabbed my arm. "Do you like her?" he asked.

"I like her a lot," I said.

"Good," he whispered. He closed his eyes and sat there for a couple of seconds, holding my arm, before finally letting go.

HUSH

Harold Barnes presented a more convincing Teddy Roosevelt then I did a Hindu swami: blunt mustache, squinting eyes behind round glasses, teeth like piano keys, stocky build draped in a black suit. He wasn't exactly a Rough Rider when it came to the personality though. It was easy to see how hard the loss of his daughter had been on him. His complexion was ashen, and he more dragged himself around than walked, as if he hadn't slept since she'd disappeared. Another man might have been frantic and filled with anger, but Barnes was mild as a lamb and spoke so low I often had a hard time hearing him.

We wound up, after navigating the extensive hallways of his enormous mansion, in a solarium on the ground floor in the western wing. Barnes sat behind a desk and Schell and I on cushioned chairs facing him. Outside, the sun beat down on the last few rose blossoms in the garden his child had been snatched from.

Schell made the introductions. There was always a moment when he relayed my lineage to the clients during which I held my breath and waited for a sign that they'd bought our bill of goods. Many of them, I could tell, viewed me as some exotic but not very inviting necessity of Schell's occupation, sort of like Morty's snake, but Barnes was truly interested and seemed pleased to have the input of the exotic East in his corner.

"Mr. Barnes, we were devastated by the news of your daughter's disappearance and thought it only right to volunteer our services to help locate her," said Schell.

"You come with excellent credentials, Mr. Schell," he said. "George Parks, the widow Morrison, the Vincents, Mr. Goshen, have all vouched for your abilities and your professionalism. Your concern is appreciated."

"When a child's well-being is at stake . . . ," said Schell.

"How did you become aware of our situation?" he asked.

"To tell you the truth, I was conducting a séance for Mr. Parks a week ago, and your daughter's image came through to me in the midst of it. This was before I'd even heard of her disappearance. When I read the newspaper and saw her photograph, I realized she'd been calling out to me for help."

"Astonishing," said Barnes. "Do you think . . . ?"

"I'm uncertain. I've received a few more vague signs, but I needed to come here and try to pick up her vibration in order to get a clearer signal."

"I can show you around, if you like," he said.

"That'll help me immeasurably. I'd also like you to tell me anything you know, including whatever the police have discovered."

"I will," he said.

"The images I'm receiving from the spirit world are suggesting to me that you have not been contacted for a ransom payment, am I correct?" asked Schell.

"That's right," said Barnes.

"I'll need a list of all those who visited your home in the last month or so. Can you have that prepared for me?"

"The police asked for the same thing. I can give you a copy."

"Very good. I've had a premonition that your daughter didn't wander off but was abducted by someone who knows you. In other words, I don't believe this is an instance of a random kidnapping."

Barnes nodded.

"And I will need to meet your household staff."

"Very well."

"One more thing . . . I ask that you not mention the assistance we're affording you to the police, as they're suspect of our abilities and will most likely interfere in our own investigation."

"The police have been less than useless," said Barnes, and for the first time I saw a hint of ire. "They've come up with nothing."

"They're limited by their reliance on the physical, whereas Ondoo and I take our cues from the unseen universe," said Schell.

"There's only one demand I have, Mr. Schell," he said.

"Please," said Schell.

"I'll need you to work in concert with another gifted individual I've hired. She's a psychic, can foresee the future and look into the past. She's impressed my wife tremendously, told her things about us and our lives she would have no way of knowing. I'll introduce you to her in a few minutes. She's upstairs with Helen right now."

"We'd be delighted," said Schell, barely skipping a beat. Of course, he felt the opposite. Barnes would never have noticed it as a sign of distress, but I caught a minute downturn at the corners of Schell's lips.

"Is there anyone you can think of who might wish harm upon your family?" asked Schell, quickly recovering.

"Mr. Schell, I'm in charge of enterprises totaling in the millions. I have none of your special insight, but I can assure you, I know my enemies better than my friends. They might try to beat me to a deal, pull an underhanded financial trick now and then, but this kind of thing is far too messy and, frankly, unnecessary for them."

"Of course," said Schell.

Barnes then looked up and his expression softened. "Hello, dear, I'd like you and Miss Hush to meet Mr. Schell and his associate," he said.

I turned to see the two women who had entered the room. The older woman, obviously Barnes's wife, was short with dark hair gathered into a tight bun at the back of her head. Her eyes were ringed with dark circles, and she appeared every bit as fatigued as her husband. She wore a long, black shawl over her shoulders and clutched the tails of it in balled fists. Behind her, though, like day following night, came Miss Hush, dressed all in white, her light blonde hair fanning out around her head like a frizzy aura. Her complexion was nearly as pale as her outfit, and she wore a kind of absentminded smile.

A slight ripple of consternation moved across Schell's brow, and I interpreted it as surprise that the seer in question had not turned out to be someone we already knew. It was obvious to me that he had never heard of Miss Hush before, and that was odd, because between Antony and himself, they knew just about every con in New York.

Schell stood, as did I, and offered his hand to Helen Barnes while her husband made the introductions. The older woman did not release her shawl but bowed slightly and thanked Schell for coming. "I'm very sorry about your daughter's disappearance," he said. Then it was on to Miss Hush, who shook his hand timidly and whispered a greeting I couldn't make out. Neither of the ladies bothered to take my own offered palm, but that was not unusual. When Schell gave them the capsule review of my credentials and name, the younger woman stared with large eyes and said, "How wonderful."

Schell and I gave up our seats to the women and each pulled another chair into the circle that formed around Harold Barnes's desk. The millionaire cleared his throat, and said, "Miss Hush here tells me that she believes my daughter is still on Long Island somewhere. Is that not correct?" he asked.

"She's close by," said the pale young woman.

"She needs someone to take her around the local area, to pick up the image more clearly," Barnes said to Schell. "I'd put my own driver at her disposal, but I need him here in case I'm called for."

"I see," said Schell. "My driver, Antony, can take her around.

Ondoo will accompany them also. His presence tends to open a clearer conduit with the spirit world. I think Miss Hush will find that his close proximity will increase her abilities. In the meantime, I'd like to stay here and see your daughter's room, walk around outside in the garden, if that's all right with you."

"Miss Hush?" Barnes asked.

She nodded.

"No sense in waiting to get started," said Barnes. "Every minute is precious. Mr. Schell, make yourself at home. I'll let the staff know you are to have complete access to the entire estate."

We all stood, save Mrs. Barnes, who, I just then noticed, had given herself up to silent tears. Her genuine grief made me feel ten times the impostor. Her husband moved around from behind the desk and took the seat next to her, wrapping an arm around her shoulders.

Schell and I were the first out of the room. As we walked the maze of hallways through the palatial house back to its front entrance, the boss quickly whispered to me under his breath, "Keep her in your sights constantly. She's a wild card. I want to know everything she does." I nodded, and then he dropped back and waited for our passenger.

As I reached the Cord, Antony stood holding the door open on the passenger side. Eventually, Schell and Miss Hush exited the house and walked down the drive to the car. She gathered up her dress but, before slipping into the backseat, requested that she be allowed to ride up front. The big man opened the front door, and she slid in. Schell held the door open instead of letting Antony close it. Antony then went around, got in behind the wheel, and started the car.

"Follow Miss Hush's directives to the letter," he said to us over the turning of the engine.

"Gentlemen," she said, "please, call me Lydia."

"Thomas," said Schell and again shook her hand.

"Thomas, from what Mr. Barnes has told me of your reputation, you must already be aware that the girl is dead."

"No," said Schell. "I hadn't picked that fact up."

"I wouldn't tell Barnes and his wife until we find her."

"Naturally," said Schell.

"We'll find her, though," she said. "I've seen it. Henry and young Diego here will be with me when I do."

Upon hearing our real names, I squirmed a little beneath my turban, and Antony's head whipped around.

"You've done your homework," said Schell, smiling.

"No work at all," she said.

Then he shut the door, Antony gave it the gas, and we were off.

SLEIGHT OF MOUTH

The Cord sat at the edge of a field that had been burnt brown by the summer sun and now was strewn with fallen leaves from the woods that bordered it in the distance. The sky was bright blue, and there was a cool and steady breeze. We had the windows rolled down, and both Antony and I sat in the front seat. The big man was smoking his third cigarette since we'd stopped forty-five minutes earlier. Off to our left, halfway across the field, Lydia Hush traipsed slowly in wide circles, talking to herself. It was the fourth such stop we'd made since leaving Barnes's place.

"This detail's a snooze and a half," said Antony, blowing smoke.

"Miss Hush's powers seem somewhat less than startling," I said.

"Well, one thing's for sure, not that we should talk, but that name's phony as a three-dollar bill."

"I thought it was poetic," I said.

"Poetic, maybe. Phony, for sure. Besides that, though, Miss Hush is a fine-looking woman, even if she's got the complexion of a snowball."

"She must live under a rock," I said.

"Did you see the boss's face when she coughed up our real names?"

"I doubt she could see his surprise, because he covered it with that smile."

"Yeah, the business smile," said Antony. "Sleight of mouth."

"Maybe his best trick," I said.

"Do you think she pulled that information out of a dream?" he asked.

"I don't know. She seems like she could either be a con or the real thing, if there's any such thing as the real thing. Schell's pretty much convinced me there isn't."

Antony blew a smoke ring, then flicked his cigarette butt out the window. "Once I was with this traveling show in Georgia for a few weeks, wrestling a bear—"

"Here we go," I said.

"No, it's true. The sorriest fucking bear in the world. It was sort of like rolling your grandmother, like moving furniture. Had to quit; I felt sorry for the bear. Anyway, with that show, there was this old hag, and I mean hag. She sat in a tent and you went in and paid your dime and she'd tell you your future. And for an extra nickel she'd tell you the day you were gonna die."

"Sounds like fun," I said.

"We're talking the loneliest of occupations," said Antony. "But in the short time I was with that crap outfit two people actually took her up on the nickel special. One was a local guy in a little town outside of Atlanta. She told him he had two days to live. Two days later, sure as shit, he's walking home from work and gets struck by lightning. Blood boils, head pops like a grape."

"She got lucky," I said.

"That's pretty damn lucky. Well, not for the guy. But there was another guy too. A midget who was with the show. He went to see her after the first guy got hit by lightning. The midget's show name was Major Minor. He dressed in a military outfit; was a real self-important little prick. The hag gave him a date in six years. So what? Right? Who's gonna remember that? But about maybe eight years later, I ran into Bunny Franchot, the Alligator Girl, one of the most screwed-up-looking broads I ever knew, in a carnival in South Jersey. She'd been with the outfit in Georgia when I was there. We got to talking, and it came out that the Major, who had this Model T rigged so he could drive it standing up, went out one night, got loaded, and ran himself into a tree. He'd forgotten the prediction, but Bunny never did. It was the exact day she predicted."

I shook my head.

"There's more bullshit in heaven and earth, than you can dream up in your scenario," said Antony.

"Well put," I said.

"Now," he said, "go out there and tell Miss Hush it's time for lunch."

I adjusted my turban, opened the door, and got out. My legs were stiff from sitting all morning, and it felt good to be out of the car. I took my time crossing the field. As I approached, she turned to face me.

"Are you feeling anything, Miss Hush?" I asked as I drew near. I didn't bother with the Indian accent, since she already knew who we were.

"Cold," she said, and I could see she was shivering slightly.

"Does that mean we're close?" I asked.

"No, it just means I'm cold," she said and smiled. It was a real smile, not that vague one she'd flashed at the Barnes place. This time I thought I caught a glimpse of her true self.

"Antony wants to get something to eat," I said. "Is that all right with you?"

"Okay," she said and walked up beside me. She was beautiful in a kind of fairy-tale way, and I thought about a story I'd once read called "The Snow Queen." Her closeness to me made me nervous to begin with, but when she put her hand on my shoulder as we walked, I had to swallow hard.

Of course, the silence was too much to bear, so I said, "And what will it be like when you discover the location?"

"I'll feel very tired, very tired. In my mind, I'll begin to dream, standing straight up, and I'll see poor Charlotte. Maybe she'll tell me where she's hidden. Or I might see the place in my mind before I see it with my eyes."

"Why do you talk while you're walking around?" I asked.

"I'm not talking. I'm singing to pass the time until something happens."

"Have you found lost people before?" I asked.

"Everybody's lost in some way," she said. "I found you, didn't I, hiding beneath a turban?"

I'd been reminded of my identity once too often in recent days and the frustration of it made me bolder. "What are *you* hiding, Miss Hush?"

"Plenty," she said and removed her hand from my shoulder. "And it's Lydia."

"How's the fishing?" asked Antony as we drew near the car. He began to open the door to get out and do his chauffeur thing.

"Nothing yet," she said, smiled, and waved for him not to bother getting the door for her.

We drove out to Cedar Swamp Road, and Antony bought a few sandwiches and Cokes at a little market. Behind the place were a table and chairs set up beneath a huge oak tree, where we sat and ate. Miss Hush had nothing but a crust from one of my sandwich halves and a sip of Coke. No one said anything for the longest time until, at one point, out of the blue, she just started singing a Ruth Etting tune, "Ten Cents a Dance." Antony sat staring at her with his mouth open and a glazed look in his eyes. She sang the whole song, and when she was done, she bummed one of the big man's cigarettes.

After Miss Hush sang that song, Antony never complained about the boredom again. There were three more fruitless stops that afternoon, two more fields and a wooded lot. When the sun started to go down, we headed back to the Barnes estate.

Schell was waiting for us on the front steps of the mansion. As we pulled up and parked, he descended and walked over to open the door for Miss Hush.

"Anything?" he asked.

"Nothing today," she said. "But soon. I'd say in the next day or two."

"Will you need Antony and Ondoo tomorrow?" he asked as she stood up and stepped past him.

"If you would be so kind," she said.

"Shall I have them pick you up at your own address?" asked Schell.

"No, here will be fine. Ten?"

"Very good," said Schell.

Before heading toward the mansion, she turned and leaned over to look into the car. She waved to us and called, "I had a delightful day, gentlemen. Thank you."

Antony and I both waved back.

"You're quite a cozy trio," said Schell as he got in the car and shut the door.

"Boss," said Antony, giving the Cord gas and pulling away down the long driveway, "that Miss Hush is a cupcake."

"Anything else?" asked Schell.

The big man thought for a moment as we passed a long line of hedges. "She's probably crazy."

I noticed that up ahead another car, headlamps on in the twilight, had entered Barnes's drive and was headed toward us.

"And you, Diego? Did you find out how she knows who we are?" asked Schell.

"No," I said, and as I spoke, I turned to look into the passing car. There were three large shadowy forms in it beside the driver—two in the back and one in the passenger seat. I caught a clear glimpse of the driver, not noticing his face in any detail but focusing on the fact that he wore a large, broad-brimmed hat. The car passed quickly, but that hat looked awfully familiar.

SHE'S A CON

The air in the Bugatorium was very still that night, moths splayed out on the walls and butterflies closed tight on branches and stems. Only one two-tailed swallowtail drifted in circles up near the skylight.

"I'm sorry we never got to Barnes before his daughter disappeared," said Schell. "He and his wife are true believers. They've had spiritualists, cold readers, psychics, in their parlor. The missus claims to be an adept at the technique of automatic writing. The house is littered with talismans and volumes on the occult. We could have made a small fortune on them."

"How's Barnes strike you?" asked Antony, setting his wineglass down on the table.

"I have to question either the intelligence or sanity of anyone who goes in for the mystical to the extent he does, but otherwise he seemed a man distraught at the loss of his daughter. He showed me around the garden from which she was taken and then had to leave to attend to some business. After that, his wife did the honors. She's very quiet and clearly heartbroken."

"Well," said Antony, "anyone who can make the kind of money he does legally can't be completely stupid."

"Did you find anything in the garden?" I asked.

Schell shook his head. "Nothing there. We went through the entire house. Of course, I had to stop every now and then and make believe I was picking up an impression from the country of spirits—a shiver, a nod, a gasp. It was a pitiful thing to see the expectation bloom in the eyes of Mrs. Barnes and then wilt again when I had nothing substantial to offer."

"This whole thing gives me the creeps," I said.

"The charity angle, the fact that we're trying to do something real, has me all bollixed too," said Antony, nodding.

"Either of you can back out if you'd like," said Schell. "For me, I have no choice but to continue until there's nowhere left to turn or I've found the girl."

"Yeah, yeah, Johnny, save it," said Antony. "What *did* you find?"

Schell laughed. "I met the staff, questioned them a little, but detected no signs of dissembling. Then Mrs. Barnes led me to her daughter's room. It's on the first floor with a huge bay window, and has a view of the grounds at the back of the house. A lovely room for a child—dolls, a dollhouse, a canopied bed, rocking horse, just beautiful.

"I looked around, but found nothing remarkable until I got to a desk in the corner and began going through a stack of drawings Charlotte had made. It was the first time I got a sense of the child as a person and not merely an image. Mrs. Barnes told me that in the days prior to her disappearance, her daughter had complained about seeing a ghost at night walking the grounds, staring in her window. She'd cried out in the middle of the night two evenings before she was abducted, and Mrs. Barnes remembered going to her room."

"Did the mother see anything?" I asked.

"No, but the girl did three pastel drawings during that time, trying to capture what she'd seen. A male form, glowing in the night, head like a big white potato, and crystal blue eyes. In one, it crouches in the bushes, in another it's back by the tree line. The last is the most startling because it's a full-on portrait of the face at the window. As Mrs. Barnes attested, the child was a wonderful little artist and drew quite often."

"What kid doesn't see things in the dark, though?" said Antony.

"Maybe somebody was casing the place at night," I said.

"I thought both these things myself," said Schell. "Some of the girl's other drawings hung on the walls of her room—portraits of her parents, her kitten, and the like. I would say she had a knack more for realistic depiction than for fantastic imagining. Also, Barnes has two night watchmen who patrol the grounds, and a guard at the front gate."

"Did the mother seem to think there was a connection between the drawings and Charlotte's disappearance?" I asked.

"In the Barneses' view everything has some kind of supernatural connection," said Schell. "But she was visibly rattled by the drawings. She didn't use the word *ghost* when talking about them. The term she used was 'dybbuk.'"

"What the hell's that?" asked Antony.

"I don't know," said Schell, "but she used it in a way that indicated she expected me to understand. Not to shake her confidence in me, I simply nodded as if I did."

Antony lifted his wineglass and drained it. "What do you say, Boss, can I have a cigarette in here?"

"No," said Schell.

"Okay, I'm just gonna lip one." He took a cigarette out and held it in his mouth without lighting it. "The whole deal's screwy, and the one thing that makes no sense at all is that there's been no ransom demand."

"We don't know enough about Barnes," I said. "He might have enemies."

"We don't know enough about a lot of things," said Schell. "I got that list of names from him of people who had visited the house in the last month." He reached into his shirt pocket and pulled out a folded sheet of paper.

"Anything stand out?" asked Antony.

Schell unfolded the paper and scanned it up and down. "It looks like mostly society women, and five or six men's names. Our friend, Mr. Parks, is among them. I'll start looking into them tomorrow while you two are driving Lydia Hush around."

"Did you find out how Miss Hush came to the Barneses' attention?" I asked.

"All Mrs. Barnes would tell me was that she showed up at the mansion two days after the girl disappeared, suggesting she might be able to help. Hush instantly convinced Barnes's wife of her abilities by revealing things about the family's personal life. That's it. I didn't want to seem too nosy on that score."

"I think Antony's fallen for her," I said.

The big man looked over at me and slowly shook his head.

"She's a con," said Schell. "She's a con and a lousy con at that."

"You think she might be involved in the girl's abduction?" I asked.

"I considered it," said Schell, "but basically I think she's just making hay while the sun shines, so to speak."

After a long pause in the conversation, Antony said, "I'm going to go have a smoke in the kitchen and then turn in. I've got a long day tomorrow with junior G-man, here, and Madame Snowflake."

We wished Antony a good night, and then Schell leaned back and closed his eyes, as if he was trying to figure out how all of the pieces of the puzzle fit together. The whole thing was too confusing for me to sort out. I let my mind wander, first thinking about Lydia Hush putting her hand on my shoulder, then about her singing at lunch. Somehow these thoughts bled into a memory of Isabel and the night we sat on the boulder by the sound. I wanted to see her again.

The next thing I knew, Schell's eyes were partially open, and he was staring at the yellow and black flutter of the two-tailed swallowtail hovering above the table between us. He smiled wearily, and said, "The Aztecs called that specimen Xochiquetzal, which means 'precious flower.' There was a goddess who followed warriors into battle, and when they were mortally wounded and lay dying, she'd copulate with them while holding one of those swallowtails in her mouth."

"I remember my mother telling me that *mariposas* were the souls of the dead," I said.

"Do you think about Mexico often?" asked Schell.

"I didn't till I met Isabel," I said. "Now I'm starting to see pieces of it in my dreams. I'm remembering little bits and pieces. Funny thing is, I was just thinking about her when you mentioned the Aztecs."

"Maybe we need to take a trip back there for you to remember," he said. He turned his left hand over, and there was a bridge deck in it. Where it had come from, I'm not sure. As he began manipulating the cards, he said, "Maybe it was wrong of me to want you to forget Mexico, but I did. I thought if you carried it around your whole life, it would weigh you down with sorrow for all the things that had happened."

I smiled, not wanting to trouble him, and waved my hand. "I'd say I've been pretty lucky."

"I wonder if," said Schell, "when a caterpillar becomes a butterfly"—here, he fanned open the deck—"and gains the ability to fly, it remembers what it was like to be a caterpillar?"

"It's probably just happy to be free," I said.

"Or," said Schell, closing the deck, "perhaps all of its restless movement from blossom to blossom is merely an attempt to return to and regain its caterpillar nature." He raised his eyebrows and then shrugged.

While continuing to work the deck, now with both hands, Schell eventually closed his eyes again, returning to his thoughts. His musings struck me at first as insightful and profound, but the longer I sat there the more something bothered me about what he'd said. I couldn't precisely put my finger on it, but it had to do with his equating Mexico with a caterpillar.

THIS MOVING WORLD

The next day, in between stops to let Lydia Hush get out of the car and psychically sniff the surrounding area, I entertained her and Antony with select stanzas from the Isa Upanishad. Using my swami voice, I recited the lines with a heightened solemnity that both honored and mocked the material.

"When once one understands that in oneself
The self's become all beings
When once one's seen the unity
What room is there for sorrow? What room for perplexity?"

Antony laughed and pronounced the holy utterances "doubletalk," and Miss Hush praised me for my ability to memorize. She said that she could almost make out what the words were getting at. Like a child vying for attention, I milked the act for a solid hour until I began to bore myself. Afterward, we traveled in a peaceful silence broken only by Lydia's occasional whispered requests for Antony to pull over. A little while after lunch, for no apparent reason, she offered a breathy rendition of "As Time Goes By."

Her perfume carried the scent of fresh-cut lemons. It filled the car and dazed the big man and me, so that even while we waited by the side of the road for her, we kept to our own thoughts. Her pale beauty was bewitching, and it made me think of marshmallow, cream, clouds, and snow. Whenever she put her hand on Antony's shoulder to get his attention, I noticed that it caused him to shiver slightly, and I felt a stab of jealousy with each touch.

Not until the end of the day, the sky growing overcast as twilight came on, when we'd pulled over at the edge of a wood in a little town named Mt. Misery, did her spell dissipate. I sat in the front seat next to Antony, who had begun humming the tune she'd sung earlier. More than an hour had gone by since we'd last seen her drifting like a ghost amid the gray trunks beneath the darkening sky. Only then did I recall something I'd meant to tell him first thing that morning.

"Oh," I said, "yesterday, after we picked up Schell and were driving out of the Barnes place, do you remember the car that passed us?"

He took a drag of his cigarette, flicked the ash out the car window, and said, "Yeah, now that you mention it."

"I tried to get a look at whoever was in that car. I'm pretty sure it was four men—big guys too. I couldn't get a look at any of their faces, but one thing I could see was that the driver was wearing a hat."

"So?"

"I think it was *that* hat. You know, the one you wore when you were Parks's mother."

Antony sat still for a moment, taking in what I had told him. Then he turned to me, eyes squinting, brow furrowed. "Why?" he said.

"Same style, same color, same big brim. If I remember when we bought it at the thrift store, it was actually a man's hat."

He turned and stared out the windshield. "Oh shit," he said. "I wonder if Barnes is bringing booze in from Canada."

"Why would he?" I asked.

"I'll give you a million guesses," said Antony. He held up his right hand and rubbed his thumb and first two fingers together. "If you have a big enough operation, there's a fortune in it. You bring it in on Long Island, less cops, and you've got the city close enough to unload all of it and then some."

"Would he do something like that?" I asked.

He laughed once and rubbed his chin. " 'Illegal' takes on a whole new meaning when you're loaded like Barnes. The rich have a separate rule book. To them if it makes money, it can't be wrong."

"The only thing is, we have to tell Schell," I said.

"Damn it," he said and smacked the steering wheel. "We *are* gonna have to tell him. I've got nothing against bootlegging. Prohibition is complete bullshit anyway, but this shows us something about Barnes that could be important. Are you sure it was that hat?"

"No," I said. "But I'm mostly sure."

"Jeez, trapped in my own spiderweb," he said. "My con is busted."

"I don't think Schell's going to care," I said. "He'll be happy to get the news about Barnes."

"Yeah, but if we tell him, you better be right," he said. "I'm gonna look like an ass."

"Why should this instance be any different?" I said.

I managed to open the door and get out of the car before Antony could grab me. He let himself out and stretched. Then he looked over at where I stood and said, "If I catch you, kid, I'm gonna wrap that turban around your neck."

"Whatever moves in this moving world, abandon it and then enjoy," I said in my swami voice.

"Enough of that," he said. "It's gonna get dark in about fifteen minutes. Where's Miss Hush?"

"She's been gone a long time," I said.

"Too long," said Antony. "We better find her."

"I think she went this way," I said and pointed at a path that wound among the trees.

We followed the path for a few minutes, looking all around, but saw no sign of our passenger.

"Miss Hush," I called out. There was no response.

We walked on a bit more until we came to a fork in the trail. "Lydia," he roared. We listened for her voice but heard only the sounds of crows in the treetops and a squirrel running through the brambles. Red leaves fell around us, joining others that littered the ground.

"Okay, kid, you go that way," he said, pointing to the right. "I'll go this way. Just keep calling her. If you don't see anything by the time it gets dark, get back to the car."

"All right," I said and took off down the path, calling her name. We yelled at intervals, and I heard Antony's voice for a good distance as I walked along. Darkness was falling quickly, and I wondered where she could have gone.

About fifteen minutes later, when I was just about ready to turn back, I thought I heard something. When I looked around, I saw a crow lift off a fallen tree and fly up between barren branches. That's when I caught sight of a small structure sitting amid a thicket of pines. It was a dilapidated old shack with a tar paper roof. There was a broken window to the left of the door, which hung crookedly from a leather strap-hinge at the top; the bottom one was torn. The place was small, and looked like it had once been a toolshed or woodshed.

I made my way over to it, and as I approached, I called Miss Hush's name, a little more quietly than before. I heard nothing but silence. I stepped up on the cracked, moss-covered concrete block at the entrance. Anxiety was building in my chest. I reached out and pulled the crooked door back, and the leather hinge just sort of crumbled and broke. The door fell away, almost clipping my shoulder, and hit the ground with a crash. What meager daylight was left, rushed in, lessening the gloom. As the light poured in, a smell came out—a horrid stench of mildew and bad meat. There was a buzz and flutter as flies and moths rose from something lying on the floor.

I knew it was her before I could even focus on the pale form at my feet. There was the Barnes child, maggots in her curly hair, naked, and white as Lydia, a small square of material with a bizarre circular design on it covering her from waist to midthigh. She was staring hard with rotting eyes, and the sight of her made my knees buckle. Suddenly, the smell registered with full force, and my stomach heaved. I turned away from the door, tripped on the concrete block, and hit the cold hard ground with hands outstretched. I vomited, supporting myself on all fours. I don't know how long I stayed like that, but all I could hear above the buzzing in my ears was the wind in the trees, the sound of the leaves blowing along the ground.

The next thing I knew, I was being lifted bodily onto my feet and it was night. Antony whispered to me, "Take a deep breath, kid." He let go of me, and I knew he was going to look in the shack. From behind me, I heard him give a giant sigh, and then say, "Jesus fucking Christ." An instant later he was beside me, arm around my shoulders. "Let's get out of here," he said.

"What about Miss Hush?" I asked.

"Forget her. This could be a setup," he said. "Come on, kid, you've got to run." He gave me a push. "Move your ass."

I did. Once I located the trail, I broke into a sprint, running as if to escape the vision of the girl's corpse. Behind me, I heard Antony lumbering along, wheezing with the exertion.

We made it back to the car in only a couple of minutes, got in, and Antony started it up. He pulled away, tires screeching, without turning on the headlights. Rain started to hit the windshield. About a mile down the road, once we'd caught our breath, he turned on the lights and slowed down.

"You okay, kid?" he asked.

"No," I said. I tore the turban off my head and flung it in the backseat. There were tears in my eyes.

"I know what you mean," he said. He drove on for a few more seconds and then added, "This shit just got about a mile deeper."

SHARDS OF EVIL

Upon arriving home, I went immediately to the couch in the living room and curled up in the corner, my head on a pillow and my knees pulled nearly to my chest. Only then did I realize I was trembling. I still felt faintly nauseated, and every time I'd focus on that indelible image of Charlotte Barnes in death, the sensation would intensify. Even though my eyes were closed, I could feel Schell's presence enter the room. Then I heard Antony address him.

"Boss, we found the Barnes kid," the big man said in a voice so weary it came out a whisper.

"Bad?" asked Schell, and I could hear him sitting down in the chair next to the couch.

"Real bad," said Antony. "She's dead."

Schell made no reply. I heard Antony slump into the chair directly across the coffee table from where I lay.

"Lydia Hush?" Schell finally asked.

"Sort of," said Antony.

"Tell me everything," said Schell, and Antony did, beginning with when we pulled over next to the woods late in the afternoon. I listened, reliving the entire scenario, and as I drew closer to the shack in the retelling, I began to sweat. When it was over, I breathed deeply and opened my eyes.

"She led you to the body," said Schell.

"Yeah, and then vanished," said Antony. "Once Diego found the girl, I thought it was best to run. I was afraid it might be a setup—the cops are tipped off and just happen to show when the two of us are standing over the body."

"It was good thinking," said Schell.

"One thing," I said. "Antony said the girl was naked. She was, mostly, but there was some kind of cloth draped over her lap."

"That's right," said Antony. "The kid's right."

"There was a design on it too."

"Of?" asked Schell.

"I didn't catch it," said Antony.

"A symbol," I said. "I've never seen it before and can't quite remember it. A circle was part of it and there were other things involved, but . . ."

"Well, not right now," said Schell. "But later on, try to remember the image."

I nodded.

"What kind of shape was the body in?" asked Schell.

"I don't know, Boss," said Antony. "The poor kid was dead. I didn't look that closely. All I can tell you is the place stunk of death, and my guess was that she'd been there for a couple of days."

"Any marks? Wounds? Bruises?" asked Schell.

"Nothing," I said. "Just white, and her eyes, flies and moths, maggots . . ." I gagged, unable to finish.

Schell reached across the arm of the couch and put his hand on the top of my head. "Okay," he said.

"I guess we just call the cops and let them take it from here, right?" said Antony.

Schell lifted his hand off me and leaned back. "Wrong," he said.

"Tommy, forget it. It was a mistake to get hooked up in this to start with," said Antony.

"There was a point at which I could have backed out but not now.

That little girl's come to life in my mind. Something stinks about the entire mess."

"Yeah, something stinks," said Antony. "A kid's been murdered, probably by some lunatic. Let the cops find him."

"What about Lydia Hush?" said Schell.

"What about her?" asked Antony.

"She obviously knew where the body was. What else do you think she knows?" asked Schell.

"Maybe she's really got the gift," said Antony.

"Bullshit," said Schell. "If you feel that way, then why did you suspect a setup?"

"Kid?" said Antony.

"I don't know," I said. "Her method of finding the girl seemed pretty suspicious. But she did lead us to Charlotte. There was something about her . . ."

"You two are wifty. I'm going to find her, then I'm going to find out what happened."

"All right," said Antony, "Whatever you say, Boss."

Schell looked over at me. I nodded. "I have to know," I said.

"Our first order of business is for me to anonymously tip off the police to where the body is. Then I'll call Barnes and tell him we found her. I'm going to beg him not to tell the cops that we were involved. That way we can hopefully avoid trouble and stay in his confidence. We're going to need to talk to him again, I'm sure." Schell stood up and took a deep breath. "This'll be rough," he said.

"Don't forget, you've only got a couple minutes before they can trace the call," said Antony.

"Yeah, I know," said Schell. "Come with me. I need you to give me the directions to the body."

Antony stood and headed out of the room. He stopped midway to the hall entrance, turned, and said, "Sorry you had to find her, kid."

"I'm better," I said.

After they left, I didn't want to be alone and thought of following, but a great weariness came over me. I thought, I'll just rest my eyes for a second and then go listen in. I woke hours later, surprised in a dream by the appearance of Charlotte Barnes. The room was dark. I heard a voice.

"Are you okay?" asked Schell.

"Just had a dream," I said.

My eyes adjusted, and I saw him sitting by my feet at the end of the couch. I wondered how long he'd been there.

"Did you talk to Barnes?" I asked.

"Yes."

"What happened?"

"He wept," said Schell and patted my shin. "Go back to sleep. It's late. Everything's fine."

The next morning I woke to find the nausea gone, replaced by a subtle sense of dread. I took a bath and changed my clothes, and got ready to lie low. That was the directive from Schell. We had to wait a few days for the furor to die down before we could dive back into the investigation. Antony had gone out early and picked up the newspaper. Pictures of the shack and partial shots of the body were all over the front page. "Barnes Girl Found Dead" was the headline. I passed on reading it, wanting to keep my breakfast down. It wasn't that the newspaper photos were so explicit, but I was afraid they'd awaken the image of her that, for the time being, slept in my memory.

I returned to my studies. Mrs. Hendrickson would be arriving in two days to discuss Chaucer's *Parliament of Fowls*, and it would get pretty unpleasant if I didn't know what I was talking about. Since we'd begun looking for Charlotte Barnes, I'd done no book work. I went to my room to get my notes and the huge copy of Chaucer. In the bookcase I saw another book I hadn't opened in years. I took it, instead, off the shelf and opened it. Very old and somewhat tattered, it was one of the first books that Schell had read to me from—*Fabulous Tales from Around the World*. On the title page, a previous owner, one Luciere Londell, had inscribed her name. I paged through until I found the illustration for "The Snow Queen," a woman who, in her paleness, could have passed for Miss Hush.

I turned back to the beginning of the tale and read the first few paragraphs. It had been many years since I'd read about the demon who had created a mirror, the special nature of which reflected all of the true and good things in the world so that they seemed distorted, absurd, frightening. When the demon tried to take his mirror to heaven to show the angels their warped reflections, he dropped it and it fell back to earth, shattering into a million tiny particles. The wind blew these infinitesimal shards of evil into the eyes of two children who loved each other, and their views of the world and each other turned dark and disturbing. The image in my mind's eye of Charlotte's corpse was a shard from that demonic mirror.

BLESSING THE MANSION

The more I tried not to think of Charlotte Barnes, and the more I thought of Lydia Hush, the more desperate I became to again see Isabel. I had no means of contacting her to set up another rendezvous on the beach or to even let her know I was thinking of her. I lived in hope that she might call, but when the phone rang and I'd go to answer it with a feeling of nervousness in my stomach I'd be met by the voice of Sal, or the fake signature bark of Hal Izzle, or Vonda, the Rubber Lady, calling for Antony. It was frustrating, to say the least, and I began to plot, which was a perfect diversion from recent events.

As Schell had taught me, "a con starts when there is something you want and you are blocked from attaining it by certain obstacles. The good con artist elicits the assistance of those who mean to stand in the way of one's attainment by appealing to their vanity, pride, jealousy, ignorance, or fear. One must first throw into a pile the expected rules of engagement, morality, society, and thought, set them on fire, and then proceed. Think big, have confidence." I did just that.

I knew Schell had the list of all the visitors to the Barnes estate in the months leading up to the disappearance of the girl. I was also aware that Parks was on that list. Schell wanted very much for us to pay another visit to Katie at the newspaper office to research the biographies and associations of the people in question. He was prevented from doing this by his own cautionary rule that we should lie low for a period, have nothing to do with our investigation until the hubbub died down and the reporters and police had somewhat withdrawn from the scene. With this in mind, I went to see him in the Bugatorium.

He'd been doing some reading about one of his blue butterflies and wanted to tell me about what he'd read. "Were you aware of the fact that when this specimen is in its caterpillar state, it's protected from predatory wasps and generally tended to by ants?"

Of course I didn't know that, but I sat and heard the whole lecture out, nodding in the appropriate places, affecting a look of great interest. I learned that these servile ants perform their duties to the exclusion of just about all else because the caterpillar exudes a chemical known as "honeydew," which the ants are mad for. Schell went on for nearly twenty minutes, and when his enthusiasm had finally run its course, I tried to change the subject.

"It's kind of frustrating just waiting around for things to blow over," I said.

"I know," he said, standing. He moved toward the large work table at the rear of the Bugatorium. I followed.

"When you get around to looking into the people on that list Barnes gave you, who are you going to start with?"

He bent over and peered into the screen cages he used to house caterpillars in their molting stages. "I'll start with the gentlemen, although that might be shortsighted on my part. I suppose any one of the women could be as culpable. You just don't hear many stories of women kidnapping children to whatever end. I'll play the odds on this one."

"Isn't Parks on that list?" I asked.

"Yes, but as of now I don't really suspect him. From what we found, he and Barnes are old college chums."

"He might know the other fellows, though," I said.

"Good point," said Schell.

"Maybe we should pay him a surprise visit. The police wouldn't have to catch wind of it, and we might be able to get a jump on the information we need from Parks. He's been a cinch for you to manipulate so far," I said and then stood very still, as if to make the slightest move might give away my hidden agenda.

Schell straightened up, having seen that all was in order with his tiny charges. When he turned to me, he said. "Not a bad idea. I'll go out there this afternoon."

"Perhaps I should go with you," I said.

"Don't worry, it won't be necessary. I know you have to catch up on your studying."

My mind was racing quickly to find a rejoinder that might make him reconsider. I was so frantically scheming I didn't, at first, notice the smile on his face. It wasn't his business smile, but a broad grin. When I finally noticed it, I gave up and laughed.

"Conning the con?" he asked.

I nodded. "I need to see Isabel," I said.

"Need?" said Schell, raising his eyebrows. "This girl has *you* conned."

"I'm a true believer," I said.

"Okay, we'll go. It isn't a bad idea to pump Parks for some information. I just want you to know one thing. Even though honesty is rarely the best policy, you can always tell me the truth."

"I know," I said, thinking about the fact that we still hadn't told him about the episode with the hat.

Three hours later, Schell and I sat before Parks, who was perched on his throne in the parlor, cigarette holder in hand. He'd been delighted that we'd come by to see him and had the guard send us right up to the mansion. Upon greeting us he patted Schell on the back as if he were an old friend and even shook my hand.

"Poor Barnes," said Parks, "I doubt he'll ever recover from this loss."

"As I understand it, they're burying the girl tomorrow," said Schell.

Parks closed his eyes. "Yes, I'll be there. I spent yesterday evening at the wake. Dreadful."

"I'd very much like to go, but I can't be seen at the funeral. I'm afraid the police would find out it was us who'd found the body. We'd then become suspects. I'd prefer if you didn't mention our involvement to anyone."

"So, it was you," said Parks. "I should have known that once you were on the case things would move more rapidly. Say no more." He waved his free hand. "I understand the dilemma. I'm just pleased I was able to put you in contact with Harold. If it wasn't for your special gifts, the police would still be looking for her."

"Ondoo and I are here for a specific purpose today," said Schell. "I've obtained a list of names from Barnes of everyone who visited his home in the last month before Charlotte's disappearance. I need to know whatever you know about them."

Parks was obviously pleased with himself as now being the man with the answers, and he showed it by swinging his legs. "I probably know them all," he said.

"The first is Stephen Trumball, do you know him?"

"Of course," said Parks. "He's . . ."

Schell held up his hand and said, "Excuse me for a moment. I just remembered that I'd intended to have Ondoo clear your house of any evil manifestations while we were here. As a favor, of course, for your having helped me to contact Barnes. Do you have any reservations about Ondoo walking the hallways of your house and blessing it?"

"None whatsoever," said Parks. "In fact, I'd appreciate it. Ever since the séance I've felt some ill sensations, cold breezes and so forth. I believe my wife has left some of her spirit behind. If your boy can whisk that away, I'd be delighted."

Parks smiled at me, and I smiled back, although his use of the phrase "your boy" rankled me. Schell was obviously opening a window for me to go and find Isabel, so whatever small complaint I had was swamped by gratitude. I put my hands together, like a Catholic in prayer, and slowly stood. Taking a step forward, I began gibbering my fake swami language, low and guttural, driving away the evil spirits before me. Parks's eyes were wide with an appreciation of the power I was employing on his behalf, and Schell wore his business smile. They watched me inch my way toward the door of the room. As I stepped out into the hallway, I heard Schell say, "This fellow, Trumball, what's he about?"

Once out in the hallway, I dropped my arms and quickened my pace. The Parks place was enormous, and I had no idea where Isabel might be. I surmised that Schell could buy me almost an hour, and that would have to be sufficient. It wasn't long before the opulence of the rooms and decor put me in a kind of trance. I met two maids in my travels, but neither of them was Isabel. I passed through a glassed-in patio with an indoor swimming pool, a vast ballroom, a kitchen big enough to hold supplies for an army. It seemed everything was made of gold or sterling silver, glittering quartz or smooth teak.

I'd searched for the better part of a half hour and was beginning to think that all of my elaborate scheming would go for nothing when I passed into a long hallway. There was Isabel at the opposite end on her knees, scrubbing the tiled floor with a brush. I was startled to finally find her, and for a moment I simply watched. At first, I noticed the graceful, purposeful manner with which she worked, leaning forward and employing the brush in hard, measured strokes, occasionally rinsing the brush in a pail of soapy water. Somewhere during my observation, my attention was distracted from the laudable scrub job she was doing to the curves of her body, and it was at that moment she looked up.

"Here to rescue me from my drudgery?" she said and smiled, sitting back on bent knees. She reached up with the back of her forearm and wiped the sweat off her brow.

"I needed to see you," I said.

She stood up, her expression growing serious, no doubt in reaction to mine. "Is something wrong?"

I nodded as I walked toward her. She dropped the brush into her pail and then lifted it by the handle. "Come," she said and waved me toward a door to her left. We entered a kind of anteroom, and then went through another door to an inner office furnished with a desk and bookcases, filing cabinets, and a separate table with a typewriter. She set the pail down beside the door, which she closed behind us.

"¿Qué pasa?" she said.

I wanted to tell her about the Barnes girl, but knew, in all fairness to Schell, that I couldn't. Instead I slowly put my arms around her. She didn't push me away but fell softly forward against me, and we kissed. This was no parting kiss to initiate a romance, as the last had been, but an urgent, passionate one. I had no idea what I was doing, but I was doing it with everything I had.

DEMONIC ESSENCE

I wanted to call you, but there was never the chance," said Isabel. As she spoke she stepped backward, pulling me along by the shoulders. She came to rest against the edge of the desk, and then hopped up to sit on top of it.

"We've got to find a way to be together without relying on the phone," I said as she hiked her skirt somewhat and lifted her legs to encircle my waist. We kissed again, this time for at least five minutes, and I felt her tongue enter my mouth. This was all wonderfully new to me. I could feel my temperature, among other things, rise.

"Do you have any days off?" I asked when our lips finally parted.

She reached her hand down between my legs and rubbed me through the gauzy material of my swami trousers. "El domingo, por la mañana, I walk to the church in Oyster Bay. Meet me there after the ten o'clock mass."

"I'll be there," I said and started kissing her again.

She pulled down the waistband of my trousers, releasing my swollen member, and said, "¿Quién es el encantadór de serpientes ahora?"

I brought my hand up to her breasts. My mind was reeling. At the same moment that I was frantically engaged, all the time I was thinking, I can't believe this is happening.

Then she pushed me gently back away from her, reached up under her dress, and drew her underpants down to her knees. "Take them," she said, none of her sly humor in her voice, only a genuine urgency. I pulled them down around her ankles and off over her shoes. With them still balled up in my hand, I moved back toward her, my own trousers at midthigh, my erection arching upward as if trying to escape my body. As I stepped up close, she opened her legs and began to lift her skirt, and then I stopped dead, for in my mind rose the image of the cloth covering the lower portion of Charlotte Barnes's body. I saw it clearly, and saw as plain as day the symbol that was emblazoned upon it.

My erection instantly wilted as the memory of the dead girl blossomed to fill my mind. There was no time for Isabel to complain, because just then came the sound of someone entering through the door from the hall to the anteroom. "Sunday," she whispered, leaped off the desk, ran around behind it, and ducked for cover. I lifted my trousers a mere moment before the door to the inner office opened. When I turned around, Schell and Parks were standing there, staring at me. I lifted my hand to straighten my turban and realized I was still holding Isabel's underpants.

"Gentlemen, you've found me," I said in a slightly shaky swami singsong.

"One of my people said she saw you heading toward this side of the house," said Parks. Both he and Schell looked expectant—Parks hopeful, Schell somewhat bemused.

"Find something there?" asked Schell, pointing to the balled-up contents of my hand.

"Most certainly, good sirs. I have discovered the culprit. Mr. Parks, when we were last here and brought forth the spirits, your mother left you a toy bear, but it seems your wife is more mischievous and left you her undergarment. No doubt a curse upon your house." I held up the offending article and let it unfurl. I noticed then for the first time that they were pink.

Parks gave a violent shudder. "The bitch," he said. "Even in death she taunts me."

"Good lord," said Schell, "I can't imagine the damage this item would have eventually done to you had it gone undiscovered."

"Excuse my language, please, Mr. Schell, but I feared her spirit was still out to do me in."

"You'll be all right for the time being, but we'd better schedule another séance in order to solve this problem once and for all. I believe we can effectively rid you of her demonic essence."

Parks nodded. "Please, I'd pay anything to get rid of her for good."

"To clear the entire house would be somewhat more expensive, but for a valued patron like yourself, we can make the price reasonable," said Schell.

I went to the desk and lifted a pen that stood upright in an elaborate inkstand. Hooking the pink curse upon one end of it, I walked forward and handed the other end to Parks. He took it but grimaced horribly and held the pen with the tips of only two fingers. "Revolting," he said and shuddered.

"Do not wait, but take them immediately to your closest fireplace and burn them. Then collect the ashes, mix them with chopped garlic, and bury them no less that three feet deep in the ground. This you must perform without the help of another," I said.

I saw the merest corner of Schell's dour expression crack, and he had to look away from me for a moment to collect himself. "Don't worry about us, Parks, we can show ourselves out," he said. "Best to see to the task at hand immediately."

The millionaire turned and headed out the door. "I owe you a great debt of gratitude. Call me as soon as you can to set up that appointment."

"Will do, sir," said Schell.

I waved my arm to indicate to Schell that he should exit first. He did. Then I followed. We walked back to the Cord in silence. I wasn't sure if Schell was amused by my antics or upset with me for playing so recklessly. Once we were in the car and had left the estate, I looked over at him. His body was jerking up and down as if he was quietly convulsing. Then I looked up at his face, saw a smile on it, and knew he was laughing. He shook his head.

"Diego," he said, "I might as well just turn the business over to you now."

"Did you see his face when I handed them to him?" I asked.

Schell pulled the car over, parked, and gave himself up to mirth. When he dried his eyes a minute later, he said, "Can you imagine what that poor woman had to deal with?"

"Thanks," I said to him.

"Yes, well, you're welcome, but let's keep our wits about us, shall we? I'd like you to proceed at a somewhat slower rate with this young lady."

"I know," I said.

"It wouldn't pay at your age to have to get married," he said, putting the car back in gear and pulling out onto the road.

The conversation was getting embarrassing, and then it came to me how to quickly change it. "I remembered the symbol from the cloth on the Barnes girl," I said.

Schell took the bait. "What was it?" he asked.

"A large circle, outlined in red. Inside it was a cross, equally dividing the circle, outlined in black. At the center of the cross was another circle all of white, and at the center of that circle a red teardrop."

WHY THE TEARDROP?

The day we went to see The Worm, the city wore a disguise of jangling excitement over its normally grim features of unemployment and destitution. On the previous afternoon, in Chicago, during the seventh inning of the World Series, score tied 4 to 4, Babe Ruth had come up to bat. There had been a season-long, bitter rivalry between the two clubs. Ruth was met by calls of derision from the opposing bullpen. His only reaction was to calmly lift his bat and use it to point out into the distance at something or someone only he could see. The pitch came from Charlie Root, and the Babe blasted a home run that broke the tie and gave the Yankees the momentum to win the game. The city's predominantly downtrodden inhabitants feasted on this feat of confidence, and we overheard people talking about it on the train, in the station, and on the streets. None of us, Antony, Schell, or I, cared much about baseball, but the feeling was infectious, and the entire city seemed to be swaggering.

Around the corner from the main branch of the New York Public Library, across the street and down an alleyway littered with ash cans and junk, was a plain metal door in the side of a brick building. Antony stepped forward, rapped twice, waited a second, rapped again three times, and then took a step back and joined Schell and me. The door squealed open a quarter of the way and a small, old woman with a nearly bald head covered in a hairnet, wearing a pair of thick-lensed glasses, appeared.

"What do you want?" she said in a nasty tone.

"Which way to Paradise?" asked Antony.

She opened the door wider and beckoned for us to enter. Her look of anger melted into a smile, and she said, "Get in here, Henry Bruhl."

Once we were standing inside a dimly lit foyer and the door had been closed and locked, Antony leaned over and kissed the woman's wrinkled cheek. She then turned to Schell and said, "How are you, Tom?"

"Pleasure to see you again, Grace," he said. He lifted her hand and kissed it.

"Still full of shit, I see," she said.

"At your service," said Schell.

She turned to me and eyed me up and down, focusing on my turban. "Who's this, Genghis Khan?" she asked, holding her hand out to me.

"This here is Ondoo," said Antony. "He's a swami."

"Halloween isn't till the end of the month," she said and grabbed my hand and squeezed it.

"Nice to meet you," I said.

"Is this your boy, Thomas?" she asked Schell.

He nodded.

"God help you," she said to me.

"We're looking for The Worm," said Antony.

"Well, you know, he's always either here or over at the library. You're in luck, 'cause he's back there right now, three sheets to the wind and diddling some Columbia professor's wallet."

"Thanks," said Schell.

"I'll bring you back a round of drinks," she said.

We left the foyer and walked down a dark hallway that ended in a short downward flight of steps. The place had obviously been the basement of an old warehouse; the bricks of the walls were crooked, and some had fused together over time. The stairs led to a large expanse crammed with tables and booths beneath a low ceiling of thick wooden timbers. There were candles on the tables and one electric light behind a makeshift bar made of sawhorses and old doors, covered with tablecloths. It was still early in the afternoon, and besides the bartender, who sat on a chair behind the bar, there were only three or four other customers.

I followed Antony and Schell toward one of the booths in the shadows of a rear corner of the room. As we drew closer, I could see the booth held two men sitting across from each other.

"Emmet," said Schell, "when you're done, we'd like to do some business."

The man he was addressing, whom I supposed was "The Worm," waved and said, "Hey, Tommy, give me another minute here." He had a bushy gray beard and wore a rumpled overcoat, tattered hat, and fingerless gloves, like some kind of hobo.

We waited while he finished talking to the other man, who was as neatly dressed as The Worm was slovenly. The fellow in the suit, tie, and small circular glasses finally stood up, reached into his pocket, and handed over a wad of bills to The Worm. Then he lifted his hat off the table, placed it on his head, and walked away.

"Okay, you guys, the shop is open," said the hobo.

Antony and I took the bench across the table from Schell and his odd acquaintance. I was introduced to the man and learned his name was Emmet Brogan. Schell gave him a brief run-down on my story, to which he nodded and said, "A swami, nice touch."

"How's New York these days?" asked Schell.

"Well," said Brogan, "they kicked Walker out at the start of last month. He's off in Europe spending all the money he bilked from the citizens of the fair metropolis. La Guardia's in. The usual ball of crap keeps spinning. Same old, same old."

"Has business been good?" asked Antony.

"Business is always good," said Brogan. "Information's more valuable than gold."

Grace appeared, carrying a tray, and set four drinks on the table. Schell handed her a bill, which she crumpled and stashed in her apron. "Drink up, boys," she said before retreating back into the shadows.

I took a sip from my glass, expecting it to be beer. Whatever it was lit a fire in my mouth and throat, and I coughed.

"Business is good, but the coffin varnish never gets any better," said Brogan, downing a sizable gulp.

"What is this?" I asked Antony.

"Bathtub gin," he said, taking a sip.

An image of the old lady, Grace, sitting in a tub of the stuff, came into my mind, and I couldn't shake it.

"Grain alcohol with a mixture of *special ingredients*, so to speak," said Brogan. "Drink enough of this shit and it'll make you go blind. I'm surprised I can still see."

"Two questions for you today," said Schell, turning to The Worm.

"I'll give you one for free," said Brogan. "I'm in a good mood 'cause the Yanks won."

"What's a dybbuk?" asked Schell.

"A dybbuk?" said Brogan. "Hold on a second." He sat as if thinking, staring into the distance. "Hey, Henry, you got a cigarette?" he said.

Antony took two from his pack, put both between his lips, and lit them. He handed one across the table. The Worm nodded his thanks, took a long drag , and went back to thinking.

While we waited, Schell tapped my arm to draw my attention. "Emmet's mind is like a camera. Whatever he reads, he can eventually remember like it's sitting right in front of him," he said.

"A dybbuk," said Brogan, obviously smiling with pride at Schell's description of his powers. "It's Jewish. Hebrew occult."

"Is it a ghost?" asked Antony.

"Not exactly," said Brogan. "I remember now. It's a kind of demon. When the spirit of a dead person, wicked, of course, enters and controls the body of a living person, you get a dybbuk. In the folklore, when this happens, the spirit's out to harm the living in some way."

"Jewish you said?" said Schell.

"Yeah, definitely," said Brogan.

Schell nodded. "Okay, here's the second question," he said. He looked at me. "Diego, do you have the drawing?"

I reached into my vest pocket and took out a square of paper. Unfolding it, I laid it on the table and smoothed down the creases. On it was the symbol I had rendered from my memory of the cloth draped over Charlotte Barnes. I pushed it across the table toward The Worm.

"Oh, I know this," he said. He tapped the paper with his index finger, and with his free hand lifted the glass to his mouth. "Yeah." He nodded to himself.

"I thought it might be religious," said Schell, "because of the crosses."

"You could say that," said Brogan. "This is from the Klan."

"What clan?" asked Antony.

"There's only one Klan," said Brogan. "The Ku Klux Klan."

"The Klan?" said Schell. "This came from out on the island."

"No shit," said The Worm. "The Klan was all over the island a few years back."

"I had no idea," said Schell.

"June 1923, over twenty-five-thousand people gathered in a huge field to hear the message of the Klan," said Brogan. "Guess where? We're not talking Alabama, we're not talking South Carolina or Mississippi."

Schell and Antony shook their heads.

"East Islip, Long Island," he said and slapped the tabletop.

"Sure, I did a whole workup on this stuff for a guy from the federal government a few years ago. One out of every seven or eight people on the island belonged. White hoods, burning crosses, the works."

"In my traveling show days down south, we heard about colored men being lynched by them," said Antony.

"This was a *new* type of Klan. They were still race haters, but they sold themselves to the populace on the platform of law and order. Imagine. There weren't enough colored people out there on the island for them to get that worked up about, so they kind of transferred their energy into hating the Catholics, the Jews, the immigrants. They were down on what they considered the dissolution of the white race by all of the foreigners coming into this country. And they were heavy supporters of Prohibition." Brogan lifted his glass, as if making a toast, and took a drink.

"What part of the island were they located in?" asked Schell.

"All over the damn place. They formed these little bands to guard the shoreline against bootleggers and would prevent them from landing. Shoot-outs, lot of violence there. White supremacy is what they've always been about, and that's basically what they're still about. Eventually, their own political infighting undercut their power. By the end of the twenties a lot of it disbanded, but I'm sure it's still there. There were times during their heyday, we're talking less than ten years ago, when they'd be allowed in churches and schools to give speeches, hoods and all. Lot of pastors were big supporters. Some shameful shit."

"That's a scary group," said Antony.

"Scary, yeah," said Brogan, "but mostly just a bunch of ignoramuses. There's guys a lot scarier than them out there."

"Who's that?" I asked.

"Guys with the same philosophy, but with real power, brains, and money. I hate to say it, my friend, but you'd be mincemeat with these bastards whether you were a swami or . . . where are you from, Guatemala? Mexico? Anyway, you'd be finished."

"Why the teardrop?" I asked.

"That's no teardrop, chum. That's a drop of blood. It's all in the blood. Their big fear is the mixing of the white race with, quote, unquote, inferior blood."

MURDER AT A PARTY

Schell paid The Worm, who thanked him kindly and used some of the money to order another round of drinks. I passed, my first still unfinished. For a few minutes, Schell and Brogan exchanged facts about butterflies, and then the conversation moved on to acquaintances and old times, and Antony jumped in. Before we left, Schell inquired as to a name, someone he could contact on Long Island who might have been or still was seriously involved with the Klan.

Emmet went through his usual thinking phase where you could envision him flipping through the stored pages in his mind. "Of the klaverns that haven't broken up, they've all pretty much gone underground. I remember reading about a guy who was a big deal with this mess. Stephen Andrews. He's an old guy, might be dead by now. He was out in Freeport. Check out this title he had—he was a Grand Exalted Cyclops. I suppose in the land of the blind, the one-eyed man is king. He might still be around. If he is, and he'll talk to you, you might be able to get some more out of him."

Antony, Schell, and I stood up, and Emmet slid over to the edge of the booth to shake each of our hands. "Great to see you guys again," he said.

"I may be back for some more," said Schell.

"If you need to get something quick, call the library and leave a message for me at the desk. They all know me."

Brogan bummed one more cigarette off Antony and then turned to me and said, "Listen, son, the future's in information. That's where the money and power are going to be. By the time your kids reach your age, they'll have machines that do what I do. And they'll be free. Only one problem."

"What will that be?" I asked.

He waved a hand in the air. "Don't worry about it. First we have to get through the next war."

We bid good-bye to Grace, who told us to come back and see her soon. Then we were out in the alley.

"Brogan's crazy as a loon," said Antony as we traced a path around the ash cans and junk.

"Yeah," said Schell. "He knows his facts, but when he starts to talk about the future, it's time to inquire as to how many of those piss gins he's consumed."

"I guess they call him The Worm because he's a bookworm?" I said.

"No, kid, they call him The Worm because he's a fucking worm," said Antony.

"What do you mean?"

"Can you imagine hanging around with that guy for any length of time? He's murder at a party."

"Emmet can't turn it off," said Schell. "The world to him is merely an accretion of facts. After a while, he burrows under your skin, and you just want him to shut up. Hence, The Worm."

"Does he live in a freight car or something?" I asked.

"He's got a place up on Park Avenue. Nice place," said Schell. "You wouldn't believe the people who hire him. The guy has dough."

"He dresses like a bum," I said.

"Life of the mind," said Antony.

After leaving Grace's Paradise, we went back to the station and caught the two o'clock train out to Port Washington. For the first part of the journey, no one spoke, but after Jamaica, Schell bent forward, resting his elbows on his knees, his hands clasped together, and said, "Why would the Klan want to kill Barnes's daughter?"

Antony and I sat there in silence, waiting for the answer.

"Well, if the Klan killed her," said Schell, "considering it was a group, and a group with a political agenda, no matter how screwed up, I'd say it would have to be either revenge for something or to make a statement. Otherwise, why leave a calling card? Obviously, the girl couldn't have done anything to warrant it."

"Does the mother's use of the term 'dybbuk' indicate that she's Jewish?" I asked.

"I'm wondering about that," said Schell. "Not necessarily, but it's a strong possibility."

"So maybe they killed the girl because she was half-Jewish?" I asked.

"Why, though? There's a good-size population of Jews on Long Island. Why pick this girl?" asked Schell.

"Emmet said they don't like the blood to mix," said Antony. "Maybe, like the kid said, it was because she was half-Jewish."

"But Barnes and his wife didn't seem really up-front about her being a Jew. I'd bet in that blueblood landscape he travels, that's not the best advertisement. If she is, most people don't know, so how would the Klan find out?"

"What do you want the guy to do, put an ad in the paper? Headline: 'My Wife's a Jew,'" said Antony.

Schell cocked his head to the side and vaguely nodded. "Good point. It just doesn't seem to make sense, though. From what Emmet said, it doesn't wash with the law-and-order façade of the Long Island Klan."

"There's one other thing," I said.

Schell looked over at me and sat up straight.

"The hat?" asked Antony.

I nodded.

"Okay, go ahead. We'd have to spill it sooner or later," he said.

"What hat?" asked Schell.

"Remember that hat I wore when I was Parks's mother?" asked Antony.

Schell nodded.

Even though he'd told me to relate the story, the big man jumped in and proceeded to lay out the entire adventure of the hat, our attempts to recover it, and our overall deceit. As much as I cringed as Schell told the tale, I was thankful to Antony for ending with the statement, "Don't blame the kid, Boss. I put him up to it."

"Deception seems to be the order of the day," said Schell, looking over at me.

"Sorry," I said.

"Make that two, Boss," said Antony. "I just didn't want you to think I was losing my professional edge."

Schell laughed. "Your professional edge?" he said.

"I didn't want you to think I'd try to do anything but a good job."

"Okay," said Schell, "let's move on before this slides into the mawkish. You've told me you lost the hat the night of the séance, then you went to retrieve it from the girl, and Diego lost it again when he was attacked by bootleggers on the beach. You two live an eventful life. But my question is, what does this have to do with the murder of Charlotte Barnes?"

"After that, the hat turned up again," I said.

"The kid saw it on a guy at the wheel of a car we passed on the drive when we were leaving the Barnes place the day we met Lydia Hush," said Antony.

"The same hat?" asked Schell.

"I think so," I said.

"I figured maybe Barnes was running a bootlegging operation, bringing booze in from Canada, and those guys in the car worked for him," Antony said.

"A guess," I whispered.

Schell took it all in and then answered me by saying, "No, no." He held his hand up. "That makes sense actually. So you two think the girl was murdered in revenge for her father's rum-running operation? That makes a lot more sense than a random kidnapping and murder. Emmet said the Klan are strident Prohibitionists."

"Seems a rather severe punishment," I said.

"I don't think making sense is their strong suit," said Antony.

"This means that we're going to have to pay a visit to the Exalted Cyclops," said Schell. "He might know if there's that kind of bad blood between Barnes and the Klan. When we get back to the house, Antony, I want you to get the Broomhandle out and get it ready."

"Boss, really, the Mauser?" said the big man. "Do we need the stock?"

"No, it's got to be concealed."

"What's the Broomhandle?" I asked.

"This old pistol," said Antony.

"A gun," I said. "I didn't know we had one."

"Oh, yeah," said Antony.

"Have you ever used it before?" I asked.

"Once," said Schell.

"Do we really need it? Guns make me nervous," I said.

"People who'd kill a little girl wouldn't think twice about offing two con men and a Mexican."

"You have a point there," said Antony.

"Just think, Mr. Cleopatra, if you hadn't lost that hat, we'd have never suspected this connection," said Schell.

"I try to do what I can," said Antony.

DOWN THE TOILET

The next day, using the simple means of a local phone book covering Freeport, we found the home of the Exalted Cyclops on the outskirts of that town. It was an unremarkable, one-story dwelling, painted brown, with a lawn and rosebushes, at the end of a cul-de-sac.

"I thought somebody so exalted would have a bigger place," said Antony as we drove past to give it the once-over. "I guess cyclopping doesn't pay a hell of a lot."

"That's probably him right there," I said, pointing to an old man, thin and slightly bent, heading slowly around the side of the house toward the backyard.

"Go back around," Schell said to Antony. "Diego, you and I'll find him. Antony, you wait a minute and set yourself up at the side of the house."

Antony nodded, turned the car around, and passed the place again. This time he pulled over to the curb ten yards beyond the edge of the property. We got out, closing the doors quietly. Schell and I took the lead, and the big man followed. We didn't head for the front door but strolled around to the backyard. The old man was there, sitting at a picnic table, smoking a cigarette. He didn't hear us approaching and only looked up at the last minute.

"What do you want?" he asked when he saw us. His head looked like a dried apple; his hair was an afterthought—a few strands blowing around in the breeze. Behind big glasses, his eyes shrunk down to slits, and he made a face like he was chewing glass.

"Mr. Andrews," said Schell. "I need to ask you a few questions concerning the Klan."

"Well," said the old man, "I'm not answering any questions, and I think you'd better get out of my yard."

"I'm afraid that won't do," said Schell, and he sat down across from him at the picnic table.

Andrews looked over at me and his eyes widened. "What the hell is that?" he asked Schell, pointing to me.

"Ondoo, spiritual savant of the subcontinent," said Schell.

"May the scales fall from your eye, my most exalted one," I said and gave a little bow.

"That's border nigger," said Andrews. The veins in his scrawny neck bulged and his hand shook.

"'Border nigger?'" said Schell. "Mr. Andrews, I have to inform you that Ondoo is considered a prince in the mystical realm."

"Listen, mister," said Andrews, launching his cigarette butt at Schell with a flick of his finger, "my boy is just inside that house, and if I call him, he's going to come out here and break your neck."

The cigarette hit Schell's shoulder and bounced off, dropping ash on his sleeve. Schell swiped the ash off himself and said, "Call him."

"Calvin," yelled Andrews.

"Yeah?" we heard from the kitchen window.

"Get out here, we've got trouble."

Two seconds later the screen door opened with a squeal and there appeared on the back steps a young man with a crew cut and a baseball bat. He wore a white T-shirt beneath which his muscles bulged. "What's wrong, Dad?" he said.

"Remove these two assholes from the yard," said Andrews with a smile.

"What the hell's this one?" asked Calvin, pointing the bat at me as if he was the Babe, indicating a home run.

"I'm not sure," said Andrews.

Calvin took a step toward me, and I backed up. Schell didn't need to call for Antony because he was already in the backyard.

"I brought my own," said Schell.

Calvin shifted his sights from me to focus on Antony. Andrews's son was big, but Antony dwarfed him. "Put down the bat, sonny," he said.

There was a tense moment or two, and then Calvin grunted and ran at Antony, cocking the bat over his shoulder. The big man went into a sort of half-assed crouch, and when Calvin swung, Antony came up with his left hand and caught the fat end of the bat in midswing, stopping it with seemingly little effort. The right fist followed, catching Calvin on the temple and dropping him to his knees. Then Antony lifted his own knee and caught his attacker directly under the jaw. The young man, blood leaking from his nose and mouth, fell backward, flat out on the grass and leaves.

The old man started to stand up, but Schell leaned across the table and pushed down on his shoulder, returning him to his seat. "Ready to talk, Mr. Andrews?" he said.

"Go to the devil. I've got nothing to say." He trembled with anger, and I thought for a moment he was going to keel over.

"Blow his brains out," Schell said to Antony.

The big man dropped down to his knees, straddling Calvin. From within his jacket, he drew the Mauser out of a shoulder holster, cocked the trigger, and lightly pressed the end of the long barrel against Calvin's closed right eyelid.

"Okay," said Andrews. "What do you want to know? Tell him to stop."

Schell held his hand up, and Antony pulled the gun back a few inches. I breathed a sigh of relief. This was a side of Schell and

Antony I'd never witnessed before. My stomach churned. I felt a little dizzy and walked over to take a seat next to Schell on the picnic bench.

"I need some information about the Klan," said Schell.

"You a cop or a reporter?" asked Andrews. He took a pack of cigarettes out of his sweater, his hand still shaking.

"Neither," said Schell. "And the information you give me stays with me."

"Okay, what do you want?" asked the old man, putting a cigarette to his lips. He brought up a silver lighter and sparked it.

"Back in the mid twenties, the Klan ran their own operations to stop bootleggers along the shore of Long Island."

Andrews blew smoke and nodded.

"You must have known who the money was behind the illegal imports," said Schell.

"Some of them," said Andrews. "We stopped a lot of it from coming in."

"Does the name Harold Barnes ring a bell?" asked Schell.

"Barnes," said the old man. "Yeah, Barnes and Parks. They had one of the biggest deals going. We tried to get the law on them, but they had too much money. We stopped their shipments more than once."

"Do you remember any particular vendetta against those two?"

"They were a couple of the worst. Some of my people got involved with some of their people in a shoot-out one night up by Matinecock Point. They killed a constable who was part of our organization."

"You know Barnes's daughter was recently kidnapped and killed?" said Schell.

"I read about it," said Andrews. "But look, Mr. . . . what's your name?"

"Forget the names," said Schell.

"What happened that night they killed one of our own happened a long time ago. That murder was avenged pretty quickly. It's all ancient history. You can't pin this girl's death on us."

"Did you know that there was a Klan symbol found with the girl's body?"

"You don't know what you're talking about," said Andrews. "That's impossible."

"So you say," said Schell.

"Whatever theory you've got cooking is bullshit, mister. The Klan's finished here on the island. Been finished for some time. You've got little groups here and there, glorified social clubs where the only thing burning is hot air. I'm not going to live much longer, and to tell you the truth, I don't mind. This country's going down the toilet. You've got all kinds of heathens mixing in here. The blood of our nation is corrupted to the point of being poisoned. That socialist dupe, FDR, is going to get into office, lift Prohibition, and then you'll see. Straight to the bottom."

Schell stood up. "Thanks for the hospitality, Mr. Andrews," he said. "It's been a pleasure."

"You better hope I never find out who you are," said the old man.

"I'm the Exalted Cyclops," said Antony, releasing the trigger of the gun. Calvin had come back to consciousness and was lying motionless, eyes wide with fear. The big man stood up, holstered the gun, and stepped away from him.

Once we were back in the car and driving away, Antony said, "Pleasant fella, that Andrews."

"You guys scared the hell out of me back there," I said. "I almost puked."

"There's all kinds of cons," said Schell.

"Do you believe him?" I asked.

"I think so, which means whoever killed Charlotte Barnes is working their own scam. We'll see."

THIS CASE IS CLOSED

After we'd gone to see Andrews, our pursuit of Charlotte Barnes's killer hit a stone wall. Schell judged the situation as still too hot to interview the other people on the list or go back to her father's estate to try to glean more clues, the Klan deal seemed to be a dead end, and Lydia Hush had melted like the snow queen she was.

Schell resumed his zombie act, drinking too much at night, and I tried to return to my studies. The days were beautiful and clear and the nights were long. All of our hours were underscored by the magisterial dirges the boss spun on his Victrola. Antony, proclaiming himself "bored shitless," fled to the city to spend two days with Vonda, the Rubber Lady.

On the morning he returned on the early train, he entered the kitchen and threw a folded newspaper onto the breakfast table so that it landed faceup, the headline showing. He took his coat off, hung it on the back of his chair, and said, "According to the cops, this case is closed." He tossed his hat onto the counter and headed for the stove.

Schell and I, who had been wearily sipping coffee, sat up and focused on the words—"Arrest Made in Barnes Case." The big man returned to the table and sat down with his cup.

"What's the dope?" asked Schell. "My eyes aren't awake enough to read yet."

"They picked up a guy, Frederick Kern, a hophead, connections to the Klan, a record of minor burglaries—one for assaulting an off-duty cop in a bar some years back. He's done some time, a couple of months here and there. The cops tell, I think for the first time, that the girl was found with that Klan rag. They say the cause of death was strangulation. The story they're telling is that Kern was a nut job on a lone mission to revive the local Klan. He picked on Barnes, because, as they put it in the article, back in the twenties it was falsely believed by the Klan that Barnes was behind a good deal of the rum-running on the North Shore. Of course, they go on to say that Barnes had been cleared of these false allegations a long time ago. I love what money can do."

"Do you buy it?" I asked.

Antony shook his head.

"Obviously a railroad job," said Schell. "No doubt Kern's a lowlife, probably not all that smart. They needed a quick arrest in this case, so they went through their files after finding out about the symbol, came up with this loser, and dragged him in. Case closed. Everybody looks good."

"I'd love for this to be over," said Antony, "but I have to agree with you, Boss. This reeks."

"Strangulation," said Schell. He looked over at me. "Do you remember any marks on the girl's neck when you found the body? There'd be bruises."

Now that some time had passed, I was able to think back to the image of the body without feeling I was going to get the dry heaves. I steeled myself and let the image come into my mind. "The light wasn't good," I said, "but what I remember is that she was very pale and that was it. No marks, no bruises."

"I don't remember marks around the neck," said Antony. "But like I told you before, I was in a hurry to get out of there."

"Maybe we could take that fed badge and papers I lifted off that guy a few years ago in Penn Station and put it to good use here," said Schell. "We go visit the coroner and tell him there's an investigation going on above the level of the local cops and see if we can get him to spill something. If he can prove to me she was strangled, I'll reconsider and drop the whole thing."

"Not a bad . . ." Antony started to speak, but at that instant the phone in the office next to the kitchen rang.

While Schell went to answer the phone, I asked Antony what Schell had meant when he'd referred to Penn Station.

"Oh, that," he said. "We were signed up to do a séance for this rich old hermit in the city. The guy's life was a real mystery, murder to find anything we could use when we did the job. Schell was desperate for information on the guy. We knew some people who could tell us a few things, but he'd paid them off really well or had scared them into keeping their mouths shut.

"Anyway, we decided we needed to pose as cops in order to get them to sing. We were in Penn Station talking about it, and right there, we spotted this guy. We knew he was a bull, undercover. I mean he was the flattest flatfoot you ever saw. Anyway, we worked out a plan. We passed by the guy, arguing. I pushed Schell, he bumped into the guy, apologized profusely, et cetera. The guy was going to say something but takes one look at me, and I give him my bear wrestling stare, and he lets it go. We walk away, and Schell, of course, has the guy's wallet. When we opened it later, we found out he wasn't a cop, though. He was a federal agent, FBI."

"What happened with the rich old hermit?" I asked.

"The fucking guy died before we could jerk his chain. If we were ever going to see him again, it would have to have been at someone else's séance."

"Have you used the FBI stuff since then?"

"No, it's not the kind of thing you want to play with if you don't have to. Posing as an agent carries a stiff sentence. If those guys catch wind of a scam, they'll find you by hook or by crook. We let it sit after that."

Schell came back into the kitchen. "Okay, gentlemen, let's move. Ten minutes, in the car. I've got a line on something good," he said. He'd already turned and started down the hall to his room to get dressed when I called after him, asking what it was.

"Lydia Hush," he called back.

No more than ten minutes later, Antony had the Cord rumbling at an idle, and Schell and I got in.

"Where to, Boss?" asked Antony.

"Head down toward Syosset," he said, "then take Berryhill Road to Eastwoods going west."

Once we were on our way, I asked Schell if he'd spoken to Lydia Hush.

"No, not her. It was Tremaine. He just got back from a stint in Philadelphia."

"Who's Tremaine?" I asked.

"Abel Tremaine, King of the Cold Readers," said Antony. "The guy's a real pro, smoother than a gin shit."

"He said he'd been meaning to call me for a while," said Schell, "but that it had slipped his mind, and then he had to take off for a job in Philly. Anyway, he just got back last night and he remembered. He said this guy in the business, Lester Brill, had called him a while ago and asked about us, wanted to know whether we could be trusted, etc. So Abel tells the guy he knows us and that we're trustworthy. Answers a few questions, you know, professional courtesy. Told him we had Diego working with us now and so on. You know how Tremaine likes to talk."

"So, you think this is how she found out about us?" asked Antony.

"More than likely," said Schell. "Tremaine said the guy told him he needed to check up on us because he was going to do a job with us. Later on, though, he realized that this guy is a lightweight, not bad for tea parties and rotary club gigs but not a real con. Then he started to thinking that it was highly unlikely we'd be working with him. By then, though, Tremaine was off to Philly, but he made a note to call us as soon as he got back in town just in case it wasn't on the up-and-up."

"Have you ever heard of him before?" I asked.

"No," said Schell. "You ever hear that name before?"

"Never heard of him, Boss," said Antony.

"We'll pay him a visit and find out why he's so interested in us," said Schell.

"I hope he doesn't have any kids who play baseball," said Antony.

The address Tremaine had given to Schell turned out to be the Immaculate Redeemer Nursing Home, a sprawling one-story building set back from the road among scrub pine. As we pulled into the parking lot, Schell said to Antony, "I don't think you have to worry about a repeat of yesterday's drama."

"I don't lean on cripples or feebs," said Antony. "That's where I draw the line."

"Admirable," said Schell.

As it turned out, Lester Brill wasn't a cripple or a feeb but a sharp-looking older gentleman with silver hair, a trim goatee, and a cane. We found him in a dayroom, playing cards with some of the other residents. When Schell introduced himself, Brill seemed to know immediately why we were there and excused himself from the game. He led us to his room and, once we were inside, closed the door. As he seated himself in a rocking chair, he waved his hand at the bed and invited Schell and me to sit down. "Sorry, Goliath," he said to Antony, "but I don't think my bed can handle the strain."

Antony nodded, folded his arms, and leaned his back against the door.

"Mr. Brill, you called Abel Tremaine and told him you'd be working with us and asked for information concerning our operation. Why?"

"I love this young man's getup," said Brill, pointing his cane at me. "I bet that disarms the marks."

"Who was it that wanted to know about us?" asked Schell.

"I remember Tremaine telling me stories of your exploits," he said to Schell. "You're quite famous in the community." Brill spoke calmly, smiling as he went on, as if we were all old friends, but no matter how many times Schell tried to move the conversation back to his main question, the old man went off in another direction.

Finally Schell switched tactics, and I was surprised by his approach. "Miss Hush, the young woman you were helping out," he said, "is in some very deep trouble." Brill's composure cracked ever so slightly, a line of worry forming on his brow. Still he continued to smile. Then Schell launched into a protracted description of the entire Barnes case and our involvement in it. I'd never before witnessed him reveal so much about our methods and secrets.

When he was done, he said, "I'm taking a very big chance telling you all of this, Mr. Brill, but I have a reason. Miss Hush's life could be at stake, and if you care anything for her, you'll want us to find her before the people who killed Barnes's daughter do."

The old man began rocking in the chair, tapping his cane on the floor. He looked out the window once and then back at Schell. "Her name is Morgan Shaw," he said. "I'm the one who concocted the moniker Lydia Hush for her."

"Very effective name," said Schell, and Antony seconded this affirmation, as did I.

"She works here a few days a week as an aide," he said. "We became friends and I taught her cold reading so that she could make some extra money for herself. She's gotten very good. An excellent student. Please, Mr. Schell, don't let any harm come to her. She's like a daughter to me."

"We'll watch out for her," said Schell.

"I'm sorry I dropped a dime on you and your friends here, but she was desperate to work those Barnes people, and she was worried you'd outclass her and she'd lose the job. She thought if she got the jump on you, had a little edge, you'd be convinced of her skill. Actually, I suggested the tactic to her when she told me Barnes was bringing you in on it."

"It wasn't a bad strategy," said Schell. "Can I trust you to keep our secrets?"

"I'll make you a deal," he said. "If you treat Morgan well, what you've told me will stay in this room. If anything happens to her, I'll sing like a nightingale to the press about how you tried to dupe Barnes in his time of tragedy."

"Fair enough," said Schell. "Now, where does she live?"

CABIN NUMBER SIX

Due west of Syosset was a tract of woods in a place called Muttontown. Brill told us all we had to do was continue on Eastwood for five miles and it would take us through the pines. Along that road, amid the trees, there were some old cabins that had at one time been summer places. Since the Depression had hit, the owner had begun renting out the few that were still in decent shape for a few dollars a month. Morgan Shaw, alias Lydia Hush, supposedly lived in one of those places. No running water, no electricity. As he explained, it was merely a roof over her head. She walked to work, and showered and ate when she could at the nursing home.

We found the half dozen or so old run-down structures, spread out over an area of about three acres and hidden beneath the deep shade of tall pines. Antony pulled the car off the road and in among the trees. We got out, and Schell motioned for us to follow him. He picked the first place we came to that had a trail of smoke issuing from its chimney, walked up to the front door, and knocked. A woman in a plain cotton shift answered. In her arms was a baby, and there were two other little kids standing behind her. She wore that blank, stunned expression that seemed to me to be the mask of poverty. I'd seen it in the city on men standing around a trash bar-

rel fire and in newspaper photos of whole families out west, trapped
in the Dust Bowl.

"Sorry to bother you, ma'am," said Schell, "but I am looking for
a young woman who lives in one of these cabins. Her name is Morgan Shaw. She's got long very blonde hair, almost white. Do you
know her?"

The woman stared for a moment as if she didn't understand. "I
might," she finally said. "Who wants to know?"

"Mr. Lincoln is inquiring," said Schell, and a five-dollar bill appeared in his hand.

I was somewhat put off by the crassness of this approach, playing on the woman's situation, but I'll admit it was successful. Her
eyes lit up, and she snatched the bill from his hand.

"Cabin number six," she said. "All the way in the back. The one
with the yellow curtain." She then shut the door, and I could hear
the lock bolt slide home.

"Five dollars must go a long way here," I said to Schell as he
started toward cabin six.

He looked somewhat sheepishly at me and said, "It all doesn't
have to be difficult, does it?"

I wasn't quite sure what he meant.

"You probably could have gotten away with three," said Antony.

A few minutes later, we stood in front of the cabin with the yellow curtain. Schell put his finger to his lips and motioned with his
hand for Antony to go around back in case she tried to escape that
way. Then he reached in his pocket and retrieved his key ring. Sin-
gling out the one long thin key with a tiny hook at the end, he held
the skeleton key up for me to see. He tossed the set to me and
pointed at the door. I knew what to do. He'd let me practice with the
key on the lock of the Bugatorium door since I was ten.

I worked the lock like a pro, and in a minute the door was open a
sliver. Schell grabbed me by the shoulder and pulled me away before I could enter. He pushed on the door, letting it swing slowly in-

ward. Only after he had looked around the interior of the cabin did he step over the threshold. "Okay," he said to me and waved me in.

The place was tiny, barely enough room for a bed, a little wood-burning stove, a chair, and a desk. There were no closets, and who-ever lived there, I supposed it was Lydia/Morgan, appeared to store her things in cardboard boxes. Even though the one window over the bed let in some light, it was still dim and somewhat dank as well, smelling of mold and the pine scent of the trees outside. There was a tattered, well-worn old rug, rumpled and lying askew on the floor, bearing a faded maroon and green floral design. Two candles in old-fashioned copper holders sat on either side, and a hurricane lamp rested on the floor between the end of the bed and the desk. A small anemic-looking plant grew in a clay pot on the windowsill.

"A tidy little ship," said Antony from the doorway, having just come around from the rear of the cabin after finding no evidence of Lydia/Morgan.

"This place reminds me too much of the shack we found Char-lotte Barnes in," I said.

"Yeah," said Antony, "I know what you mean."

"Well, perish the thought, gentlemen," said Schell, "because I think our best bet of finding Miss Shaw will be to stake this place out. We might be here for a while."

"Boss, I better go hide the car," said Antony. "She knows it, and if she sees it, she'll run."

"Good idea," said Schell.

After Antony left, I took a seat on the desk chair and Schell set-tled down on the bed, the springs of which squealed unmercifully beneath his weight. "The yellow curtains are a nice touch," he said.

I nodded. We sat in silence, and I listened to the sound of the wind quietly whistling through a small crack in the corner of the window, the boughs of the trees outside creaking. I could imagine how cold and lonely it must get there late at night and began to feel a measure of sympathy for our quarry. It also struck me, as I looked around, just how well Schell had provided for me from the time I had first come to stay with him.

Antony returned after a few minutes and closed the door behind him. Seeing Schell on the bed, he turned to me and pointed his thumb over his shoulder, evicting me from the only other seat. "Curtain call, junior," he said. I got up and sat on the floor in the middle of the musty rug, crossing my legs Indian style. As Antony eased into the chair, I told him I hoped the legs broke.

"You look like a real swami now," he said.

Schell looked over and smiled vacantly, then turned his gaze back out the window. He had a silver dollar in his left hand that he was rolling across his knuckles from pinky to thumb and back again.

"One thing I want to know," said Antony, "is what we are going to call Lydia Hush now. I'm confused."

"We'll ask her what she prefers when she shows up," said Schell.

That was the last thing any of us said for a long time. An hour, passed, and eventually I lay down on my side and used my turban as a makeshift pillow. Closing my eyes, I was heading for a catnap when I heard something odd, something very faint below the whisper of the wind and the soughing of the branches. It was slow and regular, like the sound of someone breathing. I sat up and looked over at Antony but soon realized that the noise wasn't coming from him, nor was it coming from Schell.

"Have a bad dream?" asked Antony, who sat leaning back in the chair with his hat pulled down over his eyes.

I lay back on the floor, and after a moment or two heard the rhythmic sound again. This time I could place it. There was something or someone under the rug. I got slowly to my feet and kicked Antony in the bottom of his shoe. He sat up and looked at me, was about to speak, but I motioned for him to be quiet. Schell turned around, and I put my finger to my lips. With my other hand, I pointed at the floor. He gave me a quizzical look, so I walked over to him and whispered in his ear, "There's someone under the floor. I heard them breathing."

Schell stood up. Antony was already on his feet. I stepped off the rug, and each of them leaned over and took a corner. They folded it back to reveal the outline of a small trapdoor. At the midway point, along the edge on the left-hand side, was a brass ring handle sunk into a small recessed metal square that lay even with the level of the floor. Schell moved around the folded rug, crouched down, and pulled on the handle. As the trapdoor opened, Antony and I stepped closer to look in.

There, in a four-foot-by-four-foot square shallow depression in the ground, lay Lydia Hush. A blanket covered the bare dirt beneath her, and she rested on her side, her knees gathered up close to her chest, her head bent forward so that her chin touched her knees. She wore nothing but a man's flannel shirt. The paleness of her long legs and the brightness of her hair seemed to glow in the dark hole.

"Okay, Miss Hush, or should I say, Miss Shaw, come on out of there," said Schell.

Her eyes opened. She turned her head to look up at us, and she smiled. "Gentlemen," she said.

Schell reached a hand down to her. She grasped it and with a little maneuvering managed to stand up. Antony went over to the bed and stripped the cover off. As she emerged from underground, stepping up into the light, he draped the quilt around her as if she were royalty preparing for a procession. She thanked him and then stepped over to the chair and sat down. After I had closed the trapdoor and replaced the rug, we stood around her like three children waiting to hear a story.

"Perhaps we should start at the beginning," said Schell.

Morgan Shaw's bottom lip began to tremble and tears formed at the corners of her eyes.

NOTHING TO HIDE

Schell handed her his handkerchief, and we stood by while she vented her sorrow. Antony looked like he was on the verge of tears himself by the time she finally stopped crying and began to dry her eyes.

"I'm sorry," she said. "It's just that things have been so hard lately. I'm scared."

"You've got nothing to be frightened of with us," said Schell.

"They're after me," she said.

"Who's after you?" I asked.

"I don't know, but since the Barnes thing, some men have been after me. They've come here, looking for me. I live so far back from the road, I can hear when someone's coming and I hide."

"How many times have they been here?" asked Schell.

"Three times," she said. "I thought you were them."

"What do they want?"

"I don't know," she said, shaking her head.

"If you don't mind my asking," said Antony, "how do you manage to get in the floor and have the rug lie down on top of the secret door?"

"Oh, I worked that out a while ago," she said. "I figured out a way to roll the rug back halfway and lightly tuck it under the edge.

I only open the door enough to just about slip in, and when I let it fall back down, the impact loosens the rug and it rolls down flat."

"Ingenious," said Schell. "But now let's get to the real question. How did you know where the Barnes girl would be?"

"Yes, the real question," she said. Even wrapped in that blanket with her hair a tangle from having been under the floor, she was beautiful. She turned to Antony and put her first two fingers up to her lips.

The big man reached into his jacket pocket and took out his cigarettes. With a flick of his wrist, one slid a quarter of the way out of the pack. She took it, put it in her mouth, and he had the lighter ready. She took a drag, flicked an ash onto the floor, and said to Schell, "You don't know the half of it."

"I'll settle for any part of it," he said.

"Charlotte Barnes wasn't the first child killed," she said. "Two years ago there was a little boy down in Amityville who was found murdered too. You can check it out with the newspapers, but it wasn't on page one. In fact it wasn't even on page three. It was buried back in the paper, in a tiny little article. The kid's father was a Negro, so he was picked up and charged with the murder. I don't think he was guilty. It was at that time that I got the first note."

"About the murder?" asked Schell.

"Not the murder but where the body was going to be. I had just moved into this dump, after leaving the city. I was here no more than two weeks when, one night, I heard someone moving around outside the cabin. I can't tell you how scared I was. From then on, I slept with a butcher knife I stole from the kitchen at the nursing home.

"I asked my neighbor if she ever heard strange noises at night. She told me it was probably just deer—but deer don't leave bouquets of wildflowers on your doorstep now do they? Sometimes I'd find flowers, or little broken toys or pennies. It was bizarre. I couldn't go to the police because there were certain people from my past who I didn't want to find me. Then one morning, I found a piece of paper with a scrawled map on it and some words. The words made no sense, but the map had a crude picture of an old house, busted windows, door hanging off, and a three-digit number written with two backward numeral. Okay, just strange, right?

"About a week later, I was at the nursing home, having my lunch, and reading the paper. I was reading about this kid who'd been kidnapped in Amityville. They'd found his body in an abandoned house, and they gave the address. The three-digit number was the same as on the map that had been left."

Antony whistled.

"There's more," she said. "There was another kid earlier this year from out east on the island. Her parents were migrant workers, you know, for the potato farms out in Patchogue. Again, nothing much was made of it. I forget who took the rap for that one, but I knew where they were going to find her before they did."

"The same happened with the Barnes girl?" asked Schell.

"When Charlotte Barnes went missing, I knew it wasn't just an isolated thing. I might have been the only other person who knew besides the killer, because the cops sure weren't onto it. I'd been learning the cold reading from Lester, and I thought that maybe I could save the Barneses a little grief by showing them where their daughter was and test out my skills . . ."

"And make some money in the deal," said Schell.

"You, of all people, aren't going to give me the holier-than-thou line now are you?" she asked.

Schell shook his head.

"You can see where I'm living; I needed the dough, and they needed to find their girl. Lester taught me well, because I was able to convince both of them that I had the gift. When you gentlemen came on the scene, you presented me with a chance to lead them to the body and not have to be involved if there was an investigation."

"You buy that, Boss?" asked Antony.

"It's kind of far-fetched," said Schell.

"I don't care if you believe me or not. I've got nothing to hide," she said.

"Well, you're a better con than I gave you credit for," said Schell.

"That whole wifty act was part of my Lydia Hush routine," she said. "I don't want to go into what I was involved in when I was in the city, but I know how to string someone along."

"How do I know you're not lying to me now?" said Schell.

"Look, I admit I played them, but at the same time, I felt for those people and their kid."

"We have to figure out who's leaving you these messages," said Antony.

"That's the thing," she said. "There was a new one two nights ago. Let me get it." She turned around to the desk, leaned over to open the bottom drawer, and pulled out an envelope. Swiveling back around, she pulled a folded piece of paper from within it. As the paper came forth dried flower petals drifted to the floor. "This one's different from the others. It's just a map," she said, "and you can make out some of the road names, even though there are some letters backward and missing. It's also got a picture of a big house, but nothing about whether it's a boy or girl this time."

"May I?" asked Schell. He looked at it. "Antony," he said, "do you have a map in the car?"

"I'm on it, Boss," said the big man, already heading for the door.

"Now, gentlemen, I want you two to go outside for a minute while I get changed."

"You won't disappear on us again, will you?" asked Schell.

"Where am I going to go, up the chimney?"

Schell and I stepped outside and closed the door behind us. By then it was late afternoon, and it was starting to get cold. Leaves from the occasional oak tree fell here and there.

"I believe her," I said.

"I do too," said Schell. "For some reason it's hard not to."

"Obviously, whoever is leaving her the notes must know her," I said.

"Or know about her," said Schell. "She referred to her time in the city. I can imagine what that was about."

"What do you mean?"

"Forget it," he said.

A few minutes passed and then the door opened and she called to us. She had dressed in a gray skirt and jacket, a violet blouse, and simple, flat shoes. Her hair was pulled back, and she reminded me of a librarian. As we traipsed back into the cabin, Antony returned, and I held the door for him.

"Let's see your note," the big man said to Morgan, and she handed it to him.

He sat down at the desk, opened the map from the car, and spread it out in front of him. Then he pulled one of the candle-holders close, and lit the wick with his cigarette lighter. A warm glow rose in a small circle around him, and he carefully laid Morgan's note next to the larger map. Out came the cheaters. He ceremoniously positioned them on the bridge of his nose and affixed them behind his ears. Schell and I each leaned over a shoulder.

It took Antony a long time to figure out what part of the island he should be looking at. He'd crane his neck forward, so that it was almost touching the paper, and then back away a little and squint. He'd follow the line of a road with his big thick finger and then retract the finger and say, "That's not it."

Fifteen minutes later, all of us having grown weary of waiting, we were spread around the room, leaning against the walls. "Oh shit," he finally said, and Schell moved across the room toward him. "What is it?" he asked.

"You're never going to believe this, Boss. But if I'm not mistaken, this drawing would lead you up by the sound."

"What area?" I asked.

"Forget area," said Antony, whipping off the cheaters. "Straight to Parks's place."

KILL THE LIGHT

If there was one thing that Schell couldn't stomach, it was fast, reckless driving, and, when called upon, Antony was a master practitioner. As his foot increased its pressure on the gas peddle, a steady string of foul language issued from his mouth, increasing in intensity as the Cord picked up speed. He cursed the other vehicles, the bumps in the road, the twilight. As scared as I was, I wanted him to go even faster, as my thoughts were consumed with Isabel's safety.

The boss sat in the back with Morgan Shaw, and I sat up front, my fingers dug into the cushion. Although there were times when I wanted to close my eyes, they remained open, as if welded so, out of morbid curiosity, not wanting to miss the tree or car that would ultimately be our end.

We arrived at the front gate sometime after seven. The headlamps showed the guard's booth to be empty. Schell and I got out of the car and walked up to the gate. There was no one in sight, but Schell called out, "Hello?" It was then that I saw something lying on the ground, only partially visible, behind the guard booth.

"There," I said to Schell and pointed to the body.

He took a quick look and called for Antony. The big man got out of the car, followed by Morgan.

"You're going to have to be a ladder for Diego here," said Schell. "Let him get on your shoulders."

I looked up at the top of the gate, which was at least nine feet high, and inspected the tips of its pointed bars. The thought of scaling it made me weak in the knees. "I don't know if I can do this," I said.

"Come on, kid, climb aboard," said Antony as he crouched down to make it easier for me to step up onto his shoulders.

I hesitated, and in that moment, Morgan had slipped off her shoes and was lifting a leg high to get a foothold on Antony's left shoulder. He reached up and took her small hands in his giant mitts. Clasping them tightly, he slowly stood. Morgan settled her other foot on his right shoulder as they rose.

"We oughta join the circus," said Antony as he moved closer to the gate.

She had to stand on her toes to reach the base of the spikes above the last crossbar. I doubted whether she would have the strength to pull herself up, but once she called Antony off and he stepped away, I could see her arms tense, and though they were thin, you could easily make out their long cablelike muscles.

"Good God, watch those spikes, Morgan," said Schell.

"Thanks," she said as she pulled herself straight up, and swung a leg out to the side to rest her toes on the crossbar. Once she managed to get a foothold, she made the rest seem easy. I looked over at Schell, and his mouth was agape as she lowered herself, hand over hand, to the ground.

"Get the keys off the guard," I said, but she was already at the task.

In less than a minute, she had opened the gate. Antony and Schell each took a side and pushed it back enough so that the car could pass through. I went to check on the guard to see if he was still alive. As soon as I crouched down next to him, I sensed something was terribly amiss. I had reached for his wrist to find a pulse and then suddenly became aware that, although he was lying on his back, his head was turned facedown. Calling to the others, I stood and stepped slowly away from the corpse.

"Broken neck," said Schell.

Morgan grunted, turning away from the sight. "I never even noticed."

"Somebody'd have to be pretty strong to do that," said Antony.

"Do we go on, or turn back and call the police?" asked Schell.

"I've got to go to the house," I said. "Isabel's in there."

Schell didn't hesitate. "Okay, let's go," he said.

We piled back into the car, Antony started it, and we cruised slowly up the drive. There were no lights on in the mansion, and the grounds were pitch-black.

After parking, we made our way up the steps to the front door, which we discovered was slightly ajar. Antony took out his lighter and flicked it on. The flame came up and offered a little respite from the darkness, illuminating an area of only about four feet around our huddled group.

"Let's head for the parlor," said Schell.

Antony nearly tripped over the butler in the foyer. When he held the lighter close to the body, it became evident that the man had been strangled. His eyes were huge, his tongue hung from the side of his mouth, and there were angry black-and-blue marks around this throat. Schell knelt and checked the man's pulse. "Forget it," he said.

Everything was happening so fast, and I was at least partially in shock from the sight of the bodies. Every second, I expected someone to leap out of the darkness and wrap their fingers around my throat. As we inched forward into the shadows, I tried to clear my mind enough to think what part of the house Isabel might be in.

We stumbled through the dining room, and it was there Morgan spotted two candles, which she appropriated. Antony lit them and gave his lighter a rest. Schell took one and gave me the other.

"I think the servants' quarters are on the other side of the house," he said. "You'd better go and find Isabel. Antony, go with him."

"Don't know if we should split up, Boss," said the big man.

"Time could be important," said Schell. "Miss Shaw and I will see if we can locate Parks in that parlor where we always met with him. We'll be careful, and believe me, if we need you, you'll hear me scream."

Antony shook his head, still unhappy with the arrangement. I didn't think it was such a great idea myself, but I knew Schell was right. In the time we would spend trying to find Parks, something could be happening to Isabel. We moved through the dining room and came to a main hallway that connected the eastern and western sides of the mansion.

As Antony and I were inching along, listening for sounds of an intruder, he whispered to me, "I'll bet you wish I'd brought the gun."

"From here on out, I'll never try to dissuade you from carrying the gun," I said.

Passing through the indoor swimming pool area, the candlelight reflected off the water and the large glass panes of the floor-to-ceiling windows, creating a dazzling display. Beyond that, the ballroom was a vast, echoing box of blackness. Eventually we came to the hallway that held the door to the room in which Isabel and I'd had our tryst. We'd taken no more than two steps down that corridor when I thought I heard something at the other end.

Lowering the candle so that my vision would not be disturbed by the glare of the flame, I peered into the shadows.

"Did you hear a noise down there?" asked Antony.

"Yeah," I said, and as I spoke, I caught sight of something moving, like a blur. It darted from one side of the hall to the other. I stopped, and Antony walked into me. "There's something down there," I said.

"Kill the light," he said, and when I was too slow to carry out his order, he leaned over my shoulder and blew out the flame.

Smoke rose up in front of me, and for a second that's all I could see, but when that cleared, I saw it again—a white form, like a ghost. It leaped across the hall.

"Shit, I see it," he said. "What the hell is that?"

Next thing I knew, it was moving toward me at an incredible rate, as if flying just above the ground. I was going to warn Antony, but before I could get the words out, a very material fist struck me square in the face and sent me sprawling sideways against the wall. I dropped the candle and very nearly passed out from the blow but held on, teetering in a crouch halfway between standing and falling.

I blinked once, twice, to clear my vision, and when I could see straight again, what I saw was Antony's shadow wrestling with the white form. They moved from one side of the hall to the other, banging into the walls, and the sound of the big man's grunts was interspersed with those of fists hitting their marks.

My eyes began to adjust to the darkness in time to see Antony's silhouette cock back its right hand and land a haymaker directly into what should have been the phantom's head. The white form was driven back by the blow, but it seemed unhurt as it sprang forward again. Some small object hit me in the chest.

"Kid, the lighter. Find the candle and . . ."

I dove down and scrabbled on the floor to find the lighter. When I sparked it, I noticed the figure had its hands around the big man's throat. I wanted to believe it was just a man, but I wasn't convinced. It was nearly as tall as Antony, pure white, and disfigured in some way I couldn't focus enough to discern. The two were ever moving in and out of the glow from the lighter's flame, and I couldn't get a clear view for more than half a second at a time.

Antony was trying to say something to me, but his words came forth as a kind of gurgling, and judging from the position of the shadowed figures I could tell the thing was strangling him. I forgot my search for the candle, leaped up behind the phantom, and set the flame of the lighter against its back. There followed a high-pitched squeal, like the cry of a wounded animal, and then its elbow shot back and caught me in the chest. I was knocked off my feet by the incredible force of the impact and lay gasping for breath.

I lost consciousness for no more than a few seconds, and when I came to, I managed to prop myself up on my elbow and again flick the lighter to life. Just then another form appeared in a frantic whirl from behind the phantom, who had Antony up against the wall and was obviously wringing his neck. This new presence lifted something high in the air and brought it down on the head of the attacker. There was a dull thud. The phantom dropped its arms, staggered back, and Antony recovered enough to lash out with a right and then a left, landing two punches, either one of which would have put a normal man in the hospital. The thing retreated, turned, and ran into the darkness at the other end of the hall. A moment later there was a sound of glass shattering, and without turning to look, I knew the phantom had smashed through the window at the end of the hall in order to escape.

"Fuck," I heard Antony say in a hoarse whisper. "Kid, you still alive?"

Then there was a hand holding the candle up to the flame of the lighter that was still lit in my hand. I turned and saw Isabel's face. She was leaning down to kiss me.

TALK TO ME

Isabel and I had to help Antony along for a good part of the journey to the opposite side of the mansion. I got under one arm, she got under the other, and I know he must have been in pain and perhaps dizzy, because there were times when it felt like he was bearing down on us with his full weight. I wanted to know how he felt but didn't want to ask, as every time he tried to speak it came out as a rasping cough. Eventually, he let go of us, straightened up, and croaked, "Okay." Still he moved slowly, and we had to wait up for him.

We finally saw light ahead, emanating from the parlor where we'd had our initial meetings with Parks. I called out for Schell as we approached the room. He came to the door, holding the candle, and waved us on. As we entered, he said to me, "Parks is dead."

"How?" I asked, trying to see into the shadows beyond the bubble of the combined candlelight.

Morgan Shaw appeared behind Schell like a specter of some kind herself, her face and hair aglow. "Horrible," she said with an anguished expression.

"It looks like someone drove their thumbs into his eyes. His face is a bloody mess; empty eye sockets. There's nothing we can do here," said Schell.

Antony sidled past Isabel and me. "Boss," he said in a harsh whisper, "we've gotta scram."

"Yeah," said Schell, and then the sound of Antony's voice registered, and he looked up at the big man's face. "What the hell happened to you?"

"We ran into the killer," I said. "I'll tell you in the car. Let's go."

Schell's gaze remained locked on Antony for a moment as he addressed Isabel. "Listen, the butler and the guard are already dead, are there any others still in the house?"

"No," she said, shaking her head. "The other maids live in town. They go home at night." For the first time since she'd rescued Antony and me, there were tears in her eyes. Her bottom lip trembled, and I put my arm around her.

"Go," said Schell. Finding our way by the light of the candles, we moved quickly toward the front of the mansion with Isabel leading the way and Antony bringing up the rear.

It was a great relief to finally stand outside in the cool night air where there were no dark corners to conceal murderous things. I took a few deep breaths while waiting for Antony to catch up. When we got to the car, the big man handed the keys to Schell and waited for Morgan, Isabel, and me to squeeze into the backseat. As soon as the Cord was running, Schell put it in gear and took off, driving as fast as he could bear, down the long driveway. We passed the dead guard, lying next to his booth, and two minutes later were out on the road, making for home.

Schell eased off the gas once we had escaped the grounds of the estate. "Talk to me," he said.

I filled him in on our meeting with the phantom, describing as best I could the look of it, the way it moved and its strength. When I was done, Antony, who'd been resting with his eyes closed, sat forward and said, still having trouble speaking in a normal tone, "Whatever he is, this guy's strong, like an animal. I hit him with shots that could crack stone, and he just kept coming. If it wasn't for Isabel here, me and junior would have been up shit creek."

"Can you tell us what happened?" Schell asked her.

"It had been dark outside for only a little while. Then, suddenly, all the lights went out. I left my room and went to find Mr. Parks to see if he needed my help. I found him in the parlor. He'd lit a candle and was sitting at his desk, looking at something. 'The phone line is dead too,' he said to me when I came into the room. I asked him if he wanted me to get Mr. Quigley, the butler, but he said not to worry about it, he'd find him in a few minutes.

"I was heading back to my room, when something passed me in the hallway—like a ghost. I ran back to warn Mr. Parks something was in the house. When I got to the parlor entrance, he was fighting the thing. It had his head in both its hands. Mr. Parks saw me at the doorway and yelled for me to run. As I ran, I heard him screaming for his mother, and I knew he was dying. I hid, and the fantasmo was trying to find me. Then I heard Diego's voice in the hall, came out, and saw them fighting with it. I went to help."

"The police are going to be looking for you," said Schell. "First they'll be looking for your body, and when they don't find it, they'll be looking for you. You and Morgan had both better stay at my place for the time being."

Schell's proposal was met with silence, and eventually he said, "Okay, that's settled."

"Did the killer leave anything behind in the parlor?" asked Antony.

"No," said Schell, "but I took a framed photo that was sitting in the middle of Parks's desk. His body was slumped on top of it. It may or may not be important."

"He was looking at that picture earlier," said Isabel. "I brought him tea in the late afternoon, y el sujataba esa foto, mientras charlaba por teléfono. Later, when I went to tell him dinner was ready, he was still on the phone, still looking at the picture."

"Here," said Morgan and held up the picture I hadn't been aware she'd been carrying. In the thick shadows of the backseat, I could barely make out the scene. It looked like a group of people standing in a black rain. Then a car passed us, and the fleeting illumination from its headlamps revealed the precipitation in the photo to actually be blood splattered on the glass of the frame.

"Who are they?" I asked Schell.

"Well," he said, "Parks is one of them. Who the rest are, I don't know. It could very well have nothing to do with the killing. What we can be relatively certain of is that the person who offed Parks is the same person responsible for the deaths of Charlotte Barnes and the other children."

"The same person who left me the notes," said Morgan.

"Yeah," said Schell. "There's something going on here, and it's got nothing to do with ghosts."

Schell's statement put a cap on the conversation, everyone no doubt mulling some piece of the puzzle or, as in my case, wondering what in God's name it was that Antony had done battle with. Ghosts may not have been a part of it, but this creature seemed far worse than any airy spirit. I was reminded of The Worm's definition of the dybbuk.

After a while, there came a sound from somewhere in the car. At first I thought it was Antony, moaning slightly from his wounds. Eventually, though, it became clear that someone was humming. The moment I realized it was Morgan Shaw, who was sitting to my right, she broke into song—a subdued, sleepy version of "Wrap Your Troubles in Dreams."

I noticed Schell turn his attention from the road and give a quick glance into the backseat. His face was lined with consternation and his brow was furrowed. Antony turned profile then too, and I saw Schell flash a quick glimpse at him and give a brief elevation of the eyebrows, as if to say, What the hell is this? Antony gave a slight shrug, and his face broke into a smile. I'm not sure whether Morgan saw their reactions, but either way she continued unfazed, carrying on to the end with genuine feeling.

Isabel, who had rested her head on my left shoulder, put her lips to my ear and whipered, "La señora blanca está loca." Her hand was in mine, and I gave it a squeeze to indicate my agreement. When the last line of the song had come and gone, there was an awkward silence, which was eventually broken by Schell.

"Nicely done, Miss Shaw," he said.

"Thank you, Mr. Schell," she said and then leaned back and closed her eyes.

When we got within a half mile of the house, Schell turned off the headlamps and slowed down to see if we were being followed. We hadn't seen another car for quite a while. He pulled into the drive and around the back, hiding the car from the road.

CHANGE

Once we were in the house, Schell drew me aside and said, "You let Isabel have your room, and I'll give mine to Morgan. I'll sleep in the living room, and you can take the couch in the Bugatorium. When the girl gets situated, come and see me."

I nodded and took Isabel down the hall to my room.

"Are you tired?" I asked her. From the look on her face I could tell she was exhausted.

"Yes, but I don't know if I'll be able to sleep," she said. "Everything is too strange."

"You'll be safe here," I said, pushing open the door to my room. "No one knows where you are."

She swept the strands of hair that had come loose from her braid out of her eyes and nodded. I realized that she had nothing to wear to bed, so I went to my closet and took out one of my undershirts and my first pair of swami trousers, which I'd recently outgrown. She thanked me and laid the clothes on the end of the bed. As I turned to go, she put her hand on my shoulder and pulled me back. We kissed, briefly.

"Come see me later," she said.

"If I can," I said.

"Promise," she said.

I nodded and closed the door behind me as I left.

Antony, Morgan, and Schell were in the Bugatorium, sitting around the coffee table. In the lighted room, it was easy to now see the bruises on the big man's neck and a welt on his left cheek. Schell must have been feeling badly for him, since Antony, in addition to drinking whiskey from a beer glass filled to the brim, was also smoking a cigarette. He had his jacket off and his shirt open halfway.

Schell was holding a glass of wine, and Morgan had a teacup on a saucer in front of her. They'd been discussing something when I came in, and as soon as they saw me enter, the conversation died. The butterflies were in a turmoil that night, swirling and swarming, a frantic storm of movement that was a metaphor for what was going on behind my eyes. Schell waved me over.

"Diego, take a seat," he said.

I did, opposite him.

"We have to talk about Isabel. I'm afraid she's in quite a bad situation. I started to mention it in the car, but I wasn't exactly sure how to proceed, and I thought I'd run it by you first to see if there was something you could add or that I was missing. The main thing is, the police are going to want to know what happened to her."

My mind wasn't working too well, what with everything we'd been through. "Should we take her to them tomorrow?" I asked.

"I wouldn't," said Antony.

"If we take her in, that implicates us, which isn't good for any of us, because if they start digging, they're going to find that we were all working for Barnes," said Schell. "Honestly, if I thought it would help her, I might be persuaded to do that. But if she shows up, she's going to be a suspect. Now, I don't think the D.A. could possibly make a case that she did to those men what happened to them."

"She's not strong enough," said Antony.

"She's an illegal, though. And it wouldn't surprise me, if they can't come up with an answer that they might try to pin the rap for all three of tonight's murders on her. Possible or not, given the right circumstances, it might not matter whether she's strong enough."

I shook my head, barely able to take it all in.

"Even if they treat her as just a witness, when they're done with her, they'll deport her for sure. If she wants to stay, she's got to go underground for a while and leave the area. You see? No good solutions."

"What can I do?" I asked him.

"Well, you can start by explaining this all to her. After that, I guess it's up to her what she wants to do. I hate to say it, but I think her best bet is to go back to Mexico for a while, on her own. Does she have family there?"

"Her mother's dead," I said. "Her father's been sent back, but she doesn't know where."

"That's a bum deal," said Antony.

"I'll talk to her," I said. "Not tonight, though. She's too upset."

"Okay," said Schell. "She can stay here as long as she likes."

"Thanks," I said.

Morgan Shaw reached over and put her hand on my forearm. "Things will work out," she said, and I cringed, hoping she wasn't going to sing again.

Antony reached for a second cigarette, but Schell held up his hand and said, "My sympathies have been exhausted."

Antony laughed and put the pack away. He tilted his head back and drained off the sizable portion left in his glass. "Okay, Boss," he said, looking a little bleary but nearly back to his usual self. "I'm going to bed. I have to rest up. If I get another chance at that fucking . . . you know, that thing, I know exactly what I'm going to do."

"Run?" asked Schell.

"Oh, don't say that," said Morgan. "Henry was very brave."

Antony shook his head. "I'm getting old, Tommy."

"Yeah, I know. We all are. It beats the alternative, though. Just ask Parks," said Schell.

"Have you ever been beaten in a fight before?" I asked.

"Who says I was beaten?" he asked, laughing. He stood up, weaving slightly. "Once when I was younger, I was in a bar in San Francisco. I was shooting my mouth off, being a real jerk. Anyway, I got in a fight and this little Chinese guy, no bigger than Miss Shaw, kicked the crap out of me. That was the last time until tonight."

"That's a good record," I said.

"No," he said. "Next time I meet this thing, I'm going to give him my secret punch. It'll stop his heart and he'll shit blood."

"In that order?" asked Schell.

"What is it?" I asked.

"The Stunner," Antony said.

"You're a stunner," said Schell. "Go get some rest. I'm glad you're in one piece."

Antony smiled and bowed to us. As he moved toward the door, his bulk caused a disturbance in the atmosphere that rippled throughout the room, its current made evident by the motion of the insects.

Once the door was closed, I got up from my seat and went to the couch where Antony had been sitting and lay down, propping my head on the end pillow next to a perching, closed pipevine. I exhaled, and the specimen beat its wings and was gone.

"Will we disturb you if we sit for a few more minutes?" asked Morgan. "I'm still too wide awake to turn in."

"No," I said. "I'm almost asleep." I closed my eyes. There was silence for a little while, and then she and Schell continued speaking in whispers about the events of the night.

I dozed off for a little while, no more than a few minutes it seemed. They were still talking, but in even more hushed tones now. When I opened my eyes a sliver, wanting to see but not wanting to interrupt them, I noticed that someone had turned off the lights. Morgan Shaw, glowing like a full moon in the autumn sky, lifted a wineglass from off the table, and I realized that at some point when I was out she'd switched over from tea. I lay there with my eyes closed, breathing as shallowly as possible so I wouldn't give myself away.

"You have a very nice voice," Schell said, "but I never expected a song at quite that moment."

"You mean, in the car?" she asked.

"Yes."

"I sing to calm myself."

"I liked both your voice and that song," said Schell.

"'Wrap your troubles in dreams,'" she said. "It's a nice idea, but somehow they have a way of unwrapping themselves and escaping."

"I've noticed," said Schell.

"So I have my songs, and you, Thomas Schell, have butterflies. I'd never have suspected it. Why?"

"It's a hobby," he said. "Keeps me off the street at night."

"Collecting stamps is a hobby," she said. "This is something much more."

"I'm fascinated by a good trick when I see it," he said "Sleight of hand with a deck, a magician's illusion, a con's scheme. The butterfly has the best trick in the world. They wrap their naked selves in a blanket, taking nothing with them, you can check if you'd like. They work alone and never leave that cocoon while they perform their magic. Time passes and as it does they transform themselves with only what they have, which as I've said is nothing but themselves. And when they break out, they have become something entirely different. A flying enchantment."

"And what have you learned from them?" she asked.

"Simplicity and subtlety make for the best con. A distraction should lead the mark's attention upward, either toward the sky or to some better vision of himself. Color signals danger. Try to appear to have as many eyes as possible."

"Very good," she said.

"Almost," said Schell. "There's one thing I haven't gotten yet, though, and it keeps me studying them. It's the one thing that's the heart of their art, and it still escapes me."

"What's that?" asked Morgan.

"Change," he said. "They change, but I can never move beyond myself."

"That's the bitch," she said. "It'll make you want to sing to yourself."

I dozed again, and when I next woke, it was still dark, and they had left the Bugatorium. As quietly as possible, I got off the couch and moved across the room to the door. Down the hall I went on my toes, being careful not to bang into anything and give myself away. When I reached the kitchen, the light was still on, and I prayed Antony wasn't up, as he was sometimes, called from sleep by the need for a smoke. Luckily his seat was empty. Finally, I reached the door to my room, opened it slowly, and when there was just enough room, slipped into the darkness, closing it behind me.

"Who's there?" Isabel whispered.

"It's me," I said.

"I knew you would come back," she said.

"Haven't you slept at all?"

"A little, but the dreams keep waking me." I could make out her silhouette sitting up in the bed. She threw back the edge of the covers and patted the spot next to her, as she had on the boulder when we met by the sound. I climbed into bed, and she put the cover up over my shoulder. Then we settled back, our arms around each other. I felt her pressing against me. My hand moved down her side to rest upon her hip. We lay like that for a long time, and though I meant to kiss her, instead I fell into a deep sleep.

THE BULLET'S IN THE CHAMBER

The next morning I was the last in the house to rise. Apparently, Isabel had gotten up early, dressed, and gone to the kitchen to make eggs, bacon, and coffee for everyone. When I finally pulled myself together and went out to join the others, they were all nearly done eating. I poured myself a cup of coffee and sat down. The first two things I noticed were Isabel's smile and Schell's stern countenance. He gave me an icy stare but said nothing. It was clear to me that he had discovered I had not spent the entire night on the couch in the Bugatorium and was not happy about it. I knew, though, that his sense of decorum would prevent him from making a scene over it. There would most definitely be a lecture coming later on.

At first, I was embarrassed by his look and wouldn't make eye contact with him. This only lasted for a short time and was circumvented by my seeing Isabel talking and laughing with the others. I knew I was in love, and I wasn't going to deny it. Schell will have to accept it, I thought to myself. After that, I became defiant, and when he looked at me, I stared back and smiled.

Antony had, as usual, risen early and gone to get the newspaper. There, just as we found the news about the discovery of Charlotte Barnes, we found the headlines announcing the shocking murders of Parks and his staff.

158 / JEFFREY FORD

"I guess we're on the low profile here for even longer now," said Antony. "It's gonna get cozy."

"You're right. We have to continue to lie low for a while. Diego and I are going out this evening," said Schell. "It's probably not a good idea, but I need more information."

"Where?" asked Antony.

"We're going to see the coroner," said Schell.

"You going G-man?" asked Antony.

Schell nodded.

"What about me?"

"I want you to stay here and rest up," said Schell. "Practice the Stunner."

To my surprise, Antony agreed to stay put. He still must have been hurting from the previous night.

"How'd you find out about the coroner?" asked the big man.

"I called Katie and got an address," said Schell.

"I'm surprised she didn't charge you for it."

"Who says she didn't?" asked Schell.

"Wait a second," said Morgan, "I need clothes. I'm sure this young lady needs a few things also. I know you can't stop at the Parks place for her things, but I have plenty of clothes in those boxes back at my cabin. How about stopping there tonight and picking some of them up for us, seeing as we'll be here for a week or more?"

Schell thought for a moment, considering her request, and then shook his head. "I don't want to take the chance. I'll risk shaking down the coroner for some information, but I don't want to run into whoever has been casing your place. One of us will have to go shopping for you," said Schell.

That ended the conversation, and soon after we left the table. The issue of stopping or not at the cabin was far from decided, though, as I observed Morgan Shaw go to work on Schell. Isabel and I were sitting in the living room, but we could hear them talking in the kitchen as they washed and dried the dishes together.

"I see some woods out there, Thomas. I think you should take me out for a walk and show me your property."

"I never go out there," said Schell.

"Never? It's a beautiful day. I'd like to see your place. We wouldn't be seen from the road. This house seems very secluded."

"I was going to do some work with the butterflies," said Schell.

"Forget the butterflies for a while," she said. "I'm your guest. I'll go crazy if I have to stay indoors the entire time I'm here."

There was no response from Schell.

"Is there a view of the sound through those woods?" she asked.

"I think so," he said. "I've never been back there. Diego could tell you."

"Diego's busy," she said. "I'd like you to take me."

I could picture Schell in the kitchen, staring into the dishwater. He said nothing we could hear, but a few moments later, Morgan started humming a tune, which turned into a song. The next thing I knew, the water stopped running and the back door opened and closed. I got up and went to the kitchen window and watched as Schell and Morgan Shaw headed out across the grass toward the path that led through the trees.

While I stood there, Antony came through the kitchen and stopped to glance out the window to see what I was looking at.

"Is that the boss?" he asked. "Taking a walk in the woods?"

"So to speak," I said.

"Between the two of them," he said, "it's hard to figure who's the mark and who's the con."

"She's got him," I said.

"Or is he letting her think she's getting him?" said Antony.

"Or is she letting him think that he's letting her think she's getting him?" I said.

"Romance," said Antony. "A con so crazy that by the time the bullet's in the chamber, you don't know if you've taken someone or you've been taken."

"Romance?" I said. "That's a little premature."

"Call it whatever the fuck you want," he said.

When we turned around from the window, Isabel was standing, leaning against the entranceway to the kitchen with her arms folded. I wondered how long she'd been listening to us. Antony went to the table and grabbed his newspaper. "I'm gonna check the morning line," he said. He held the paper up as he left the kitchen, saying, "Adios," and padded off down the hall, past the office, toward his room.

As soon as Antony was gone, I sat with Isabel at the kitchen table and explained to her the predicament she was in as it had been explained to me by Schell. She already had a fairly good grasp of the situation and knew she was in a tight spot. I told her that Schell thought she should head for Mexico and try to find her father.

"Are you sure he just doesn't want me to be as far away from you as possible?" she asked.

"What do you mean?" I said.

"Did you see his face when you came out of the room?"

"Yeah," I said. "I never thought of that. He does have big plans for me. He wants me to go to college."

"He doesn't want you getting mixed up with an illegal," she said and gave me a sarcastic smile.

"I don't think Schell has anything against you," I said. "I just think he's protected me for so long, he's having a hard time accepting that I've grown up."

"Creo que él tiene dificultad con que te vuelvas mejicano otra vez," she said.

"That I'll admit," I said.

"And what do you think I should do?" she asked.

"Stay with me," I said.

"No es possible, en realidad," she said. "And if I did, we'd have to leave Long Island and find somewhere else to live."

"True," I said.

"I don't know," she told me. I could see the sadness creeping into her expression.

"Schell said you could stay here for as long as you liked. We don't have to decide right now. Maybe if we think about it for a few days, we can come up with a solution."

She bit her bottom lip and nodded.

"Hey," I said, changing the subject. "Come, I'll show you something incredible." We both stood, and I took her by the hand. I led the way down the hallway to the Bugatorium. When we came to the door, I told her to close her eyes, and she did.

Once she was in the middle of the room, I told her to open them. "Behold, the Bugatorium," I said. The butterflies seemed to perform on cue. She spun around to take in the entire sight, giggling nervously.

"This is Mr. Schell's?" she asked.

I nodded. "What do you think?"

"I don't know," she said and took a seat at one end of the couch, her gaze darting about.

I sat down at the opposite end. "He says he studies butterflies because they are masters of deception, but I think there's more to it than that."

She nodded, and I wished I'd owned a camera so I could have captured the look of enchantment on her face. We spent the next few hours telling each other our childhood memories. She'd grown up in a town in Zacatecas, an old colonial town in the highlands, where her father had labored in the silver mines. Her mother's family was Huesteca, originally from northern Veracruz, and they spoke a form of ancient Mayan as well as Spanish. We recalled relatives and games, mole poblano and chilaquiles, and I told her about the men in the Plaza Santa Domingo who composed love letters and wills for those who could not write. The tide of memories increased the longer we talked.

When finally it was time to leave the Bugatorium, I asked her again what she thought of it.

"Una cárcelita muy preciosa," she said.

I was disappointed that she didn't love it, but at the same time her words planted a seed in my thoughts, and I wondered if I would ever see that room again in the way I did before she'd spoken them.

TRUTH IS BEAUTY

By the time Schell was finished with the makeup kit, we each looked ten years older. He now sported a trim goatee and fuller eyebrows. My complexion was nearly white, and I sported a bushy black mustache and round-frame glasses. He told me that government agents don't usually have facial hair, but that we needed to take the chance in order to thoroughly confuse the coroner's memory.

His belief was that the most important aspect of any costume was the shoes, and he had pairs and pairs of them he'd picked up on the cheap at the Salvation Army to add the right touch to his false incarnations. "A G-man's a cop with greater jurisdiction," he said, "but still a cop." With this in mind, he chose two pairs of simple black shoes that appeared slightly scuffed, with well-worn heels. We dressed in three-piece suits, each outfit topped off with a fedora and a trench coat.

Schell was agent Barlow, as stated on the false ID he and Antony had lifted in Penn Station, and I was agent Smith. The county coroner, a Dr. James Cardiff, lived in a nice, old, two-story place off Middle Neck Road in the town of Great Neck. We arrived at his house precisely in the middle of the dinner hour, as Schell had planned it. The sun had already set, and the night felt more like winter than autumn. There were lights on in most of the houses on the block and the air was laced with the smell of frying onions. As we walked up the path to the front porch, Schell advised me, "No pleasantries. Just stare at him as if you believe he's guilty of something."

I nodded.

We climbed the steps, and Schell rapped rather long and hard on the front door. A plump woman in late middle age, with graying hair, impressive jowls, and wearing an apron, answered. She was a little startled to see us standing there, but she composed herself and asked, "Can I help you?"

Schell flashed the badge and ID quickly and then pocketed them. "Federal Bureau of Investigation," he said. "I'm agent Barlow and this is agent Smith." I quickly touched the brim of my hat as a greeting to the woman but did not alter my blank expression. "We're here to speak to Dr. Cardiff."

"Please come in," she said and pulled the door back for us to enter.

We stepped into the living room of the house. Off to our left was a dining room, and sitting at the table was a boy, about fourteen, and a man I figured was Cardiff. The gentleman stood, placing his napkin on the table, and came toward us. He was a heavyset fellow, balding on top, and had a kind of nervous spring in his step. Schell introduced us again and showed the ID, this time more slowly, so that Cardiff could get a good look at it.

"What can I do for you?" he said, shaking Schell's hand. "Always happy to be of service to the law." He reached toward me for a handshake as well, but I didn't offer my hand, only my look.

"Is there a place we can speak in private?" asked Schell.

His wife went back to the dinner table as Cardiff led us through the house to a small book-lined study. Once inside, he shut the door behind him and offered us seats. Schell and Cardiff sat in leather chairs. I remained standing, off to the side a little, but in a place where he could see me watching him.

That nervous energy I'd noted earlier in the coroner's step had now manifested itself in his hands as he clasped them together, then rubbed them, then flexed his fingers, only to begin again with this unconscious ritual.

Schell tipped his hat back with one finger. "We're conducting a secret investigation concerning the Barnes case," he said. "You know the situation I'm referring to? The murder of Charlotte Barnes?"

Cardiff nodded.

"You're to tell no one of our visit," said Schell.

"Certainly not, gentlemen," he said. "Mum's the word."

"You worked on this case, am I right?" asked Schell.

"Not officially," said Cardiff.

"You didn't sign the death certificate?"

"No, I signed off on it, yes, but someone else did the autopsy."

"That seems rather unusual," said Schell, lifting one bushy eyebrow.

"I'm the coroner," said Cardiff. "I sign the legal paperwork in that capacity. That's it."

"Who looked at the girl?" asked Schell.

"Well, usually I examine bodies if there's any question as to cause of death, as I'm also a licensed medical examiner."

"But you didn't handle this case?"

"No. Someone from higher up ordered a special Forensic Pathologist to come in to oversee things."

"Do you know who it was?" asked Schell.

"Never met them," said Cardiff. "I was told to take the day off when the procedure was done. At first I'd assumed Barnes had applied his significant influence, but as it turned out, I rather think his influence was blocked by someone even more powerful."

"It's stated that the girl died of strangulation," said Schell.

"That's what it says," said Cardiff. "But, to tell you the truth . . . that's fishy."

"What do you mean, fishy?" I asked.

Cardiff glanced quickly up at me. He was now obviously sweating and wiped his brow with the heel of his palm. "I looked the girl over when she first came in," he said. "There were no marks on her throat. There was no traumatic damage done to the windpipe. None of the telltale signs of strangulation. Nothing indicated to me to look in that direction at all. Instead, she was pale, her complexion slightly yellow, as if she were both anemic and jaundiced at the same time."

"No violence?" asked Schell.

"The only mark I saw on her was a puncture wound in the crook of the left arm." Here he laid two fingers of his right hand on the inside of his left elbow.

"What kind of puncture mark?" asked Schell.

"Some kind of needle, large gauge. I took blood for a test, but by then the word came down to leave her be. That's when I had an inkling it might not be Barnes who was calling the shots. Still I had the blood. I waited until the pathologist issued his report. When I read that he'd determined the cause of death to be strangulation, I couldn't believe it. I mentioned to my superior that this couldn't be, and he said to me, 'Do you like your job?' Well, these days . . . you know the way things are. I couldn't jeopardize my job."

"So you let it slide," said Schell.

"Not entirely," said Cardiff. "Even if no one else seemed to care, I wanted to know what was going on. I sent the blood to the lab to be tested under another name."

"And what did you learn?"

"The strangest thing," said the coroner. "I can't be sure, because I'd have to check the internal organs, and that's impossible now, but it seemed to me that the girl was transfused. I think she died of a bad transfusion."

"Bad in what way?"

"I know this sounds crazy, because the girl seemed to have been otherwise healthy, but I think someone pumped blood into her that was the wrong type. All the signs are there, clotting, jaundice caused by kidney malfunction, the paleness from the lack of oxygen getting to the cells."

"What happens to a person under these circumstances?" asked Schell.

"Fever, pain throughout the body, in the organs. Not a pleasant way to go. The only problem with my theory," said Cardiff, "is that there should have been some indication of the other blood in her system. Her type was A positive. There seemed to be other blood there, but it had no type as far as I could determine. Admittedly, I had only one sample and one chance at a test. If I'd had another go at it, I might have been able to determine what it was."

"Ever seen anything like it before?" I asked.

"I've heard of people getting a bad transfusion. But never this," he said.

"You've been most helpful," said Schell as he rose from the chair. "Thanks for the information. You're sworn to secrecy about this conversation. It doesn't matter who's asking. In other words, Mr. Cardiff, do you like your job?"

Cardiff nodded vehemently and laughed, as if Schell had made a joke. Neither of us cracked a smile, though, and the coroner quickly regained his composure.

Once we were back in the car and on the road, Schell said to me, "I feel as if God, in return for my years of flimflam, is working some cosmic con on me. Now we have bad blood transfusions and a conspiracy to contradict the facts. I've never been so concerned with the Truth before in my life."

"Truth is Beauty, that's what Keats said," I told him as I worked to tear off the fake mustache. I'd already ditched the eyeglasses, the overcoat, and the fedora in the backseat.

"The Truth—highly overrated," he said. "Nothing but a big pain in the ass."

When I was finally free of my disguise, I said to him, "And what about Isabel and me?" I'd been waiting all day for his lecture and still it hadn't come. All through the drive out to Cardiff's place, I'd waited for him to broach the subject. Now that our job was complete, I was more than ready to face him.

He sighed and smiled. "Diego," he said, "you're a good person, a good son. I'm going to have to trust your judgment on this, but I think you're moving too quickly with Isabel. Sleeping together in the house? You know that's not right. Why get so deeply involved with her at this point? Who knows where she'll wind up? She may have to go back to Mexico. She'll definitely have to leave the state. You have too much ahead of you that you have to do. I'm expecting great things."

"I thought you would be angrier," I said.

"I was put out this morning, I'll admit, but mostly I'm worried."

"Isabel thinks it's because she's Mexican," I said.

He considered this for a moment and said, "Yes, but not in the way she probably thinks. She seems like a nice girl. She's very smart, very pretty. But I don't want you falling back into that. It's too dangerous."

"Falling back into what?" I said.

"Getting lost in the past," he said.

I didn't have the heart to tell him I was considering returning to Mexico with her if she went. It wouldn't do to heap that upon him now, with all that was happening, so I bit my tongue.

"In general," he said. "you've got to watch out for women. They work a mean con."

"How?" I asked.

He pulled a slip of paper out of his pocket and handed it to me.

"What's this?"

"A list of the boxes that we have to pick up from Morgan's cabin," he said.

I started to smile, but he held his hand up. "Please," he said, "spare me the indignity."

A SWEET DEAL

It was black as a kettle in among the trees near the cabin. Schell had pulled off the road and hidden the car behind a natural wall of brambles some way off from number six. We stumbled through the dark, avoiding trunks and trying to steer clear of the other cabins. Somewhere high above us an owl sounded every half minute. I'd left my trench coat in the car and, wearing only my suit jacket, was freezing.

"I think this is it up here," said Schell as he struck a wooden match to life. The momentary flame showed us the way to the door of the place, and once we were standing in front of the small cabin, he lit another so we could check the number.

"Yeah, you found it," I said.

Reaching into his pocket, he retrieved the key Morgan had given him. He opened the door and we stepped inside. That dank mildew smell made me gag slightly, bringing to mind Charlotte Barnes's body in the tumbledown shack. Schell lit one of the candles on the desk, and the light chased the bad memory from my mind.

"Can you imagine living here?" I said to him, my breath coming as steam in the cold.

"Better yet," he said, "how about hearing someone prowling

around outside and having to climb into a hole under the floor-boards?"

"She's resourceful, I'll give you that. But she's also . . ." I was try-ing to think of a way to describe her eccentric nature without being derogatory.

" . . . a loon?" said Schell and laughed quietly.

"As a matter of fact," I said, "I think she's very nice, but the singing . . ." I shook my head.

"My favorite part is the singing," said Schell. "You have that slip of paper?"

I handed him the list. He looked it over and shook his head. "Box with tartan jumper," he said. "What in Christ's name is that?"

I shrugged.

"I'm not going through all of this cargo," he said. "We'll take four boxes, two trips to the car, and then we're giving this place the air."

I grabbed a box and so did he and we headed out. On the return trip it was easier to find the cabin with the candle glowing in the window. Schell had had the trip to the car and back to reconsider his position on the clothes. Once inside the cabin, he took the list out of his pocket and lifted the candle off the desk to get a better look at it.

"Okay, maybe we can actually find some of this stuff," he said.

I walked over to where the boxes were stacked and waited. Even-tually, he said, "Here's one that sounds simple enough—box with black dress."

I went to work, moving boxes off the stack onto the floor, reach-ing in and flipping the folded clothes back to look. I was going to tell him to bring the candle closer when I heard something outside. Schell looked up from the list and turned his head. I froze. A second later, the door, which was unlatched, began to open. The first thing I saw was the muzzle of a gun. An instant later, I could see it was a machine gun. The man who held it, dressed in a black suit, yelled, "Don't move."

Before the gunman could get completely into the cabin, Schell jumped to the side and kicked the door as hard as he could. It caught the stranger in the side, and he went down, the weapon flying from his grasp. Schell wasted no time and kicked the fallen man in the face. At the same time, another fellow was forcing his way in, pushing the door against his partner's body. He managed to get halfway in and began to raise the pistol in his right hand. Schell reached into his suit jacket pocket, took out a handful of something, and threw it in the air. Flash powder. The intruder was about to pull the trigger when Schell tossed the candle into the miasma of powder floating in the air. There was a dull bang and a bright explosion. The second man reeled backward, his gun going off, and the slug hit the ceiling.

"Now," Schell yelled to me, and I leapt across the narrow cabin and followed him out the door. As I passed the machine gunner on the floor, who was scrabbling to his knees, I kicked him again, this time in the ribs. Outside, the other fellow, temporarily blinded by the flash, was furiously rubbing his eyes. He heard us running past him and he squeezed off two shots that went high above our heads. We ran out, around, and behind the cabin, sprinting full tilt.

We'd run for about a minute, luckily not slamming into a tree or tripping on a branch, when something hit me from behind, and I went down. It was Schell who'd knocked me over. "Cover your head," he whispered. And then it came, a storm of machine-gun fire, chewing up the landscape all around us. Bark splintered off the trees and dirt and stones kicked up to the right of us.

By the time the barrage ended, I was dazed and shaking. Schell got up, shoved his arms beneath mine, and lifted me. He offered no verbal command, but I instinctively began running. I couldn't see a thing. Branches were whipping my face, and I tripped and caught myself from falling more than once. We'd gone another twenty yards when we heard the machine gun come to life again. I didn't need Schell to tackle me. We hit the ground, and this time the gunman's aim was even farther to our right. When he stopped firing, in the accentuated silence that followed, I could hear distant footsteps on the fallen leaves, drawing closer.

A voice called then, not from behind us but off to our right. "Hurry, they're coming," it said, and a few seconds later, "This way," from even farther off in that direction. As the machine gun blared again, I realized the voice had been Schell's; he'd projected it in an attempt to confuse our pursuers, a classic séance technique. The shooting stopped, and we heard the men pass only ten yards from where we lay, heading in the direction of Schell's projected voice. Two or three minutes passed, and we heard the machine gun spray again, but this time at a good distance. The smell of gunpowder was everywhere.

Schell tapped my shoulder, and we got to our feet. He whispered, "Don't run." We moved in the direction of our parked car, cautiously pacing, trying not to make a sound. A single shot from a pistol rang out in the distance, and I imagined a dead raccoon or deer. Wandering through the dark was like a nightmare, and it was only by blind luck that we found the Cord.

Once we were in the car, he said to me, "The minute I start this up, they're going to come running, so stay down." Then the engine turned over and it sounded louder to me than ever before. Without turning on the headlamps he backed out of the hiding place behind the undergrowth, whipped the wheel to turn the car around, and hit the gas pedal. We made the turn onto the road so sharply, I thought the car was going to tip over.

A few yards down on the left-hand side of the road, we saw their car. Schell stopped. He reached down somewhere near his shoe and came up with a switchblade. Pressing a tiny latch on the side, a long thin blade snapped out. "You've got to hurry," he said. "Slash a tire."

I grabbed the knife, jumped out of the Cord, and was beside their car in an instant. I plunged the blade into their right front tire, and the air came hissing out. Schell hit the gas the moment I jumped back into our car, and we took off so quickly the tires squealed.

A shudder ran through me as I handed the knife back to Schell. He folded and locked the blade against his thigh and said, "How I almost died for a tartan jumper," as he finally switched on the headlamps.

"So far I've been chased on the beach, beaten up by that thing at Parks's place, and now shot at with a Thompson," I said. "And we're not even getting paid for this."

"It's a sweet deal, for sure," he said.

"Who do you think those characters were?" I asked.

"I don't know," he said. "This thing is so . . . I can't even think of the right word for it. It makes me wonder if the girl in the glass, who started it all, wasn't actually a real ghost."

"The ghost girl's the easiest part to believe," I said.

When we arrived home, we found Antony in the living room, entertaining Isabel and Morgan with tales of the traveling carnival life. There was a haze of cigarette smoke in the air and a bottle of whiskey on the table.

I slouched down on the couch next to Isabel, and Schell took off his trench coat and jacket, tossing them on a chair in the corner.

"How was the coroner?" asked Antony.

Schell didn't answer but went into the kitchen.

"Kid?" he asked.

I waved my hand to put off the question, leaned over, and took one of his cigarettes from the pack on the table. He looked as if he was going to say something, but I suppose from my expression, he knew I needed it. Instead he silently passed me the lighter. Schell returned from the kitchen with a tumbler and proceeded to pour himself a tall drink from the whiskey bottle. Before even finding a seat, he swallowed a quarter of it in one long gulp.

"Did you get the paisley wrap?" asked Morgan.

Schell took a seat across from her. "I don't know if we got the paisley wrap or the tartan jumper," he said. "We did very nearly get an ass full of machine-gun lead, though."

"At the coroner's?" asked Antony.

"No," I said, "out in the woods, at the cabin."

"Oh, no," said Morgan.

Schell nodded, and in between sips of whiskey, he related what had happened at both of the stops we'd made that evening.

"Sorry I wasn't with you," said Antony.

"That makes two of us," said Schell. He looked over at Morgan. "Those people you were mixed up with in the city that you told me about this afternoon, could this have been them?"

"I don't know," she said. "What did they look like?"

"Two guys in dark suits, hats, with itchy trigger fingers. We didn't stay around long enough to see their faces."

Morgan shook her head and shrugged.

TAKE THIS

I was standing in cabin number six, the candle flame dancing madly, weaving wild patterns of light and shadow around me. The man in the black suit brought the machine gun up and pointed it at my chest. "Where's the fucking paisley wrap?" he said. "I don't know," I yelled. He pulled the trigger. I winced in expectation of a loud, rapid report and the pain of hot lead ripping through me. Instead, I heard the sound of a phone ringing. I opened my eyes into the darkness of the living room and sat up on the couch. It took a second for my head to clear, but it soon came to me that the phone in the office was actually ringing. I had no idea how late it was, but morning hadn't yet come. I pulled myself to my feet and went around through the kitchen.

I wasn't sure how many times it had rung and was anticipating that whoever was on the other end would hang up before I could lift the receiver. When I finally answered it, though, I heard a voice say, "Schell?" It took me a second to place the inflection: Barnes. "Schell, is that you?" he asked. I was resourceful enough to put on my Ondoo accent.

"One moment, sir, I will summon Mr. Schell," I said. I gently put the receiver down and went to the Bugatorium. When I flipped the light on, I was surprised to not find him lying on the couch. I made a quick check of the other rooms, flipping the light switches on as I went. Finally, I gave up and went to his bedroom door. When I knocked, he answered, "What?"

"Barnes is on the phone," I called.

I heard the sound of the bedsprings squeaking as he got up, and a few seconds later, he was at the door, wrapping a robe around himself. He glanced briefly at me as he passed, and I couldn't help but smile. Then he was gone down the hall to the office, leaving the door open halfway. Morgan Shaw's pallid body verily glowed in the dark. She lay, sleeping, completely naked, atop the blankets, her hair fanning out like a corona of sunlight around her head. That momentary glimpse of her burned my eyes, and I shifted my gaze, quickly pulling the door shut.

The phone conversation lasted all of five minutes. From where I waited in the kitchen, I could hear the low murmur of Schell's voice but was unable to make out his words. Finally the receiver landed in the cradle, and he appeared. Taking a seat across from me, he said, "Barnes wants a séance."

"What did you tell him?" I asked.

"I said we'd be there."

"Did he say why?"

"He thinks if we communicate with the dead, they'll tell us who murdered Parks and his daughter. He told me he'd seen his daughter's body, and he doesn't buy the strangulation story. He thinks Kern is innocent. Every attempt he's made to have the authorities launch a new investigation has been blocked."

"We could be taking a big chance going out there," I said.

"He promised me no cops. I told him to invite everyone on that list he'd given me."

"You still think it's someone he knows?"

"Not necessarily," said Schell, "but I'd like to see their reactions."

"When?"

"Tomorrow night . . . or I suppose I should say tonight," he said, glancing at the clock over the sink, which showed the time to be 2 A.M.

"Better get some sleep," he said. "We've got a lot to do. This has got to be a flawless performance."

"What happened to the couch?" I asked. "Too buggy in there?"

Schell stared hard at me for a good thirty seconds. I couldn't read his expression, and I was unsure if he was amused, angry, or perhaps even hurt by my taunt. When he finally opened his mouth, a pale muslin bombyx flew out and fluttered in a spiral up toward the light. He stood and left the kitchen. "Sleep tight," he said once his back was turned. He flicked the switch off as he went by, leaving me to sit in the dark by myself. The bright moth flew in erratic circles around the entire room three times before landing in my hair.

When I got up, I didn't return to the living room couch but went to my room. Isabel awoke when I climbed into bed beside her. Suffice it to say, Schell's advice to get some sleep went unheeded, but when we had settled down and both lay back with our heads upon the single pillow, Isabel said, "You were nearly killed tonight when you went to the cabin."

"I'm trying to forget it," I told her.

"Did you ever think your luck has turned bad because you mock the dead by what you do?"

"I never really thought about it quite as mocking them," I said. "Besides, what do the dead care once they're dead?"

"Your Mr. Schell has taught you to doubt the power of the dead?"

"Well, he doesn't believe in spirits, if that's what you mean. And his argument is very convincing."

"But he's seen the ghost of a girl, no?" she said. "Isn't that what drew you all into this?"

"You have a point," I said. "Do you believe in ghosts?"

"¡Claro!" she said.

"Have you ever seen one?"

"No."

"Then you believe only because you want to believe or you've been taught to believe?"

"No seas tan condescendiente," she said. "When I was five years old, my father came to me one Sunday afternoon and said, 'Come, I want to show you something.' 'What is it?' I asked. 'Something to help you live your life,' he said. He took me by the hand, and we left the house. We walked to the end of town and then out across the meadow and up the large hill, nearly the size of a mountain that watched over all our lives. 'Where are we going?' I asked. 'To the mines,' he said. I knew that he worked in the silver mines, but I'd never been to them.

"There were no workers at the mine on Sunday, only a guard, who we found sitting in a rocking chair on the porch of the mine office, fast asleep. My father woke him and told him we were going to take a walk in the mine. The guard smiled and nodded. 'You're taking her to number three?' asked the man. My father nodded. 'I took my boy only last month,' said the guard, who gave us a helmet and lantern.

"A few minutes later, we stood at the opening to the silver mine, a huge dark hole framed by timbers. Just inside, in the shadows, I could see a train track and a few cars, but my father told me we would be walking. He held the lantern up in front of him and I wore the helmet, which was far too big for me, and we walked down into the ground, as if we were being swallowed whole by a giant snake. As we walked, he started talking. 'Some years ago,' he said, 'there was discovered in tunnel number three, a very rich vein of silver. The discovery made everyone very happy. Five men were sent to work there. They began mining the silver, the purest quality, and so much of it.'

"All the time he talked, we continued to descend. The air got thin, and it became very warm. Still we kept walking. When we reached a place where the main tunnel split, we headed right. Then the tunnels split and split until if I had been alone I could never have found my way back to the surface. 'One day, while the five men were working in tunnel three,' he said, 'there was a terrible cave-in. Something shifted in the earth, and hundreds of tons of rock and dirt collapsed into the tunnel. There was too much debris for us to try to dig through. We called out to the men on the other side of the wall of rubble, but nothing came back, not a single word, not a whisper. They had all died.'

"Eventually we came to a particular tunnel and turned into it. It ended abruptly, though, and when my father held the lantern up, I could see it was choked with large rocks. 'Step up,' he said, 'and put your ear to the rock.' I did. 'Listen hard,' he said. Immediately I heard a sound that seemed to come from inside the pile of rocks. Many voices, screaming, yelling. I couldn't make out any words, but their sound was so frantic and frightening, I could not listen for long, for the lament chilled me to my soul. 'Now they know we are here,' said my father, and the sound of the voices grew so that we could detect them clearly even standing back.

"'Some say the sound is from a stream that runs through the ground there, some say it is the echoing of the wind blowing into the mine from some unknown opening. But no, it is haunted,' said my father, 'by the spirits of the dead miners. Men who have to work near here always bring wads of sheep wool to stuff in their ears, so they don't have to hear the cries of the dead.' 'Why do they cry out?' I asked. 'They are angry at having died,' he said. 'The mine owner knows there is much silver in there, but he will not allow the vein to be reopened, because he fears their ghosts will haunt the entire mine.' 'Why did you bring me here?' I asked. 'I wanted you to know that this exists in the world. To know this is to know something important about life.' I didn't understand what he meant at all and thought he was just trying to scare me, which he did.

"Later that day, I told my mother about our trip to the mine. 'The ghosts are so unhappy to have died,' I told her. 'Nonsense,' she said. 'Death is hard, but once you're gone there is nothing to be un-happy about.' 'There is only one reason the dead come back,' said my mother. 'They return to instruct the living.'"

"But that doesn't mean that the sound on the other side of the cave-in wasn't running water or the wind coming through a shaft that led to an opening," I said.

Isabel gently laid her left arm across my chest. "Wait," she said, "there's more. That night, I had a bad dream. In it I was being chased by some unknown evil. The only part I clearly remember was that my grandmother, who had recently died, appeared. She materialized, a ghost, her face contorted in anguish as it had been when she was laid in her coffin. She screamed at me, 'Take this!' and thrust forward a silver candlestick. I awoke and knew that the voices in the mine had given me this nightmare. Even though I was only five years old, that image stayed with me forever.

"Two years later, a rich man bought the mine. He fired everyone who worked there, including my father. The new owner was warned about tunnel three, but he said he didn't believe in superstition. When he learned that a rich vein of silver lay down there, he ordered his new men to excavate the tunnel. As they dug, the crying of the dead miners increased until it could be heard all the way to the entrance. Still, he insisted they continue to dig. On the day they broke through the debris and found the bones of the old miners, all of the new workers, eight men, suddenly died."

"A curse?" I asked.

"No," she said. "Poison gas from underground. Later it was dis-covered that the original collapse was caused by an explosion due to this gas. My mother had been right, the spirits were trying to warn the miners not to dig there. Once the gas was discovered and the mine was vented, the voices of the spirits were never heard again."

"I don't know," I said. "It's a good story, but does it prove that there are ghosts?"

"One more thing," she said. "That night you came to save me at

the mansion, and that thing was fighting Mr. Cleopatra in the hallway, I knew the phantom might be hurting you and I wanted so
badly to help. I looked around the darkened room for something, a
weapon. Then I heard my grandmother's voice, 'Take this,' it said,
"and I remembered a heavy silver candlestick that was on the mantel in that room. I used it to beat the demon on the head."

BY WAY OF YOUR ART

It was after dark when Antony parked the car at the end of a line of others in the circular drive of the Barnes estate. From the considerable number of autos present and the absence, as far as we could see, of the police, it seemed Barnes had been good to his word. Antony, in his chauffeur guise, got out and came around to open the door for Schell and me. He then retrieved the large traveling trunk that carried the props that would be necessary for that evening's séance, and we began our slow, cadenced walk to the front steps. We hadn't done a job since Parks's place, and it felt good to be working again. I gave my turban a last-minute adjustment before we began the ascent to the front door.

Barnes met us in the foyer, looking more haggard than ever, as if he'd aged two decades since last we'd seen him. He approached Schell with his hand out, but I stepped forward to intercede.

"Mr. Barnes, please do not take this as a slight, but Mr. Schell has asked me to communicate for him until after the séance. He is in the process of preparing himself to go more deeply into his mediumistic trance than he has ever gone before."

Barnes, at first, appeared disappointed at the prospect of dealing with me, but as I continued with my explanation his fears seemed to subside. "This will be a very arduous, and to some degree dangerous, foray into the spirit world tonight, and Mr. Schell has been preparing since early this morning, descending through the various levels of concentration and consciousness to reach the very quincunx of afterlife affinity."

This last phrase made Barnes take a step back, as if he feared he'd already possibly been too disruptive to the great man's preparations. Schell was turning in a command performance, his eyes closed, his lids fluttering, his Adam's apple bobbing, and his hands out in front of him, fingers splayed wide. Before we'd left the car, he'd purposely rumpled his hair, displacing it to achieve just the right look of duress.

"I've assembled everyone from the list, as Mr. Schell requested," said Barnes. "All of them, that is, except poor Parks."

"Mr. Schell has asked me to express his condolences to you for this sudden, tragic loss of your friend following so hard upon the heels of the loss of your daughter."

Barnes said nothing, nor gave so much as a nod, but stared fixedly off into the distance, as if stunned by the thought of what he'd been through. It was only the arrival of his wife that brought him back to the moment. She came up next to him and entwined her arm in his. Mrs. Barnes had fared no better than her husband. Her previously dark hair had gone completely gray in only the short time since I'd last seen her. I bowed slightly to acknowledge her presence, and Barnes explained Schell's condition to her.

"If you will gather your guests together," I said, "Mr. Cleopatra and I will begin setting up. Once the room has been prepared, I will usher in Mr. Schell."

"Very well," said Barnes. "Follow me. We're going to use the dining room, as it has a table large enough to accommodate everyone."

Mrs. Barnes went off to gather the others, and I started down the hall after Barnes, taking a quick glance behind to see Antony lift the trunk he'd momentarily set down and fall in line. When we reached the room in question, there were already a number of people there.

The place was spacious, with a table at its center that could easily seat a dozen. The men and women were dressed in evening clothes, and I scanned their faces in an attempt to memorize them.

I overheard one older woman in a blue chiffon evening dress whisper to her male companion, "I understand this savage speaks freely to the dead." "Savage" was an appellation I'd not yet heard applied to me at these events, but it very nearly made me smile.

I decided that Schell would sit in the center of the left-hand side of the table and directed Antony to lay his case down on the floor a few feet behind that chair. He did so and began unlatching it. Once it was open, lying flat on its side, I reached in and retrieved the candleholder and candle that would sit in the middle of the table during the séance. Next, Antony took out an easel with telescoping legs and a small folding stand. We brought these to the side of the dining room opposite the entrance and set them up a few feet from the end of the table.

Antony positioned a large white sheet of paper on the easel, and I put the stand in front of it, finishing the job by placing two candles at either side so that the paper would be visible to everyone at the table. The last two items to be put in place were incense burners that clamped onto the back of, and rose above, the chair that Schell would be using. Once they were affixed I filled them with sticks of sandalwood.

When the candle at the center of the table and the two caches of incense were lit, smoke rising and twining about the room, I began seating people. I held my hand to my forehead for a moment, as if receiving a signal from the spirit world, and then, with a whispered phrase of "Yes," or "I understand" sought out the guests one by one, bringing each in turn to his or her spiritually ordained chair. It was during this that I learned their names and took a quick inventory of who was who. Schell had instructed me to place the two oldest participants on either side of him. Although I offered my hand, few would take it, but one gentleman slipped me a dollar when I showed him his spot. The chair opposite Schell's was reserved for his faithful servant, Ondoo.

When the Barneses and all of their guests were seated, I bowed beside Mr. Barnes and told him that I would fetch Mr. Schell. As I left the room to get him, Antony turned out the lights. I found Schell meandering down the hallway like a simpleton, weaving from side to side, sunken deep in his mediumistic trance. I took his arm, and he whispered to me, "How do I look?" His hair was now crazier than ever, and his eyes were rolled up. "Like an escapee from the Immaculate Redeemer Nursing Home," I said. "Perfect," he said and smiled. I could readily sense his joy at being back in action.

We entered the dining room, and Antony, who had taken up a position by the door, as if standing guard, closed it behind us. Stifled gasps went up from Barnes's friends at the sight of Schell. I led him to his seat and helped him into it while holding my breath against the prodigious output of the incense burners. Before seating myself, I walked over to the easel and lit the two candles directly in front of it. Once I was situated, Schell instantly began twitching.

We warmed up with some preliminaries—the moth from the mouth, the knocking of my big toe on the underside of the table, voices thrown here and there, a couple of bangs of flash powder. The crowd was jittery, expectant, the gentlemen losing their gruff facades, the women losing their breath. When Schell was shuddering so badly it seemed as if he would soon explode, he opened his mouth wide and in a vibrating voice, the words seeming to leap from his tongue rather than being spoken, he said, "We call forth Charlotte Barnes. We implore you to pass through the vale of tears and leap the yawning divide to help us understand your departure from this world."

Mrs. Barnes, who sat to the right of Schell, began weeping. Her husband looked as if he might simply crumble to dust. The gentleman I had marked as Mr. Trumball dabbed his high forehead with a handkerchief, and the old woman in the blue chiffon, Mrs. Charles, nervously pursed and unpursed her lips, as if offering dainty kisses to the unseen. Just to the right of me, the family physician, Dr. Greaves, watched suspiciously from behind thick-lensed glasses.

"We ask you to identify your killer, Charlotte Barnes," intoned Schell, "by way of your art. Come forth and show us who took your life."

"Absurd," said Collins, a gentleman with a drooping black mustache and one continuous eyebrow.

"Please, refrain from speaking," I said, and Collins, instead of looking annoyed at my request, suddenly appeared chastened.

The voice of a young child could be heard in the room. At first it was only a murmur, but it soon grew into the clear sound of a girl's voice singing "Mary Had a Little Lamb." It wavered on a breeze that blew increasingly strong. Luckily no one seemed to notice that it came from the spot where Antony was standing in the shadows.

"The child has come," said Schell, his ghoulish demeanor taking on a look of triumph.

"My god," said Mrs. Barnes in a shrill voice. "Look, there, at the picture."

Everyone turned his attention to the easel, where a drawing was slowly revealing itself one line at a time.

"This can't be . . . ," said the oldest woman, sitting to the left of Schell.

But it was, the figure appeared incrementally, as if an invisible entity was standing before the easel, sketching. The portrait in the process of becoming was obviously that of a man, but the distinguishing features had not yet been rendered.

"Who is it?" cried Barnes. "Charlotte, who?"

The flame at the center of the table exploded with a dull pop, and sparks streamed out in all directions. All eyes were diverted, but when the effect from that had passed, and the group's attention reverted back to the drawing, what we saw, nearly completely executed, was the misshapen head and snarling visage of the phantom Antony had done battle with.

"It's a demon," said Trumball.

"Harold, it's the figure from her drawings," said Mrs. Barnes. "The figure that haunted the grounds before she was abducted."

"Yes, but who or what is it?" asked Barnes, posing his question as much to the darkness around him as to his wife and the others. "Schell, ask her for a name."

"What more can you tell us about this horror?" said Schell.

My eyes went wide, and when the others saw my expression they also looked up, for behind Schell's chair, amid the billowing incense smoke, rose the ghost of Charlotte Barnes. Her hair was in curls as it had been when she had died, and her cheeks shone with a strange waxen palor.

Mr. Gallard passed out sideways off his chair, and his wife hit the tabletop with a thud. Trumball made to lift Mrs. Gallard, but I whispered harshly to him to stay still.

The ghost of Charlotte Barnes cast down her icy stare, and her gaze swept across the assembled participants. Mrs. Barnes was breathing heavily, audibly, and clutching her chest.

"My killer moves among you," said the spirit, and the voice was high and tremulous. "Avenge my death."

Mrs. Barnes grasped at her own throat and then sprawled back in her chair. "Helen," her husband called and reached one arm out toward her and one toward the image of Charlotte. The doctor, sitting next to me, yelled, "Mrs. Barnes!" rose to his feet, and began to make his way around the table. I slipped my foot back beneath my chair and caught his ankle at the last second as he went by. He sprawled headlong onto the floor. The last thing Charlotte did was toss something down that landed on the table with a definite material impact.

"Turn on the lights now," cried Barnes. Antony did as he was told, and the lights suddenly flashed on, temporarily blinding everyone. The room was filled with sobs, gasps, and hushed comments of the guests. When we looked back, the girl was gone, and Schell was bent forward, head down, passed out on the table.

IT'S ALL RUBBISH

By the time Doctor Greaves managed to pick himself up off the floor, Helen Barnes had revived, so when he continued on around to that side of the room and passed her by, I thought he was going to see if he could assist Schell. Nothing doing. Instead, he got down on his knees and looked under the table, obviously believing that the spirit of Charlotte Barnes had been merely an impostor and was now hiding, waiting for a chance to slip out unseen. Schell came to then, looking like he'd been through the mill. He was groggy and disoriented, and when he noticed Greaves on the floor at his feet, he said, "I beg your pardon, sir."

Greaves stood up. "An effective stage trick, Mr. . . . What was your name again?" he asked.

Schell answered.

"Yes, very amusing, but complete rubbish," said Greaves. "Have you no decency? To perform this kind of whim-wham on these poor grieving people—shameful."

"Adam, please, let Mr. Schell catch his breath. He's been through a harrowing experience," said Barnes, coming more fully to life than he had all evening.

"Harold," said Greaves, "it's all rubbish."

Mrs. Barnes pulled herself up, using the table for support, and wobbled over to where Schell was sitting. "Doctor, if you can't re-spect this great man's ability, at least don't hound him after he's rendered us such a service." She put her hand on Schell's shoulder and said, "Thank you."

Schell reached up and patted her hand. "I know how difficult this must be for you," he said.

"Such a service . . . ," said Greaves under his breath and stepped away.

Antony had applied the smelling salts to the Gallards, who were spluttering their respective ways back to consciousness. Trumball stood, leaned over the table, and lifted a small object. "Look," he said, "here's what the girl threw." He held it up for everyone to see. It was a blue drawing pencil. This prompted the others to turn their attention back to the picture on the easel, material proof that the spirit of the girl had been present. Mrs. Charles, attended by Mr. Collins and a few of the others, moved across the room to where the portrait of the strange figure stood. They blew out the candles in front of it and unfastened it from the easel. Gathered round, they held it up close to their faces in order to study it care-fully.

Barnes had gone to the small bar in the corner of the room and fixed Schell a drink. He was making his way back to the table when a high-pitched scream came from Mrs. Charles. The sudden-ness of the cry startled Barnes and caused him to drop the glass. He let loose a string of curses I would never have suspected him capable of uttering.

"Good lord, Margaret," he yelled, "What ever was that for?"

Mrs. Charles turned and, holding the portrait that had been on the easel, displayed it to Barnes and the rest of us. "The drawing," she said. "It's disappeared."

"Right before our eyes," said Collins.

The large piece of paper that had held the likeness of the phan-tom was now totally blank.

"It couldn't last," said Schell, standing. "Charlotte did her best, but the spirit world reclaimed her efforts."

At this, the doctor shook his head and left the room. The rest were wrapped in a state of silent awe. Antony and I allowed a minute or two of respectful inaction to pass, and then we set to gathering together our props and putting them in the trunk. While the two of us worked quickly, Schell explained to Harold and Helen Barnes that he would phone them the next day to discuss more fully what had transpired. It was clear that they were eager to rehash the events of the evening right on the spot, but Schell cautioned that it was important to bring focused reflection to bear on the actions and words of the dead.

"Perhaps there's a clue we will miss if we rush to judgment," he said.

They reluctantly agreed.

Antony and I had the trunk packed and were ready to go in ten minutes. Schell made the rounds of the guests and shook their hands. Each and every one of them, even the Gallards, had only praise for his abilities and thanked him for the experience. The old crone, who'd sat next to Schell during the séance, even thanked *me*, nodding slightly and calling me Mr. Fondue.

Then we fell into our parade formation with Schell leading the way and Antony in the rear, lugging the trunk. We made our slow, ceremonious exit from the dining room to the hallway and toward the front door. On the way to the exit, we encountered the doctor, standing off to the side of the hall, smoking a cigar.

"Good evening, Dr. Greaves," said Schell and extended his hand.

"Keep walking," said Greaves. "I've nothing to say to you."

Schell withdrew his arm and we continued.

Two miles down the road from the Barnes mansion, Antony turned into the parking lot of a grocery and drove around behind the building, where he stopped. We all got out of the car and went quickly to the back compartment of the Cord and retrieved the prop trunk. Laying it carefully on the ground, Antony unlatched the clasps and opened it. Schell reached in and took out the easel, the folding table, the candles, etc., handing each item to me in turn.

Once the trunk was empty, Schell took out his knife. Releasing the blade, he ran its tip along the bottom side of the trunk. A moment later what had seemed to be the bottom opened outward like the cover of a book to reveal a hidden compartment filled with the contorted body of Vonda, the Rubber Lady. She looked like a woman who had fallen into a car compactor.

Antony reached into the trunk and lifted her twisted form up into his arms, holding her as one would hold a child. Very slowly at first, and then with increasing speed, she began to open outward like a folded paper figure placed in a bowl of water. While this remarkable transformation took place, Schell and I replaced the false bottom of the trunk and began refilling it with our séance implements.

Like a butterfly emerging from its chrysalis, Vonda turned into a slight but perfectly normal-size woman in Antony's arms. As soon as the metamorphosis was complete, she said, "Okay, Henry, you can put me down."

As her feet touched the ground, she reached up and whipped off the curly wig she'd worn to effect the guise of Charlotte Barnes. I'd only met her once before, and briefly at that, at Morty's funeral. Now I could tell, even through the makeup job Schell had done on her to get her to look like a little girl, that she was a good-looking woman. Her own blonde hair was gathered in a tight bun on her head. She was thin but had a fine figure, and her face was youthful for someone who I knew to be only a few years younger than the big man. Despite what seemed to be a lazy left eye, Antony had done very well for himself.

"Are you feeling good?" asked Antony, gently touching her back.

"A little dizzy," she said. "It'll pass."

"You were in that trunk for a long time," I said, "I don't know how you did it."

"It wasn't the trunk, kid," she said, "that's a piece of cake. It was that fucking stuff you guys had burning on the back of that chair. It nearly gassed me. What is that shit? It smelled like dirty feet."

Antony must have been satisfied that she was back to normal, because he smiled broadly and bent over to give her a hug.

"Great work," said Schell. "Come on, we've got to beat it."

The trunk got loaded back into the Cord, and Schell gave Vonda the front seat so she could ride next to Antony. We pulled back out onto the road and made for home.

"Diego," Schell said, "did you remember to take the drawing? I doubt any of them would figure it out, but in the event someone analyzed it, we'd be sunk."

"Yeah," said Antony, "like that doctor. I wasn't feeling the warmth from him."

"That's what happens when you're educated in the sciences," said Schell. "You lose that charming quality of naive acceptance."

"All you ever talk to me about is getting a college degree," I said.

Schell laughed. "I'm talking about our marks, Diego. It's okay for us."

"Wait a second, there," said Antony. "I think Barnes went to Havard."

"That doesn't count," said Schell. "Absolute wealth befuddles absolutely."

"I did take the picture," I said and reached up to retrieve the folded piece of drawing paper from beneath my turban.

"How about the scream that old broad let out when the drawing disappeared?" said Antony.

"I heard that in the trunk," said Vonda. "It almost busted my glass eye."

"I love that effect," said Schell.

"I know you guys were saying the drawing appears and disappears, but how do you do it?" she asked.

"The boss never gives away his secrets," Antony said to her.

"It's all right, Antony," said Schell. "Since Vonda did such a marvelous job, and she has close personal connections to the operation, I'll reveal this one, but you must promise not to tell anyone."

"Yeah, yeah," said Vonda and turned slightly to look into the backseat.

I was glad she asked, because although it had actually been Isabel who'd originally drawn the portrait of the phantom with a solution that Schell had concocted, I had no idea what that special ink had been made from.

"Cobalt oxide dissolved in nitric acid," said Schell. "You could also use hydrochloric acid instead of the nitric. You render the writing or drawing with this solution on a piece of white paper and it's completely undetectable. When it comes in close proximity to heat, like the candle flames we placed directly in front of it, the drawing appears in blue lines. Breathe on it, as Mrs. Charles and Collins and the others were doing when inspecting it, and it disappears again. I got that one from Morty."

"Jeez," said Vonda and shook her head.

"And I apologize for the ill effect of the incense, but without it I was afraid it wouldn't have been dark enough for you to get in and out of the trunk undetected," said Schell.

"Forget it," said Vonda. She turned to Antony and lightly punched him in the arm. "Baby, give me a cigarette," she said.

HERE'S A CLUE

Living with Schell often made me forget that the country was suffering the stupidity of Prohibition, for he had an endless supply of alcohol and not the bathtub swill that Grace served at the Paradise. Once every few months, he and Antony would drive over to the docks in Hoboken, New Jersey, and visit a particular longshoreman named Gallagher. It never failed that they would return with a stash of European champagne, wine, and liquor. To celebrate our successful bamboozlement of the Barneses and their guests, Schell had pulled, from some secret compartment in his room, two bottles of French cognac. We all crowded into the Bugatorium, and the party took wing.

That night my glass was refilled with each round, and I was not held to my usual one-drink limit. My role had somehow changed. I no longer felt like an apprentice but as a full partner in the séance operation, on equal footing with Schell and Antony. I could only think this was due to the presence of Isabel, looking beautiful in Morgan's paisley wrap. As simpleminded as it sounds, I had my arm around a woman and a drink in my hand, and I mistakenly thought as I'm sure many have, What, if not this, is evidence of being a man in the great United States?

My participation in the conversation was no longer merely to ask questions, to sit back and listen, to act the student, so I held forth on my own personal ideas as to the ultimate moral nature of the confidence scheme. Everyone was in a good mood, though, and when I went on too long, the others simply turned away and smaller conversations broke out around my own monologue. Eventually Antony said, "Kid, give it a rest," and I laughed. Isabel did too, and kissed me on the cheek. I felt as though I had made some definitive move toward adulthood.

Schell recounted the goings-on at the Barnes mansion for Morgan and Isabel; the whole affair and how it played out—our entrance, the trunk, the guests, etc. Although Isabel nodded with interest, I knew that privately she disapproved of our con every step of the way. Morgan had a beatific smile on her face and appeared to hang on Schell's every word. When Schell got to the part where Doctor Greaves leaped out of his seat to rescue Mrs. Barnes and I tripped him, Antony said, "That guy had a doodlebug in his ass."

Vonda broke in then and said, "Oh, yeah, you mean the guy in the photo."

Schell stopped speaking and turned to her. "What guy in the photo?" he asked.

"The joker sitting across from where I appeared, the one with the beard and the little round glasses?" she said. She made circles with her forefingers and thumbs and brought them up to her eyes.

"The photo, though . . . ," I said.

"Right back there," said Vonda, pointing over her shoulder with her thumb. "On that table in the corner. I looked at it when I came in."

I went to the table in question and lifted the photo we'd retrieved from Parks's house the night he was murdered. As I walked back toward where the others were gathered around the coffee table, I studied it but saw no sign of Dr. Greaves. "I don't see him here," I said.

Vonda reached out for it. "Here," she said, "I'll show you." She took the picture from me and held it up to the light. She looked at it for a moment and then began scraping away the stains on its glass with her long, red thumbnail. "What is this crap?" she asked.

"You see that guy right there?" said Antony. He leaned over from where he sat next to her on the couch and pointed.

"Yeah?" she said.

"That crap is his blood."

"Christ, why didn't you tell me?" She rubbed the residue off her nail onto a napkin on the table. "That's disgusting."

"But where's the good doctor?" asked Schell.

"There's the little pissant, right there," said Vonda, pointing now with her nail but not touching the glass. "Give that guy a beard and a pair of those goofy librarian specs, think of him as a few years older, and I'll bet you a sawbuck that's him."

Schell reached across the table, keeping an eye on the figure Vonda pointed to, and took the framed photo from her. He brought it up close to his eyes, a moment passed, and then he nodded. "You know, I think you're right," he said.

"I *know* I'm right," said Vonda.

"A sawbuck it is then," said Schell. He passed the photo to me, and I looked closely at the man they had singled out. Vonda was right, but had she said nothing I'd not have noticed it. There was Greaves, dressed in a suit as were the other subjects of the picture, standing a few feet behind Parks in the group of a dozen or so men.

"Let me have your knife," I said to Schell. He took it out, opened it, and handed it to me. I turned the picture frame over and, using the blade, lifted the thin nails that held the photo and mat in place behind the glass. I flipped the frame over and let the photo fall out onto my lap. After handing the knife to Isabel, I placed the blood-splattered frame and the mat on the table, picked up the photo, and studied it more closely.

"Look there," said Morgan, pointing, "on the back."

I turned the picture over, and there on the lower left-hand side, written in pencil was the date, *December 23, 1925.* Beneath that were the words *Cold Spring Harbor* followed by the letters *ERO*.

"Cold Spring Harbor's a town, we know that," I said, "but *E-R-O*, what's that?"

"How do you know they're initials and not a name, Ero?" asked Morgan.

"You might be right, but they're capitalized, which leads me to believe they're initials, each standing for its own word, perhaps the name of the group or club to which all of these men gathered in the photo belong."

"Did you ever hear of anybody called Ero?" asked Antony.

"No," said Vonda, "but I never heard of anybody called Antony Cleopatra either."

"Maybe it's a picture from a Christmas party," said Isabel.

"That'd make sense, considering the date," said Schell. "If I'm not mistaken, a number of the men have drinks in their hands."

"And they're not lined up as if for an official shot," I added, "but seem to have been milling around informally when someone interrupted and said, 'Say cheese!'"

"I think this is a job for The Worm," said Schell. "I'll call the library first thing in the morning."

"The Worm?" asked Morgan, and the conversation moved off in another direction with Schell and Antony telling tales about the incredible memory and equally incredible power to annoy of Emmet Brogan.

The cognac as well as the conversation continued to flow, and before long, the sudden discovery of my own inebriation made me content to again simply sit back, listen, and revel in the sense of the event as a kind of family gathering. Isabel, who was well lit herself, told the ghost story about the silver mine. I translated when it was necessary and was amazed at Schell's reaction to it. Whereas I'd have expected him to adopt a kind of sneering skepticism in the face of a *true* tale of spirits, he seemed genuinely interested. When she was done recounting the details, he even went so far as to say, "from my experience with the ghost of Charlotte Barnes, I know how you must have felt." Antony and I looked at each other in reaction to Schell's statement, both of us wondering if some change had begun in the boss as a result of our investigation.

There came a time later when, even though the conversation droned on, I was more interested in the butterflies, their flight patterns, and the thought of the fleeting nature of their lives. I must have dozed off for a little while then, because when I awoke, it was to the strains of a duet of "I Can't Give You Anything But Love," being sung by Antony and Morgan. Schell, cigarette clamped at the corner of his lips, was keeping the rhythm by patting his hands on the table, Isabel was humming the background harmony, and Vonda was passed out, her mouth open and an orange theope perched on her nose.

I didn't even remember going to bed but found myself there when I woke, close to noon. Isabel had already gotten up. Feeling a little shaky, I crawled out of bed and threw on my robe. Upon entering the kitchen, I found them all gathered again, save for Schell. The only verbal welcome I got was an "Hola," from Isabel. The others smiled and nodded but looked altogether bedraggled.

"Coffee?" I asked.

"Forget the coffee, kid. It's hair-of-the dog-time," said Antony.

Then I noticed the two open champagne bottles on the table. I took a seat, Morgan passed me an empty flute, and Vonda poured. "Takes the edge off," she said as the bubbles rose in the glass.

I was just going to ask where Schell was when he came into the kitchen. He took his seat and reached for the bottle. Filling his glass with one hand, he held up the other, waving a slip of paper. "That was Emmet just getting back to me," he said. "He does fast work. I called him at eight this morning. He said that the initials ERO, and he thinks they're most definitely initials, in conjunction with the town of Cold Spring Harbor, refer to the"—here Schell consulted the slip of paper again—"Eugenics Record Office."

"What's that?" asked Antony.

"Never heard of it," said Schell. "But Emmet said the study of eugenics has to do with inherited traits, like in Darwin or, more precisely, Mendel. He's going to look into it more deeply and call back later."

That afternoon, Schell, Antony, Vonda, and Morgan took off in the Cord to drop Vonda at the train station and then to take Morgan shopping for a few things that were not in the boxes we had been able to retrieve from the cabin. Isabel couldn't go, as it was still uncertain to the police if she'd been kidnapped or was a suspect in connection with Parks's murder. Even though there were no photographs of her, it was too chancy for her to leave the house yet.

She and I stayed home and lolled on the couch in the living room, talking, kissing, napping. At about two o'clock, the phone in the office rang, and I went to answer it.

"Is Tommy there?" asked the voice of The Worm.

"He's not here, Mr. Brogan."

"How about tall, smart, and handsome?" he asked.

"Antony?" I said. "He's out too."

"Who's this, the swami kid?"

"Yes," I said.

"Okay, kid, it's going to have to be you, because I don't know when I'm going to have a chance to call back. Listen good. Do you have a piece of paper and a pen?"

I sat down at Schell's desk and lifted a pen. "I'm ready," I said.

"First, take down this name. The guy's in Huntington and has written a recent article, not too complimentary, about the ERO. He used to work there . . . a doctor, Manfred Stintson." He gave me less than two seconds and asked, "Got it?"

I was still writing when I said, "Yeah."

"Well, Schell asked me about the Eugenics Record Office in Cold Spring Harbor. Your old man has a knack for sniffing out the shit, 'cause this one stinks like there's no tomorrow."

He paused for a moment, and when he began speaking again, he sounded agitated, almost angry. "Eugenics Record Office, Cold Spring Harbor, founded in 1910 by Charles Davenport and Harry Laughlin. The main purpose was to study heredity in relation to the scientific work of Mendel. It's all about breeding, and it's all about breeding the *perfect* race. They started by tracing the heredity of anomalies like your buddies on the midway down in Coney— giants, dwarfs, six-finger guys, you know. Then they got into twins and albinos, imbeciles, any trait that could be traced back genera- tions. Hey, I'll give you a hundred guesses what the model was for perfection."

"I've no idea," I said.

"Here's a clue. All of the people who support this have a heritage from northern Europe. We're talking Anglo-Saxon, white, blue eyes, get it? And there were and are some very powerful people be- hind this. The initial money came from the fortune of E. H. Har- riman, to the tune of eleven million dollars. You also have donations from Carnegie and Rockefeller. Teddy Roosevelt, Woodrow Wilson, Margaret Sanger, moneymen like Prescott Bush. All were or are solid supporters of this crackpottery. And what is it they support? A beating back of the rising tide of, as they put it, 'feebleminded- ness'; compulsory sterilization for those of less marked intelligence; distinct separation of the races; and stricter immigration and natu- ralization laws to keep the likes of you and also those of southern European extraction from sullying the lineage of the founders of the great USA. As far as these guys are concerned, the very Depres- sion itself was caused by hereditary malcontents, imbeciles, and the shiftless masses draining the life from our culture. And kid, please tell me you realize that perfection is in the eye of the beholder."

I didn't understand that he actually wanted an answer, but when he didn't continue, I snapped to and said, "Certainly."

"Shiftlessness, by the way, is something these doctors at the ERO can apparently score for. Also things like 'musical intelligence.' That's not too subjective a determination is it? Christ, to normal society, I'm as shiftless as they come. I could see these guys wanting to make me a castrati. Can you imagine how annoying I'd be if my voice was even higher? This shit's everywhere, in school textbooks, in church sermons that say only the *best* should marry the *best*, in Congress, where the real idiots are passing laws to put this plan in place. Through the efforts of these arbiters of humanity, twenty-some-odd states have mandatory laws concerning the sterilization of anyone they consider to be of subpar intelligence. There's even talk of euthanasia. You know what that means? Who needs the fucking Ku Klux Klan when you've got these guys? This very year, the International Congress of Eugenics met, and, baby, they've got plans for you. Are you with me, kid, are you with me?"

"I'm here," I said.

"I'm going to give you a little prophecy from the illuminated mind of The Worm. Follow me on this. You think you've got it bad, well you do. Mexicans are seen as a poison in the bloodstream of true America. You're a shiftless and thieving lot. That goes without saying, and that's the main reason they want to round you all up and send you back. It's political, it's social, but they pretend it's a medical condition. But consider the Jews, they have none other than Henry Ford on their keisters. Henry's a major race baiter. In the newspaper he owns out in Deerborn, Michigan, he published a piece called 'The Protocols of the Elders of Zion.' The bottom line: Jews need to be eradicated. He's spreading this stuff all over Europe as well. The Germans, who he does scads of business with, are loving the hell out of him. Take the fact that in his autobiography he claims to have gotten the concept for the assembly line from slaughterhouses and put that together with the money and influence these fools have, their desire to sweep humanity clean of anyone who doesn't look or think like them, and that equals dark days ahead, my young swami. The Worm has spoken."

The receiver went dead. My head was swimming, not only from the cyclone of Emmet's diatribe but also from its implications. A strange emotion filled me, but I was too stunned to place it. I went back into the living room and took my seat on the couch next to Isabel. I put my arms around her and held her tightly, closing my eyes. It came to me then that what I felt, like a snowball lodged in my chest slowly melting into my system, was fear. I felt as fragile as a butterfly, and no matter how tightly I held on to Isabel, I couldn't help but see, in my mind's eye, the image of a giant shoe, above me, descending.

A CHIMPANZEE IS CURIOUS

That evening, Schell tracked down Stintson's number through phone information and called, pretending to be a reporter for the *New York Times* who wanted to follow up on the professor's writings in opposition to the ERO. Apparently Stintson was eager to discuss the issue and bring his concerns to a wider audience. He invited Schell to visit him at his home the next day. I would accompany Schell and act as his assistant and photographer.

Early the next morning, as we tooled along Lawrence Hill Road, Schell told me, "I still haven't called the Barneses back to discuss the séance. I have no idea what to tell them. They're looking for answers, and this thing just keeps getting more complex with zero payoff."

"Do you think Greaves had anything to do with it?" I asked.

"I doubt it," said Schell. "We're grasping at straws, focusing in on him. But he's all we've got at the moment. Granted, he's not likeable, he was on to our con, and he belongs to an organization that, as Emmet reported, and more than likely Dr. Stintson will corroborate, is practicing a rich man's subtle genocide on the weak, the lame, the hungry, and the foreign, but that doesn't mean that he murdered Charlotte Barnes. I'm afraid we've pretty much reached the end of the line with this."

"That's not going to look good for us, is it?" I said.

"Not if Barnes gets on the blower to his cronies and tells them we failed at what we have advertised as our expertise. No, that's going to be a direct hit on our business. Barnes probably knows every wealthy truebeliever on the Gold Coast of the North Shore. We may have to relocate. I've always thought Hollywood might be a good venue for us. Movie stars seem as if they'd be easy marks."

"I suppose this is a lesson in taking jobs for free," I said.

Schell shrugged, "Not the greatest policy, but we're still the richer for it."

"In what way?"

"You've found Isabel, and I've found Morgan. Money is not the only manifestation of good fortune."

There was something definitely wrong with Schell. It wasn't the sodden depression of a few weeks earlier, before the Parks séance, but this optimism was completely unexpected. Was Schell becoming a romantic? I found it nearly as disturbing as the more mordant condition that preceded it. I mulled it over for a few minutes and was about to mention it to him, when he pulled up to the address Stintson had given him.

Stintson was a vital-looking older gentleman, who sat ramrod straight in his chair as he poured us coffee at his kitchen table. He had about him a kind of energy and a can-do attitude that, frankly, I found wearying. It was a certainty he'd been up at sunrise thinking intricate thoughts. Still, he was not at all averse to speaking with us as long as the conversation didn't flag. When I asked him to pose for a photo, he became exasperated at what he considered to be a waste of time.

"We wanted to find out about the ERO," said Schell, beginning the interview. I took out my pad and pen and began scribbling.

"Yes," he said. "I understand."

"Have you worked there long?"

"Well, Mr. Schell, I don't spend much time there anymore. I still have a membership, so to speak, but . . . my interest has cooled over the years."

"Why's that?"

Stintson winced. "I found I was working at cross-purposes with the leaders of the organization. You see, many of us who worked there hoped that our research would eventually lead to cures for inherited maladies. But as time went by I began to realize that the intended mission, of those who were supporting it that is, was to disenfranchise, to persecute, to *play God* instead of help people. I still believe the research could lead somewhere positive, but not now, not in this climate."

"Doesn't it all just fit into Darwinian theory?" asked Schell. "Survival of the fittest?"

"Yes," said Stintson. "But who or what is the fittest? It's Nature's purview to make that selection. There are so many factors, both seen and unseen, that go into that selection; it's not humanity's job. Some of my colleagues there bring an almost religious zeal to it, definitely a subjective zeal. They never consider the fact that what might seem to them to be aberrant may, in the larger scheme of things, be the next rung on the evolutionary ladder—a solution of survival for our species."

Schell nodded, and I could tell he was truly contemplating the doctor's comments and how they fit with his worldview of marks and cons, predators and prey.

I could see Stintson was getting a little restless, so I put my hand on Schell's arm to draw his attention. "The photo," I said.

"Oh, yes," he said and held up the photograph from Parks's place. "Does this look familiar to you, doctor?" asked Schell, laying the picture on the table so that the professor could study it.

He took a look at it and smiled. "Probably one of the informal gatherings at ERO," he said. "That's me, looking somewhat younger, right there," he said, pointing. I looked and it was true—a more youthful Stintson, darker hair, fewer wrinkles, stared up at us from the static tableau.

"How about this gentleman?" asked Schell, pointing.

"That, I believe, is Mr. Parks. He was a contributor to the cause. A wealthy man, who, if I'm not mistaken, recently met with a grisly end."

"You don't say," said Schell.

I saw a look of suspicion flash across Stintson's face, but Schell obviously noted it also and pushed on. "And did you know this fellow, Greaves, here?" he asked.

Stintson bent forward to get a better look. "I know him, but his name isn't Greaves."

"What?" asked Schell. "I was told he was a Doctor Greaves."

"Why exactly are you asking these questions?" asked Stintson, suddenly cold. "I don't think I'll be answering any more."

"We're simply curious," said Schell.

"A chimpanzee is curious, a cat is curious," said Stintson. "What are you after?" He pushed back from the table and began to stand up, no doubt to show us the door.

"Have you heard the name Charlotte Barnes?" asked Schell.

Stintson stopped midway in his ascent and returned to his seat. "The girl who was found murdered," he said. All of his good humor had vanished.

"Yes," said Schell. "We're investigating her death, and I think this fellow either knows something or was involved in some way. Now you don't have to help us, but an innocent man, or a man innocent of this particular crime, is going to take the rap for it and that girl's murder will have gone unavenged."

"You're not with the *Times*, I take it. Are you police?" he asked. "Federal agents?" He looked at me as if the thought of me working for the government would be a bizarre revelation indeed.

"We're working for Barnes, and I can assure you we're the furthest thing from police as one can get," said Schell.

"Can you prove it?" asked Stintson. "Say I call Barnes?"

"Barnes won't admit that we're working for him. He's promised me that. We've told him we're spiritual mediums. He thinks we're communicating with the dead to find out who killed his daughter. Actually we're con men, but I swear we aren't taking any money from him."

"That sounds fairly preposterous," said Stintson.

"Do you have a deck of cards?" asked Schell.

Stintson went to a drawer in the kitchen and brought forth a deck of cards. Schell had them out of the pack and was putting them through their paces in a flash. Stintson smiled as he watched the incredible display. When Schell was finished with the cards he set them down, waved his left hand in the air, and a monarch butterfly appeared above the table. "Lean over here and shake hands with me," he said to the doctor. Stintson warily did as he was asked. They gripped hands briefly and then the old man pulled away.

"As I said," said Schell, "we're not cops." He pointed with his left index finger at his right wrist, where Stintson's watch now resided.

The doctor's eyes focused, he looked down at his wrist, and broke out laughing. "Okay," he said. "I'm convinced you're not federal agents. That's what I was worried about."

"Why would you worry about that?" I asked.

"The man you pointed to isn't named Greaves. His real name is Fenton Agarias, and one thing I know about him is he has mysterious connections to some very powerful people, some wealthy, some in the government."

"Is there anything else you can tell us about him?" said Schell.

"He's mad," said Stintson.

BLOOD

You mean like frothing at the mouth?" asked Schell. "When I met him, he didn't seem any worse than a crank." "No, no," said Stintson. "I'm talking about the work he was doing at the ERO. Agarias was sold—lock, stock, and barrel—on the whole concept of thinning the *unsavory elements* from the country's breeding stock. A true zealot. We tried to force him out of the organization, because his practices were so blatantly immoral. He was doing some experiment that involved the interbreeding of fraternal twins. He'd found these test subjects somewhere in Pennsylvania—second-generation twins, born of an incestuous union between twins. We believed that he either paid or coerced this particular pair to mate. I never found out for sure, but it was rumored that this union resulted in yet another pair of twins—also fraternal, brother and sister, whom he'd adopted. I had a hard time believing it, for even though there is always a certain percentage of a chance that twins will result from a pregnancy, the chances that it would occur in this same family seemed infinitesimal."

"So you and some of the others questioned him?" asked Schell.

"We went above his head, to our boss, Davenport, and told him we wanted Agarias out. They either wouldn't or couldn't relieve him of his position, but soon after he got a grant, private money, and a lot of it, to build a facility elsewhere, all on his own, and continue his research."

"When was this?" I asked.

Stintson thought for a moment. "About . . .1918 perhaps, maybe even earlier. I've seen him since then, but he doesn't speak to me. He's been at the ERO on occasion, for instance the gathering in that photo. He still has an office there, and I heard that he also opened a private medical practice, catering to wealthy families here on the North Shore, although I doubt he needs the money. I don't know anything more about his present circumstances."

"Can you tell us anything more about the research he was doing?" asked Schell.

"His specialty was hematology. That I remember. He had an insane notion that racial difference was found in the blood, which has no scientific basis. It's like something out of the Old Testament. Unfortunately, the people supporting him also cull their science from the Bible.

"One other thing, and this will explain to you why I was so cautious. One of my ERO colleagues insisted on investigating Agarias on his own. He wound up dead. Shot through the back of the head while kneeling on his living room floor. Coincidence? Maybe. Then again, maybe not."

"An execution," said Schell.

"The police report called it a robbery, but according to his daughter, nothing was missing from the house. After that, no one asked about Agarias any further."

"How do I find out more about Agarias without getting shot in the back of the head?" asked Schell.

"I wouldn't confront him," said Stintson. "But you might take a look through his office. He still has one at the ERO."

"Locked up, I imagine," said Schell.

"Are you a con man, or are you a con man?" said Stintson.

We eventually said our good-byes to Stintson after getting a hand-drawn map from him depicting the layout of the ERO, in particular the location of Agarias's office and the security guard's station. His parting remark was a plea not to ever mention that he spoke to us. On the drive home, Schell admitted to me that things had finally broken open in his mind and were beginning to become clear to him. He wasn't quite ready to share his theory, but he predicted that after our trip to the Eugenics Record Office and a look at Agarias's papers, if we should find them, we'd know the full story.

"In a few hours we've gone from abandoning this goose chase to being on the verge of solving the whole thing," I said.

Schell smiled, ruefully it seemed. "Remember you were saying I never made mistakes? Well I was completely wrong about Greaves/Agarias. He seems to be the guy, though, or at least a part of it, I'm sure of that," he said.

"I see the connection between him and what the coroner told us about the death of Charlotte Barnes. Blood and transfusion," I said. "But why was Parks murdered? I don't get that."

"Think about when it happened," said Schell. "Directly following Charlotte Barnes's funeral. I'm betting Agarias, in his guise of Doctor Greaves, showed up at the funeral or the wake or both. Parks probably recognized him, tried to remember where he'd seen him before, and eventually put it together. That's why he had the photograph on his desk. As a friend of Barnes, perhaps he wanted to figure out what kind of scam Agarias was pulling, using an assumed name. Parks might have remembered that some of the other researchers had wanted to drum Agarias out of the ERO."

"So they killed him and two of his employees?" I asked.

"Agarias is covering his trail. Like Stintson said, the guy's a lunatic. And if what I'm thinking about the rest of it is even close to true, we're going to see that he's crazier than we could ever imagine."

When we reached the house, before getting out of the car, Schell put his hand on my shoulder and said, "Listen, I'll fill Antony in, but don't say anything to Morgan or Isabel about what we learned."

I nodded.

For the rest of the day, Schell was very quiet. He told me he was planning how we would gain access to Agarias's ERO office the following day, but I could tell there was something else on his mind as well. Isabel and I packed a lunch and took a walk through the trees to sit by the sound. The day was very cold, threatening a first snow, but we huddled together against the wind and watched the choppy water. In the course of our conversation she admitted to me that as soon as things blew over and Schell thought it was safe for her to leave the house, she would find a way to go back to Mexico.

"Come with me," she said.

I'd had a feeling that things would come to this, but I wanted to put off thinking about it as long as possible. If she went away and I didn't go with her, I knew I would never see her again. But if I left Antony and Schell and the promise of college behind, I would be writing off that part of my life. All I said to her was, "When you're ready to go, tell me." She smiled and said nothing more about it, and I wasn't sure if she thought I was promising I'd follow or if she knew I couldn't decide, but I didn't have the courage to contemplate the choice any further.

Back at the house, we found Antony sitting at the kitchen table, cleaning the Mauser. He was bent over the gun, whistling, amid all manner of rods, brushes, and solvents laid out.

"I haven't cleaned this damn thing in years," he said, "and it's not in bad shape—a little copper fouling, that's about it."

"Are you getting an itchy trigger finger?" I asked.

"Not me," he said. "This is by order of the boss."

"Is he expecting gunplay?"

"Beats me," said Antony. "I just clean the gun, drive the car, get strangled by the bad guys, and make the dinners around here." He started whistling again and went back to his work.

Schell and Morgan only appeared at dinnertime. I didn't inquire what they'd been up to all afternoon. During the meal, Isabel asked Schell when he thought it would be safe for her to leave the house.

"Give it a few more days," said Schell. "Where are you thinking of going?"

"Mexico," she said.

"I'll give you some money," he said.

"I couldn't take your money," she told him.

"Well, it's going to take you a long time to walk there," he said.

"Take his money," said Antony. "I would."

"We could drive you over to Jersey and put you on a bus," Schell said. "Once you get to Mexico, send the dough back to me if you want, or not. I don't care."

"Why not a train?" asked Morgan.

"More people traveling on trains read newspapers than people on the bus," said Schell.

"Don't sweat it, hon," Antony said to Isabel. "It's going to work out."

I quickly changed the conversation to the upcoming presidential election, which was only weeks away. With the exception of Antony expressing his hopes for the repeal of Prohibition, the topic soon died from overall disinterest, but it was enough to divert the discussion away from Isabel's departure.

Later that night, once Isabel was asleep, I went in search of Schell. I wanted to talk to him about my possibly leaving. Luckily, he'd not gone to bed but was sitting on the couch in the Bugatorium. Morgan, stretched out next to him, had fallen asleep with her head resting on a pillow propped against his thigh. As I entered the room, he looked over at me, and I said, "Sorry," and began to leave, but he waved me back. I walked over and sat down across from him.

Before I could speak, he whispered to me, "I've been meaning to talk to you."

I was going to tell him the same, but his expression was one of perplexity, as if he'd made himself weary from too much thought.

"What is it?" I asked.

"I've been thinking about the butterflies," he said.

"That's not exactly unusual," I said, smiling.

"No," he said, shaking his head. "I think once this present group dies out in a few weeks, I'll discontinue the Bugatorium."

"Why?"

"Recent developments have left me with a bad taste for the idea of breeding in any capacity. It's never struck me before, but now the whole thing"—here he lifted his hands in the air, the same motion he used to release butterflies during the séances— "seems to me wrought with vanity; the most self-serving affectation."

"But the study of butterflies excited you," I said.

"I think I conned myself into the excitement."

"I always enjoyed them," I said.

"Did I ever tell you how I got started?"

"No," I said.

"It was my first con," he said. "My father, the great Magus Jack, would bet on anything. He'd bet me on things and never lose—coin flips, horse races, how many times a woman at the mailbox on the corner would open and close the little door after putting her letter in. When I'd lose, he'd laugh at me. It got to the point where all I wanted to do was beat him—if only just once.

"One morning, before the sun was even up, one of the few days he ever spent with me, we were walking through the park—he was going to show me some scam—and I spotted a butterfly, closed, on a flower. I bet him I could wiggle the flower and the butterfly wouldn't fly away. He laughed his condescending laugh at me and took the bet. I got down, grabbed the flower by the stalk, and moved it back and forth, a good six or seven times. The butterfly hung on, wouldn't budge. He didn't laugh then but paid me in silver with a grim look on his face."

"Why didn't it fly away?" I asked.

"It was something Morty had read to me one of the nights I'd stayed with him. Out in the wild, a butterfly can't fly until it's warmed by the sun. It needs the heat to move its blood up into the wings. I never forgot that con. Butterflies became my good luck charm."

"You never told me that before," I said.

"Yes," he said, nodding. "It feels like a lot of things are about to change." He looked up then and followed the flight of some white specimen whose name I didn't know. As if snapping out of a daydream, he again focused on me. "Was there something you wanted to talk about?" he asked.

"No," I said. "I just came in to say good night."

"Okay," he said and leaned back, closing his eyes. His left hand descended to rest on Morgan's shoulder.

SNOW

When I woke in the middle of the night this time, it wasn't to the sound of a phone ringing but something a hundred times louder and far more ominous. I sat bolt upright in bed just as the din died, and then I recalled where I'd heard it before—at cabin number six. A machine gun.

As Isabel came to, sitting up next to me, I grabbed her around the waist and pulled her onto the floor. She struggled to get free, saying, "What are you doing?" but I whispered in her ear to stay down and keep quiet. Remaining on all fours, I scrabbled across the bedroom and out into the hallway. There was another burst of gunfire, shorter this time, and then the sound of someone kicking in the front door.

We'd left the light on in the living room, and its glow seeped back into the hall where I was and into part of the kitchen. On the other side of the living room entrance, hunkering down with his back to the kitchen wall, was Antony in his boxer shorts and an undershirt. He held the Mauser, his finger on the trigger, the barrel pointing toward the ceiling. Looking over, he saw me and motioned with his left arm for me to get back. I started to inch away, and the next thing I knew he was spinning on his heels, bringing the gun around in his right hand. He peered quickly out into the other room and squeezed the trigger. I don't know anything about guns, but the Mauser was obviously not a mere single-shot weapon. A barrage of gunfire spat out its end.

There was silence in the living room, and I was tempted to look. I felt Isabel's hand on my back and knew she had crawled out of the bedroom behind me. I cautiously moved to the corner of the wall, all the time Antony motioning me to go back. When I finally did take a quick glance, I saw a body lying just inside the door. I pointed for Antony to look and he did. As soon as he saw no one else in the doorway, he signaled for us to run across and join him.

We literally leaped across the open entrance into the kitchen. Antony stood up and grabbed me by the back of the neck, pulling me close to him. "I'm going to lay down some fire. Take Isabel, leave by the back door. If it looks clear, run your asses off for the woods. Stay there till I come for you."

I just then realized I was shaking. He let go of my head and patted me on the cheek. "You with me?" he said.

I nodded, not even considering that all I wore was a pair of pajama pants and Isabel one of my dress shirts. That's when the back door burst in with a jarring crash, shattered glass and splinters of wood flying everywhere, the chain lock whipping the air. The phantom landed on Antony's back, knocked the gun out of his hand, and drove him forward, face-first, into the wall as Isabel and I were shoved to the side. There was a great cracking noise, and the lathing showed an imprint of the big man's head. I put my arm in front of Isabel and pushed her out of the way.

We watched helplessly as Antony staggered away from the wall and clamped his hands on the arms of the phantom, which were now around his neck. He turned and, in one fluid motion, bent and heaved the creature over his back onto the kitchen table, the legs of which broke under the impact.

"Get out," Antony said to us. The back exit was wide open, inviting us to flee, but I couldn't leave him.

The phantom sprang up immediately, and before Antony could even turn again to face his attacker the thing had viciously punched him in the side of the head. Antony went sideways across the kitchen. We heard more men entering through the front door in the living room. The big man was dazed, nearly buckling from the force of the blow. The phantom advanced upon him and threw another punch. Antony ducked, and the white fist smashed into the wall.

"Diego, run," said Schell, who just then appeared in the kitchen, his robe billowing behind him. He raised his arm and threw something. Only when it struck the creature's right shoulder blade and sunk in halfway to the hilt did I see it was the switch-blade. There was an ear-splitting howl, and the thing arched its back. Schell never stopped moving but went to his knees, scooped up the Mauser off the floor, and tossed it to me. I grabbed it, turned, and aimed for the phantom's misshapen head. It saw me at the last second, and when the gun went off with, for me, an unexpected kick and explosion, it ducked and I watched as the shots hit a man in a black suit who was just then entering the kitchen. More intruders were behind him, who caught his body as he fell backward.

I grabbed Isabel by the arm and we ran over the broken glass. A wild leap from the back steps and we were off across the yard toward the woods. At the tree line, I turned to look back and see if anyone was following us. Someone had flipped on the kitchen lights, and I saw Antony punch the phantom's muscled white form in the chest as two more men grabbed him from behind. Schell was completely out of sight.

I let go of Isabel and started running back toward the house, but I'd not taken five steps before Antony dove headfirst through the doorway. He sailed over the steps and hit the ground, rolling head over heels. In a second he was on his feet and running at me. Two men ran out after him, but I brought the gun up and fired wildly.

They ducked down long enough for Antony to reach me. He grabbed my arm, nearly lifting me off my feet, and pulled me toward the trees. As we passed Isabel, he took her arm too.

Once in the woods, hiding in a thicket, we looked back and saw that no one was following us. Antony was out of breath, bent over with his hands on his knees, heaving. I was stunned, also gasping for breath, and Isabel asked the question I would have spoken had I been able to.

"What about Mr. Schell?" she whispered.

"We've got to go back," I finally was able to get out.

Antony straightened up, still breathing heavily. "Give me the gun," he said. I handed it to him, and he shook his head. "Schell thought they might be coming," he said. "That's why he had me take care of the gun. I just don't think he expected it to come so soon—or so strong."

"He's in trouble, though. We've got to do something," I said.

"He told me if anything happened I was to get you two clear and wait till things died down. So that's what I'm doing," he said.

"They'll kill him," I shouted.

Antony backhanded me across the side of the face. "Shut up," he said. "I don't get paid to second-guess him."

There was the sound of commotion in the house, coming from just about every room. "Get down," he said. "If we don't see them coming, we'll stay right here."

Antony crouched, and Isabel and I followed his lead. It was freezing out and I put my arm around her, the two of us shivering as much from fear as from the cold. It was torture waiting for the sound of another gunshot.

"What are they doing?" I asked.

"They're looking for Morgan," he said.

"¿Dónde está ella?" asked Isabel.

"Let's hope for Schell's sake they don't find her," he said.

Ten minutes passed, maybe fifteen, and then we heard the cars start up down by the road. Gravel crunched as the cars pulled away, and everything went perfectly quiet. Antony stood up.

"Okay, I'm going in to have a look around. Wait here until I give you the high sign." As he made his way through the trees and across the yard, dressed in his nightclothes, the gun held high, it started to snow; giant, wet flakes.

"Tengo mucho frío," said Isabel.

"A few minutes more," I said. In the time we'd waited for them to clear out of the house, I'd thought of nothing, but now my mind was on fire with images of what we might find in the house. I saw brief mind flashes of Schell and Morgan slaughtered on the kitchen floor. Finally I stood up and told Isabel, "I can't wait any longer."

As we headed out of the woods, Antony came to the back door, dressed in a shirt and trousers and signaled to us that the coast was clear. Before turning back inside, he called, "I don't see Schell or Morgan anywhere. They must have taken them."

The place was a complete wreck, Schell's once-orderly domain now a chaotic mess. The furniture was overturned, lamps and paintings were smashed, and dozens of butterflies had escaped the Bugatorium and floated above the debris, already perishing in the cold air rushing in through the open doorways. The first thing I did was find a blanket for Isabel and wrap it around her, but Antony warned, "No time for that. Get dressed. We're getting out of here in case they come back."

After dressing, we helped Antony perform one more search of the house, but the others were nowhere to be found. Suddenly, the big man said, "Shit, I just remembered something." We followed him to Schell's bedroom, where he went directly to the already open closet, reached in, grabbed an armload of suits, and threw them on the bed. Leaning into the closet again, he put his hand up to the ceiling. "There's a button in here somewhere," he said, groping around. This was something I'd never known about. A moment later, a panel in the rear wall of the closet slid back to reveal a compartment filled with the form of Morgan Shaw dressed in a long white silk nightgown. Antony held his hand out to her and helped her into the bedroom.

The first thing she said was, "Where is he?"

"They took him," said Antony.

Morgan began to cry, covering her face with her hands.

"No time for tears, sister," said Antony. "Get dressed. I'll go start the car."

Luckily they'd left the Cord in one piece. As we piled in, Antony said he figured that if they were coming back they'd at least have slashed the tires so we couldn't get away. Still, he insisted on leaving the house. When we were on the road, he told me that Schell kept a little place in Babylon on the South Shore, next to the bay. "It's sort of a glorified fishing shack, but it's got a fireplace and a stove," he said. This was yet another revelation to me.

"He never told me about it," I said and tears came to my eyes.

"Shit, kid, he's got secrets he doesn't even tell himself. Don't take it so personally," said Antony as he pulled out onto the road. The light from the headlamps glinted off a fine dusting of snow that had already stopped falling.

"It's not that," I said, now outright crying.

"There's one piece of good news," said Antony. "I got a clear look at that so-called phantom tonight. He's no monster. I'm sure of that from the way he yodeled when Schell threw that shiv into him. He's just a fucked-up guy with a pasty complexion, a big lumpy head, and in serious need of a dentist. He's in perfect shape, though, and strong as an ox. Must be a bitch wearing nothing but that pair of shorts he's got on in this weather. Nothing a couple of bullets wouldn't bring down, though."

"Are they going to kill him?" said Morgan, leaning forward over the front seat.

"Who, Schell?" asked Antony. "I don't know."

She sat back and started crying again. I turned to see how Isabel was doing, and she was staring quietly ahead in shock. Only Antony was operating as if it was business as usual.

The drive from the North Shore to the South Shore was fairly long. Both Isabel and Morgan eventually dozed off, their nerves frayed. I was also succumbing to a deep weariness, my eyes blinking like mad, my mind numb. I tried to stay awake to keep Antony company, but I was fatigued beyond measure.

Although he hadn't spoken for miles, the big man turned to me somewhere in the middle of the trip and said, "You awake?"

I shook my head to bring myself around and sat up. "Yeah," I said.

"Listen, Schell and I agreed yesterday that I'm good at following orders but I'm no mastermind. He said if anything happened to him, you should take over. So, kid, as of right now, you're the boss."

"What?" I said, unsure as to what I'd just heard.

"You're the man now, junior," he said.

"Okay," was all I could get out. I was too tired to comprehend the implications of my new position. My first act as the head of our operation was to slump over and fall fast asleep.

HOLY SHINOLA

By noon the next day, after having slept and eaten something, Antony and I were back at the house. We'd left Morgan and Isabel in the fishing cottage in Babylon as it seemed secluded enough to be safe. I'd also told Antony to instruct Isabel on how to fire the gun, which we'd left with her.

The weight of my responsibility had begun to dawn on me during the return trip to the North Shore, and although the prospect of calling the shots was frightening, I had to laugh, remembering how only a few nights before, I'd felt so mature, thanks to having my arm around a woman and a drink in my hand. It struck me now that growing up had more to do with others being able to count on you, and whether or not you could pull through in a jam.

Antony rigged the back door to keep it closed and nailed up an old rug over the front entrance to keep out most of the autumn breeze. I built a fire in the living room using the shattered remains of the furniture. Once the blaze was really rolling and the house had started to warm up, I made my first decision. Going to my bedroom, I fetched the turban, my pasha pants, and the high-collared blouses that had been the props, and a good part of the lie, of Ondoo, and chucked them all into the fire. Black smoke, like some evil genie, roiled upward from those garments, and the stink of them burning seemed somehow right to me.

I went to Schell's room, chose one of his silk suits (a cream-colored one with a vest), a pair of shiny black shoes, and an indigo tie. I knew intuitively somehow that these things would fit me, and they did. It was a stroke of luck that when Schell was abducted, he was in his pajamas, because that meant he'd left behind his wallet (we'd need the money) and the skeleton key, which I knew would come in handy. Slicking back my hair in the mirror, I studied my reflection, and it struck me that, like one of Schell's butterflies, I'd finally emerged from my cocoon.

I walked out into the kitchen, where Antony was making coffee. He looked up, and I know he noticed my new attire but said nothing as he turned his attention back to filling the pot.

"Did they cut the phone wire?" I asked.

"No," he said, turning off the tap.

"When you get a chance," I said, "call Hal Izzle. Tell him what happened to Schell and tell him we need him to get out here as soon as possible. We'll pick him up at the station."

"Okay, boss," said Antony. He put the pot on the stove and then went into the office to make the call.

I took my seat at the kitchen table, focused on the intricate wing pattern of a mosaic, *Colobura dirce*, that lay dead next to the sugar bowl, and took stock of what I knew and what I needed to know. My only goal now was to save Schell. I didn't care any longer if we got Agarias or avenged Charlotte Barnes.

When we picked Hal up at the station in Port Washington a few hours later, he was wearing an overcoat with extra-long sleeves, a pair of gloves, and a hat with an exceedingly wide brim he kept turned down, obscuring his face from the curious and the cruel.

"Anything from Tommy?" he asked as he settled into the backseat of the Cord and removed the huge hat.

"Nothing," said Antony.

"Kid, what's with you?" Hal said, pulling off his gloves. "One time I see you, you're a swami, and now you're a gigolo. You've got more disguises than Lon Chaney."

"The kid's in charge now," said Antony.

"Holy shinola," said Hal. "Congrats on the promotion." He reached his hand into the front seat and I shook it.

"It's not something I wanted," I said. "But you can call me Diego from now on."

I felt Hal's hand on my shoulder. "You're going to do fine, Diego," he said.

"Thanks," I said, feeling as though I'd jumped some hurdle by naming myself.

"Wait till you see what he's got cooked up for you," said Antony, smiling into the rearview mirror.

I then held up the leash and collar I'd kept out of sight on my lap.

"The old leash and collar," said Hal, his eyes widening. "You must have been talking to some of my lady friends."

"I don't know how to say this without being offensive," I said. "But you've got to play the dog."

"How could I be offended?" he said. "That's my bread and butter. You want me to bite somebody, pee on a lamppost, hump some dame's leg? Just let me know."

"You've got to get naked," said Antony.

Hal howled. "This is going to be better than I thought," he said and proceeded to take off his coat and start unbuttoning his shirt.

"I should have put a tarp down on the backseat," the big man said.

"Fuck you, Henry," said Hal. "Diego, do I have any lines, or do you just want me to act doglike?"

"All dog," I said.

"My specialty," he said.

We drove for a while, and as Hal put the collar on I explained my plan. After we crossed the Cold Spring Harbor town line, Antony asked, "What's this street we're looking for?"

I looked down at the directions Stintson had given me. "Bung-town Road," I told him. "It should be the third left up here."

It was late afternoon by the time we drove slowly past the ERO. It was a good-size building set back from the road, at the end of a straight path that led right to the front door. I couldn't help but think that it was trying to hide itself among the surrounding trees while its "researchers" did their nefarious work. I directed Antony to drive to the end of the block and park. There was a field and some woods behind the building, and it was my plan to approach the place from the back.

"This could take some time," I told Antony. "Once Hal gets back to the car, drive around for a while and then pull up on Bungtown a little ways down the street but facing the building so you can see me when I come out. We may have to move quickly."

"No sweat," he said.

"Okay, let's go," I said to Hal.

"See you later, Henry," he said and slipped into his overcoat.

"Spread some fleas around in that joint," said Antony.

Hal laughed, but the second he stepped out of the car, his entire demeanor changed. He was now a sullen mishap of nature, escaped from who knew where, as evidenced by the leash dangling from the collar around his neck. His expression had gone completely dull, and a glimmering string of drool hung from the corner of his mouth. When I started walking, he shuffled along beside me like a mindless animal. The transformation astonished me. Hal Izzle was a pro.

We crossed the field and made our way carefully through the woods at the back of the building, making sure no one was watch-ing us from inside. After stashing his coat in the woods, we dashed out from under the cover of the trees over to the left side of the building, scurrying close to the ground, below window level. When we reached the front, I took a little paper bag from inside my pocket and handed it to Hal. He opened it, put his head back, and brought it to his mouth, letting some of the white powder sift in between his lips. He chewed on the baking soda and worked up some spit, and before long he was frothing at the mouth.

"Okay," I whispered, "you're good."

I stayed put with my back to the side wall of the building, trying to imagine the plan unfolding. Hal, for his part, was to enter the foyer and stumble around, as if disoriented. Then he was to drop to all fours, growl, whimper, and eventually just lie down and curl up on the floor until the guard got out of his chair. The idea was to get the guy to follow him outside and distract him long enough for me to slip in behind them.

The wait was torture, and I started to worry that the guard might have a gun and, being spooked by the sight of Hal, draw it. Somehow twilight had arrived without my noticing its approach, and the impending darkness turned my thoughts gloomy. When I was about ready to come out of hiding and go to Hal's rescue, I heard the door open. I peered around the corner and saw the dog man on all fours, swaying back and forth. The door had closed behind him, though, and the guard had obviously stayed inside. Hal growled and barked, clawing the glass of the door, but to no avail. I realized then that if I was the guard, I might not be too anxious to get too close to this creature either, and I feared I'd miscalculated the situation.

Another minute passed and I was sure the jig was up, but then, in what could only be described as a stroke of genius, the dog man suddenly turned sideways to the door, lifted his leg, and started peeing on it. Before he even finished, he started crawling on all fours toward the other corner of the front of the building. The door swung open, and from my hiding place, I saw the guard emerge, dressed in his blue hat and uniform, holding a billy club.

"Get out of here, you filthy mutt," he yelled. Hal got to his feet and shuffled off around the other side of the building. "Jesus Christ," said the guard. He took two steps, as if to follow, but then stopped. I started to make my move as quietly as possible, walking on tiptoe. The guard was only about eight feet from the entrance, though. I'd have definitely been caught, but just as I was about to open the door, Hal stuck his big dog head around the corner again and let loose a string of vicious barking. The man jumped a little, then lifted his club and gave chase. After that I didn't see what happened. I was inside, moving through the foyer and down a hall to the left, as Stintson had instructed.

SPEAKING OF MUTATION

As I'd hoped, due to the late hour, the halls were deserted. Around the next corner, I found the office Stintson's instructions pointed to. The door was unlocked, and when I opened it, though the lights were already on, the place was empty. I went in and locked the door behind me. Three of the room's walls were lined with wooden filing cabinets and the last held a tall bookcase. There was a chair at a desk with a lamp on it, and opposite that a small couch with one window behind it.

I set to tracing the last names on the cabinets. Stintson's notes had put me in the general area of Agarias's archive, and the specific drawers holding his files were not hard to find. The first drawer I tried was locked though. Pulling out Schell's skeleton key, I went to work. A few seconds later, there came a faint click from within the baffle. The long drawer slid out with one pull on the handle, and I saw it was choked with folders, each crammed with paper.

I didn't know where to start. There were three more drawers similarly stuffed. It's going to take forever, I thought and felt a sense of panic begin to spark to life in my chest.

I took a deep breath and, realizing there was nothing else to do, reached in and pulled out a huge stack of files, about a quarter of what was in the top drawer. Carrying them to the desk, I laid them carefully to one side. I took off my jacket and draped it over the back of the chair, rolled up my sleeves, grabbed the top file, and sat down.

At first, nothing made any sense. There was a lot of scientific jargon concerning blood types, equations, formulas, and testimony concerning individuals who'd been studied. The best I could do was scan as much as I could and keep a lookout for something that rang a bell or that made things clearer.

Somewhere well into the second half hour, I started skipping files, simply glancing down whole sheets without actually reading, jumping around from file to file until the stack beside me on the desk became two stacks and then three and then just a mess of folders. Just when I thought that perhaps my trip to the ERO, calling Hal in from Brooklyn, the whole elaborate con was going to go to waste, I finally picked up on the thread of something that seemed familiar. I recalled Stintson mentioning Agarias's experiment with twins, and from the look of the text I was then scanning, I had blundered my way into the middle of that research.

I did some backtracking, found the origin of the research in question, and then moved forward. Even though my eyes were weary by then, and my back hurt from leaning over the desk, I was infused with a new energy and clarity of vision. And then I caught sight of the name *Shaw*. I read on at a rapid rate as it became clear to me that I had before me certain pieces of the puzzle.

It was precisely when I uncovered an interesting fact concerning Morgan that I heard the sound of footsteps outside the door. A key slid into the lock from outside. There was no time for me to even get out of my chair. The door opened a sliver, tentatively at first, and then swung all the way in. Standing in the entrance, smiling, was Agarias. I stood up, thinking there was going to be trouble.

He tilted his head downward to look at me over the rims of his round glasses, and said, "If it isn't the spiritual savant of the sub-continent. Ondoo, is it?"

"What have you done with Schell?" I asked.

"He's in my keeping. Safe, for now."

Seeing he was alone, I started to move around the desk. All I wanted to do was punch him.

"Please sit down," he said.

When I kept advancing, he added, "If you'd like to see Mr. Schell again, I'd sit down."

I stopped in my tracks, unclenched my fist, and backed off.

"Sit down and I'll tell you anything you'd like to know, really. I've nothing to hide. Let me warn you, though, if you can't control yourself, I've got a gun, and I wouldn't mind shooting you." He patted the side pocket of his jacket as he took a seat on the couch.

"How did you know I was here?" I asked.

"After you and Schell went to see Stintson, I figured he would lead you here."

"Stintson?" I said in a weak attempt to cover the truth.

"Yes, poor Stintson. It seems he'll be all over the front page to-morrow. A robbery, I'm afraid."

I closed my eyes momentarily at the knowledge that we had been responsible for the man's death. "Okay," I finally said. "All I want is Schell. Tell me what I need to do to get him back, and we'll forget all about you."

"Simple," said Agarias, "I want Morgan Shaw. An even ex-change."

"Why?"

"She's critical to my work," he said.

"She's legally your daughter, isn't she?" I said.

Agaias nodded. "Adopted. She and her brother. The twins of twins born of twins."

"What *is* it about twins?"

"Good question," he said, shaking his finger at me. "We know that incest begets birth anomalies, correct?"

I nodded.

"This is why it's illegal to marry, say, your sister, or even your first cousin. But I discovered this family out in the woods, where the laws of civilization were largely ignored. I waited until the children came of age and then, shall we say, *persuaded* them to couple. Imagine now, if incest between first cousins, brothers and sisters, causes mutations, just think about what the union of twins might produce. You see? When I first stumbled upon these degenerates, I noticed something in the early bloodwork, some anomaly. Over the two successive generations it has become more pronounced."

"Speaking of mutations," I said, "what exactly is that creature you sent to murder Parks and visit us at Schell's?"

"That's my boy, Merlin," said Agarias, smiling. "He's quite a physical specimen, isn't he?"

"He's deformed," I said.

"Now, now," he said. "Merlin is a very special individual. Granted, he's not the most handsome fellow. But take, for instance, his skin. He's not albino. Albino is the lack of pigmentation. His pigment is white. The other thing about him, and this is most important, he's got a blood type like none other."

"What do you mean?" I asked.

"I mean his blood type is unique. If you were to test it, it would register nothing, not A, A negative, B, B negative, AB, or O. Only he and one other person possess it."

"His sister," I said. "Morgan."

"You're shrewd for a wetback," he said.

"Not shrewd enough," I said. "Why exactly do you want her?"

"Morgan, Merlin, I'm sure you didn't catch the Arthurian reference," he said.

I shook my head, even though I had.

"I adopted them both but decided early on that I would work only with the male child. I've trained him from birth, physically of course, like a circus animal. Mentally he's of subpar intelligence. But it was his blood that interested me most.

"We need manpower in this country to save us from economic decline, but unfortunately, we're lacking in the right type of men. Those with Anglo blood, our rightful forefathers, will build a great civilization here. We need to deport and eradicate all those of weaker bloodlines. But those of mixed bloodlines, it may be possible to salvage some of them in order to create workers. My theory is that Merlin's special blood might negate, might cleanse, the tainted blood of half breeds, like the Barnes girl. In other words, wash the Jew out of her."

"And so she was part of an experiment. You transfused her, and she died. How many others have you killed with these experiments?"

"Believe me," he said, moving to the edge of his seat, "we're making progress. I think the answer lies within Morgan. I should not have ignored her and concentrated on her brother. I now believe she's got the blood ingredient necessary to accomplish my goal."

"How can anyone who treats children the way you do create a great civilization?" I said.

"Oh, do I sense you disapprove?" he said, feigning concern. "My work is far more important than individual lives."

"What if I go to the police?"

"Think through it, my boy. You're an illegal. They're more likely to deport you than to listen to you. And I have powerful benefactors."

"There's just one problem, Mr. Agarias."

"Yes?"

"I don't know where Morgan is. She took off the other day after Schell and I ran into your friends out by her cabin. She didn't want us to get hurt."

"Very sad," he said. "Poor Mr. Schell. It seems he's conned his last old lady."

"What if we can find her?" I asked.

"I can give you three days. After that, I'll rerun the experiment and transfuse Schell. He is half Jewish you know, on his mother's side."

"No," I said, "he never mentioned it."

A PATRIOT

Three days," he repeated. "I'll contact you at the end of that time. If you have her, we'll set up a meeting. If you don't, Schell gets the needle, and my boy Merlin will be out to pay you another visit. Next time I'll instruct him to bring me the head of that big oaf of Schell's."

"Agarias," I said as he rose to leave. "You know, your name doesn't exactly sound Anglo to me. What are you?"

"I'm a patriot," said Agarias and smiled.

"Call me, I'll find her," I said to him as he made for the door.

He stopped before leaving and said, "Three days, my friend. No more."

I was afraid Agarias would alert the guard that I was in the building, so the second the door closed, without bothering to return the files to their appropriate drawers, I strode across the office and climbed up on the couch. Reaching over the back of it, I opened the window and removed the screen. When I landed on the ground on the side of the building, it was already night. I didn't hesitate to see if anyone was about but just took off running toward the street. A few seconds later, Antony pulled up to the curb and I got in.

Hal was in the backseat, fully clothed now, and first thing, I asked him if he'd done all right.

"The guy chased me back as far as the trees," he said, "but once I made it into the woods, he stopped running and just yelled 'Filthy mutt' at me a few more times. He didn't want to screw with the dog in the dark woods, though. I'd have shoved that billy club up his ass."

"Filthy mutt," Antony said, laughing. "I wonder if the guy really thought you were a dog."

"I had an interesting visit while I was inside," I told them. When I told them I'd seen Agarias, Antony and Hal were both for going back and getting him. I told them to calm down and then filled them in on everything I'd learned.

"We have to get this schmuck," said Hal.

"If only we knew where they were keeping Schell," I said. "We could go and get him. My guess it's that special lab of his Stintson told us about. I was hoping I'd find an address for it in there, but it makes sense that he's not advertising its location, what with the kind of work he's doing, murdering children and raising lumpen-headed mutations like circus animals."

"You talking about Mr. Pasty?" asked Antony.

"That thing is legally his kid," I said. "Merlin is its name."

"What's he been feeding him?" said Antony.

"He's Morgan's brother," I said.

"What?" said the big man, momentarily taking his foot off the peddle. When he recovered, he said, "Makes sense, though, they're both white as milk. But Jeez, she definitely got the looks in that family."

"Do you know where this woman is who he wants to trade Tommy for?" asked Hal.

"Yeah, we've got her," I said. "But I don't think I can just turn her over to him."

"Well you're going to have to," said Hal. "Otherwise Schell takes the dirt nap."

"I know Schell would tell me not to do it," I said.

"Not exactly," said Antony. "Schell would scheme some con."

"Yeah," I said. "But we need an edge, which we don't have right now."

"Count me in," said Hal.

"Go back to Brooklyn," I said. "Get Sal to help you round up the others, anybody who'll help. Stand by. I might call at any time. I'm going to need you all to move at a moment's notice."

"You got it," he said.

"Don't go to the station," I told Antony. "We'll get some gas and take Hal all the way in and drop him at the Captain's place, not near his apartment. I'm afraid Agarias is having us followed. He knew we'd been to Stintson's place, because he told me he had the poor guy sandbagged. If they're on us, we can lose them in the city. We'll pay the toll; take the Motor Parkway."

"Okay," said Antony. "If we take them back to Babylon on our tails, we'll lose Morgan *and* Schell."

In Brooklyn we followed Hal into Captain Pierce's place and hung around a while to make sure no one was on our trail. The old Negro knife thrower had served as a scout at fifteen for the Union Army in the Civil War. That night he served Antony and Hal a mason jar each of the home brew beer that he'd concocted in a barrel in his kitchen. I explained to him what was going on with Schell, and he volunteered his services if need be. The Captain suffered from the shakes, and his eyes were starting to go cloudy, but he still had that hair-splitting aim, as he insisted on demonstrating by skewering, from across the living room, an apple he made Antony balance on his head.

We didn't get back to the fishing cottage until well after midnight. By then my fists were just about able to unclench. Antony's driving had been inspired, to say the least. The way he'd piloted the Cord, two-wheeling around corners, weaving in and out of traffic, cutting across open fields, I'm surprised my pants were still dry. If Agarias's goons had followed us after all that, they were welcome to us. I was exhausted, brain-weary from trying to think of an out for Schell and at the same time not giving up Morgan. In the morning, I knew I'd have to tell her everything, and that in itself frayed me.

Isabel met me at the door, holding the pistol.

"Don't shoot," I said and put my arms around her. She kissed me and told me it had been a quiet day. She'd gone out to the little market in town to get the things she needed to make dinner. I could smell the rich aroma all over the cottage, the scent of thick potato soup with bacon and onion that took me back to my mother's kitchen in an instant.

"No chiles," she said and shook her head. She served us each— Antony, herself, and I—a bowlful and a wedge of bread. Morgan was asleep in the back room.

While we ate, Antony and I filled her in on what had happened at the ERO. She'd never met Hal, so we had to describe him for her, and then Antony was good for a few stories from the old carny days when they'd worked the same shows. Finally the big man got up from the table.

"That meal's brought me to the conclusion that my cooking stinks," he said. He looked around the tiny cottage and then lifted the gun off the table and told us we could cram onto the couch, he was going to sleep in the car. "If I see anything going on," he said, leaving, "I'll hit the horn. We should've brought a fucking bottle from the house."

Isabel and I quietly cleaned up the dinner table, and when we were done, I sat on the couch and lay my head back. She came over and stretched out, resting her head on a pillow on my thigh. It was the exact position I'd seen Schell and Morgan in the last time I'd spoken to him.

"Morgan told me about her life in the city," Isabel whispered. "Very sad. She ran away from home and ended working for some man. You know, como puta. One day she returned to the place where he kept all his women and found him dead on the floor with a bullet in the back of his head."

"Sounds familiar," I said.

"I think she very much likes Mr. Schell," said Isabel.

"Yeah," I said, "they need each other. But what am I going to do? As it stands now, it's either one or the other."

"Pensarás en algo; duérmete," she said.

The imagery of the day ran through my thoughts in a crazy patchwork—Hal running around stark naked, Agarias's smirk, Antony's death-wish driving. It all ended with that dead butterfly on the kitchen table back at home. Suddenly, the wings of the mosaic twitched, and it began to flutter. I continued to stare as it lifted into the air, into the sky where the ceiling had been, and then I knew I was dreaming.

PERFECT

It was late morning, and I sat in the kitchen back at Schell's house. Antony came in from the newsstand but didn't, as usual, throw the paper on the table. He kept it rolled up under his arm as he poured a cup of coffee and then left it facedown on the counter before pulling out a chair and joining me.

"Stintson?" I asked.

He scratched his head and nodded. "Took one the hard way. Back of the head."

"Robbery?"

"That's what they say."

"Agarias is out of control," I said.

Antony gave a sad grunt of a laugh. "Well, think about his plan. From what you told me, he's taking the blood of some mistake of nature and using it to try to clean out the blood of what he considers to be other mistakes of nature. How's that figure?"

"My guess is the thing that attracts him, like a shiny object attracts a cat, is the whiteness of the skin. This is about whiteness."

"That and the blood," said Antony. "Nothing is ever more fucked up than when someone decides they're going to save the human race from itself."

"You mean like me," I said, "thinking Agarias has got to be stopped one way or the other?"

"Boss, make no mistake about it. In case you were thinking otherwise, he's never going to let us live if he can help it. We'll make the exchange with him, and then he's going to plug us all. So as you're dreaming up a plan to save Schell, you better keep that in mind."

I nodded. "My mind's a total blank. I couldn't dream up what to have for lunch."

"He's definitely got us by the short hairs," said Antony.

"We don't even know if Schell's still alive," I said.

From that moment on, for the rest of the morning and well into the afternoon, Antony said nothing. He read the race results, picked up around the house where items from the break-in still lay in disarray, and spent hours in the Bugatorium, carefully collecting the fragile corpses of dead butterflies. As for me, I sat at the desk in the office, pencil and paper at the ready, waiting to jot down an agenda that never materialized.

While sitting there, drawing circles, I considered the talk I'd had with Morgan that morning before Antony and I had left the cottage. She'd had a hard time accepting that she was the cause of Schell's kidnapping. I didn't think she'd really understood the implications of the entire thing, the part about Agarias and Merlin and herself. When I'd relayed to her that what they were asking for was an exchange of her for Schell, she'd said she would gladly do it but then dissolved into tears and ran to the back room. I didn't have the heart to pursue it, so I simply asked Isabel to do her best to calm Morgan down, which she said she would. And then we'd left . . . to do what?

That's the way the entire day went. Nothing but bad thoughts—the grief of Stintson's family; the innocent Kern, wasting away in a jail cell; the Barneses still wondering why their daughter had been killed. Grim reality, like some insatiable spirit, devoured every idea I might possibly have hatched. I bit my nails, banged my fists against my temples, all to no avail. As twilight came on, I called for Antony, and he appeared at the office door.

"I guess we might as well write this one off and head back down to the South Shore," I said.

"Okay, Boss," he said, and my heart sank to see his dejection.

"Maybe something will come tomorrow," I said.

He went to get his coat. I stood up and threw the pencil down on the desk. We met in the living room, and just as we were about to push back the makeshift rug of a door and leave, Antony said, "Oh yeah, I'm definitely getting a bottle for tonight."

"Good idea," I told him.

He reappeared a few minutes later from down the hall with a cloudy bottle holding an amber liquid. "The good stuff," he said. "Something ought to be good."

We left, and the rug fell back into place. As we made for the Cord, I heard, in the distance, the sound of the phone ringing.

"Hey," said Antony, coming to attention, but I was already off, running up the path to the house. I was out of breath when I reached the office and fumbled the receiver before getting it to my ear.

"Hello?" I said.

There was nothing for a second, and then a voice suddenly blared.

"Tommy?" It was Emmet Brogan again.

"He's not here," I said. I wasn't in the mood to explain everything that had gone on.

"Oh, he's a busy, busy man," said The Worm.

"Can I help you?" I asked.

"It's nothing, kid. Just a point of interest to a fellow lepidopterist. Page five in your local paper out there on the island today. Thought he'd get a kick out of it. Bottom right corner."

"I'll let him know," I said.

"What'd he think of the ERO stuff?" asked Emmet.

"Perfect," I said.

"Ain't that the fucking word for it," he said and hung up.

By then, Antony was standing in the hallway, looking on expectantly.

I put down the receiver and said to him, "Where's the newspaper?"

"In here," he said, and I got up and followed him down the hall.

I sat down at the kitchen table, the paper in front of me, and trying to ignore the photo of Stintson on the front, flipped through it till page five was facing me. "Here," I said and pointed to a small article in the lower right-hand corner.

"Boy Finds Exotic Butterfly in Fort Solanga," I read aloud and then scanned the rest of the article.

"Let's have it," said Antony.

"It says this kid caught a beautiful blue butterfly in the woods near his house yesterday. It's since died, but he brought it to his science teacher, who reported it to the newspaper. The teacher says it was bizarre finding this butterfly, which he identifies as a blue morpho, on the island, in autumn no less. His theory is that it came off a passing ship headed for New York."

"Schell?" said Antony.

"If the teacher has it right, and it's a morpho, they're from South America. Why would a ship coming up from the south circle around to the sound to approach New York? Besides, with the temperature as it is, I doubt it would have made the flight in from the sound to wherever this town is. This has got to be Schell leaving his calling card," I said.

"Where the hell is Fort Solanga?" said Antony. "Ever hear of it?"

"No," I said, "but I bet the place he released the butterfly from has to be fairly close by."

"I've got the map in the car," he said.

A few minutes later, we were back at the kitchen table, Antony hunched over the map. "Fort Solanga," he said, "what kind of half-assed name is that?"

"You've got to give me a cigarette," I said. I couldn't sit still.

Whereas earlier I'd been so depressed I could hardly think straight, a new nervous energy made my legs twitch beneath the table.

Antony reached into his jacket pocket and pulled out his butts and the lighter. With his eyes still trained on the map, he handed them over. "Light me one too," he said.

Two cigarettes apiece later, he finally said, "Okay, we're in business. Fort fucking Solanga. Quick, get me a pencil before I lose it."

He took the pencil I got him from the office and circled the location, blowing a smoke ring at the same time. "It's out east a ways," he said. "Almost due north of King's Park up by the sound, south of a spot called Crab Beach."

"Tomorrow," I said, "we'll go out there. There's an address in the article for the kid who found the blue. We'll tell him we're biologists or something, slip him a buck, and get him to show us the exact place he bagged it."

That night, after dinner at the cottage, we sat around the table and sipped tumblers of the good stuff from the cloudy bottle. Morgan joined us and seemed to be in somewhat better spirits than she had that morning. Everyone was a little high with the promise that the article about the butterfly meant Schell was still alive.

Antony described how when he had collected the dead butterflies, a breeze from the rug-covered front door must have blown down the hall and entered the Bugatorium. "It was too slight for me to feel," he said, "but when I looked down at the table where I'd laid out the dead bugs, I saw their wings start to move, and for second, I thought they were coming back to life. I swear I thought it was some kind of ghost mess; like a miracle."

Sometime during the third round of drinks, Morgan said, "I've been thinking hard today about the past, and I remember my foster mother telling me one night when she was drunk that I had a brother. Actually, when I was very young, I might have met him."

"What about Agarias?" I asked. "Did his name ever come up?"

"I'm not sure, but again, when I was young, I remember a doctor coming to the house to see me. I thought it was just a regular checkup, but for a while he came quite often."

"I have a theory," I said.

"I know what you're going to say," she told me and held up her hand. "The person who left me the clues to where the bodies were was Merlin."

"Yes," I said. "The fellow you lived with in New York was killed the way Stintson and another researcher were killed. I'll bet Agarias was keeping an eye on you the whole time. He didn't like what you were doing, so he ended that relationship for you."

"I could almost thank him for that," she said.

"He followed you out to the island, kept tabs on you, but left you alone until recently, when he decided he needed your blood. Agarias's goons would drive by and send Merlin to the cabin to get you, but instead of breaking in and rousting the place, he'd leave you the notes about the bodies and the flowers and so forth."

"Why?" asked Antony.

"Maybe old Merlin isn't as stupid as Agarias wishes he was. Perhaps he'd overheard him telling one of his henchmen that you were his sister. Who knows?"

"Which would mean," said Morgan, "he knows what Agarias is up to."

"Exactly," I said. "Even if he's a monster, he may be a reluctant monster, but I wouldn't count on it. We have to remember that he gouged out Parks's eyes, broke the security guard's neck, and strangled the butler all in one night."

"He doesn't seem to have much affection for me," said Antony. "I'll tell you right now, if it comes down to it, I wouldn't hesitate to put his lights out."

"Antony, what you say, I understand. But I feel sorry for him a little bit," said Isabel.

"I'm glad you didn't know anything about him that night at the Parks place," said Antony.

Morgan started to cry, huge glistening tears running down her face.

"I'm sorry, Morgan," said Antony.

She reached over and patted his forearm. "It's not you. The whole thing is just so sad." Antony offered her a cigarette to make amends, and, I suppose, to prove she meant what she had told him, she sang him a couple of verses of "You Forgot Your Gloves."

After that, I needed another drink.

SWEATING THE KID

With another hit from the dregs of the cloudy bottle to cure the morning funk, Antony and I set out early for Schell's place. Once we were there, I took a bath and picked another suit this time, a double-breasted, gray pinstripe. Antony also bathed, applied some of his special tear-inducing cologne, and changed in order for us to make the best impression we could with the parents of the kid who'd found the butterfly. It was Saturday, so we knew he'd at least be out of school. Before nine, we were on our way to Fort Solanga.

Maybe it was on my mind from having recently dealt with Agarias, but I decided an Anglo face would be more convincing in this situation, so Antony led the way as we took the steps to the house on Clayton Road. He knocked on the door and a young boy of around ten with freckles and red hair answered.

Before speaking, the big man took his hat off. "Is this the residence of the remarkable young man who discovered the blue butterfly?" he asked.

"Yeah," said the kid. "It was me."

"May we please speak to your mother or father?" asked Antony.

The kid disappeared and a few minutes later came back with a woman in tow. She took one look at the two of us and her expression went south. "Yes?" she asked, looking as if it might not be a better idea to close and lock the door.

"I'm Professor Cramshaft from the Royal Academy of Butterflies, and this," he said pointing over his shoulder at me, "is Dr. San Francisco, our South American specialist."

"Hola," I said and bowed.

"Dr. San Francisco?" said the woman. It was evident she wasn't buying it. Antony must have sensed that too and reached into his pocket. He pulled out a five-dollar bill.

"At the academy, we're very interested in the butterfly that your son found. We were wondering if you would allow him to show us exactly where he located it."

The woman looked hesitant. Antony flashed the cash. "Of course, we'd be willing to offer a small fee for your trouble," he said.

"I don't know," said the woman.

Antony took out another five and held the two bills in one hand, flapping them slightly. Like some sleight of hand that Schell might pull off, the woman moved so fast I could hardly track it. Next I looked, she was holding the bills.

"Jimmie," she said. A second later, the kid reappeared. "Put your coat on and take these two professors out in the woods and show them where you found it."

"Yes, Mom," he said and went to get his coat.

The kid returned again, dressed for the outdoors. Even though the mother still had a sketchy look on her face, a deal was a deal, and she kissed the kid and told us she'd be watching from the back window. "If you want to buy it from us, we can make arrangements," she said.

"I'll be in touch about that," said Antony. We smiled, tipped our hats, and took off after the kid, who was out the door and down the steps in a flash. As we moved around the side of the house to the backyard, Antony said to the boy, "Your old lady drives a hard bargain."

"That's what my dad says," said Jimmie.

He took us to the edge of his yard and into a wood of scrub pine and oaks that seemed to border the backyards of all the street's houses. We walked through fallen leaves along a path the local kids had probably worn. It wound around trees and through stands of sticker bushes.

"How far back does this woods go?" asked Antony.

"I don't know," said Jimmie. "I'm only allowed up to the sand hills."

A few minutes later, we were at the sand hills, a large clearing of small white sand dunes, surrounded by trees. "This is where I found it," he said.

"Where, exactly?" I asked.

The kid looked around, as if he was making up his mind. "Over here," he said, walking to the nearest pine tree and touching one of its branches.

"Jimmie," said Antony, moving up a little closer to the kid. "I think you're feeding old Professor Cramshaft a line of malarkey."

"I found it here," said the kid.

"I know you're not supposed to go past here," said Antony. "But let's face it, Jim, no kid is going to be satisfied for long by stopping at the sand hills."

The kid shook his head. "I'm going to go back now."

Antony leaned way down so that he was face-to-face with the kid. "You mean to tell me that you and your friends never went out there to see what was on the other side of the sand dunes?" asked Antony.

I couldn't believe the big man was sweating the kid.

Jimmie started to get nervous, but then Antony's jacket opened a little. The kid's face broke into a smile. "Hey, mister, you've got a gun."

Antony straightened up. "Of course I do," he said. "This butterfly stuff is dangerous business. You like guns?"

"Yeah," said the kid.

The big man took the Mauser out and removed the clip. "Here," he said, handing the kid the gun. "You can hold it. Lead on, James, only the absolute truth will do."

"Don't tell my mother."

"I swear," said Antony, crossing his heart. "You too, Dr. San Diego."

The kid led the way. Fifteen minutes later, after passing two ponds and winding snakelike along a less distinct path, our journey ended at a ten-foot stone wall. It stretched a good fifty yards in either direction.

"Who lives here?" asked Antony.

"I don't know," said Jimmie. "But I found the butterfly on that wall right there."

Antony took two singles from his pocket. "It could get dicey from here on out, kid," he said. "You'd better give me the gun back." As the kid handed over the gun, the big man slipped the two dollars into his hand. "You don't mention the gun, we don't drop one on you to your mom about coming out here."

Jimmie nodded.

"Run home now," said Antony. The kid took off through the trees. We started around to the western side of the wall, taking pains to walk as quietly as possible. As we crept along, Antony replaced the clip in the Mauser.

If the wall Jimmie had taken us to was about fifty yards in length, the western wall was a good seventy-five. Keeping tight against it, we followed it to where it turned another corner. The trees thinned out a little there, and we could see that halfway down the next wall of the huge rectangle there was a dirt road that led into the place.

"I'll sneak down there and take a look through the entrance," I whispered.

"I'm right behind you," said Antony.

"No, you're too big. I'll make less noise. Give me the gun; you can keep your two bucks." I took off my hat and handed it to the big man, who crouched down to wait.

I slid along the wall like a shadow, gun pointing up and ready as I'd seen Antony carry it. When I got close to the entrance where the road passed in, I saw a tall iron gate. I got down on my hands and knees and crept along only a few inches at a time, stopping to listen every now and then. Reaching the gate, I took a deep breath and stuck my head out to peer around the corner and through the bars.

The road that led into the place went straight up to a tall, old house with a wraparound porch and two gables. There was a black car, a Ford, parked at the end of the dirt drive about ten yards from the house. Sitting on the porch in a rocking chair was a man in a black suit and hat, cradling a machine gun. Another fellow, in a similar dark getup, sat on the steps. The yard around the house, with the exception of the front, which was a leaf-covered, flat expanse, was thick with trees. I was about to pull my head in and inch back to Antony, when I heard something just inside the wall.

Another man in a black suit, carrying a Tommy gun, passed inches away from me inside the gate. I was so low, he didn't notice, but had he turned, he'd have easily seen me. I waited for him to pass the gate and continue on behind the other side of the wall before making my move. With the same stealth I used to get there, I retreated. A few minutes later, I was crouching next to Antony at the corner.

"This has got to be it," I said. "I saw three of those guys in the black suits."

Antony nodded.

"Who are those guys anyway?" I asked.

"If I didn't know better I'd say they were gangsters, but I never knew any gangsters who all wore the same outfits. The black suits are like uniforms almost. Private security maybe, paid for by Agarias's wealthy friends. Who knows, maybe government issue."

As I was describing the house to him, we heard the sound of a car motor starting up. We moved around the corner, behind the wall. The gate opened a minute later, and the black Ford sped out down the dirt road, dust flying up behind it.

We made our way quickly back through the woods and to the Cord sitting parked on Clayton. I wanted to find the entrance to the dirt road leading to the compound. Leaving Jimmie's neighborhood, we drove south and then took the first road to the right. Before long, we spotted the path through the trees. Antony marked it on the map.

"I'm not sure what this is going to do for us, but at least we probably know where Schell is," I said.

"Start thinking, Boss," said Antony as he turned the car around and headed back toward our house.

Along the way, we passed through some small town; it very well could have been Fort Solanga, I don't know. There were a few shops and about a hundred yards of sidewalk along either side of the main street. Parked in front of the general store was the black, Model A Ford I'd seen leave through the gates of the compound.

As we cruised by, two of Agarias's men in those distinctive dark suits came out of the store, carrying brown paper bags. The second Antony saw them, he hit the gas, and we were gone before they could look up.

"What do you think?" he asked. "Were they getting lunch maybe?"

"They gotta eat," I said. "I doubt Agarias is cooking for them."

"You've got a smile on your face," he said to me.

Only when he said it did I realize it myself. I nodded. "I've got it," I said. "When we get back to the house, call Sal. Tell him they need to come tonight."

"Okay," he said.

"Tell him we need guns, and if he can, to scare me up a stick of dynamite."

THE FEROCITY OF MY PIGEONS

I sent Antony south to pick up Isabel and Morgan. There was no way, once Sal and the others showed up, that we could all fit in the cottage in Babylon, and I needed everyone assembled to go over my plan. It was a chance I'd have to take. I hoped Agarias would be too confident and think he had us stymied to the point where he didn't have to bother tailing us. Otherwise, once everyone was gathered at Schell's, if he sent a raiding party with Merlin and the goons, we'd be finished. Before the big man left, I'd told him to keep Morgan down in the backseat.

"Tell her to wear a long dress and a sweater with long sleeves. Have her put her hair up and wrap a kerchief around it. Dark glasses if you can find some."

I sat and waited for Sal to show up with the reinforcements from the city. In that time, I tried to polish my strategy, tie up the loose ends. There was a good chance someone was going to die when the exchange eventually went down, and that made me queasy. It would be machine guns versus the likes of myself and Hal Izzle. The deck was most assuredly stacked against us.

Morgan, Isabel, and Antony arrived only minutes before the two cars carrying Sal's recruits. Marge the Ton Templeton was the first to push back the rug and enter. Following her, and giving her a shove in the rear end to squeeze her through the opening, was Hal. Then came Captain Pierce, dressed in his parade uniform, carrying his case of throwing knives and sporting a cane. Sal was the last of the first group, wearing his cape and top hat, holding a wand in his left hand and a stick of dynamite in his right.

A few seconds passed and the next carload filed in—Miss Belinda, toting a huge crate of pigeons, Peewee Dunnit, carrying another crate of pigeons, and bringing up the rear, scuttling along on his knuckles, Jack Bunting, the spider boy. Peewee informed Antony and me that Vonda had to work and couldn't make it. "Shit, somebody's gotta work," said Sal as he passed by.

I caught Antony in the hallway, coming out of Schell's room with four bottles of champagne.

"Do you think that's a good idea?" I asked.

"Are you kidding? It's a great idea. We got to keep the morale of our forces up."

"I don't want them to get too drunk," I said.

"No," he whispered. "You want them to get drunk, so when we get to the part about the machine guns, they won't have second thoughts."

I acquiesced with a sinking feeling. For the next hour, everyone milled around and drank and talked and smoked cigarettes. I introduced Isabel and Morgan to each of the volunteers.

Miss Belinda told me she needed to find someplace to let the pigeons out, so I showed her to the Bugatorium. She nodded and called down the hall for Peewee and Antony to bring the crates. I closed the door behind me, and Miss Belinda said, "Okay, let 'em loose."

Antony and Peewee lifted the sliding planks at the ends of the wooden cages, and the birds rushed forth in a torrent of flapping wings and falling feathers. Once they settled down and found perches, a pandemonium of cooing filled the air and set the room to vibrating.

Miss Belinda took a small satchel from within the folds of her gown. Dipping into it, her hand came forth filled with golden meal, and she began spreading it on the floor like a farmer sowing seeds. The pigeons fluttered down to feed, strutting and bobbing their heads. As we left the Bugatorium, careful as to where we stepped, Antony muttered, "And I used to worry about butterfly shit."

The four bottles of champagne didn't last long, and once they were done and some of the guests were inquiring if there was more, I called for all to gather in the living room. Isabel and Hal brought chairs in from the kitchen so that everyone could have a seat. Marge took up half the couch but at least held Jack Bunting on her lap. When everyone was settled in, I took up a position near the front window, facing them. Antony stood just to the left of me, hands behind his back in his chauffeur attitude of attention.

The first thing I did was thank everyone for coming and then didn't waste any time but got right down to business.

"Okay," I said, "was anybody able to bring a gun?"

"I brought my Colt," said Captain Pierce. He held his gun up in the air to show it.

"Look at that thing," said Hal. "It's rustier than Sal's act."

"Does it even fire anymore?" asked Peewee.

"Haven't shot it since . . . ," said the Captain, trying to remember.

"Okay," I said. "Anybody else?"

"I got my derringer," said Peewee.

"No need for personal confessions at a time like this," said Miss Belinda, and the crowd broke up. As soon as the mirth died down, Marge farted, a sound like she was sitting on a string of firecrackers. "I got a Gatling gun," she said. More laughter, and Jack Bunting faked passing out.

I had no choice but to wait. When things had quieted down, I asked Sal for the stick of dynamite. He stood and rather ceremoniously handed it over to me. "My wife's cousin is a foreman on one of the blasting teams working on the subway tunnels. He snitched this stick but said it's only a half of a real stick from an old batch and is probably pretty unstable to boot."

"Just what I wanted to hear," said Hal.

"A light touch is probably a good idea," said Sal retaking his seat.

I gingerly placed the dynamite down on the windowsill behind me. "So that's it on the weapons then," I said.

"I've got my knives, of course," said Pierce.

"And I've got a straight razor out in the car," said Jack.

"Don't discount the ferocity of my pigeons should I command them to attack," said Miss Belinda.

"Excellent," I said and then launched into my somewhat prepared speech about the dangers we'd be facing. I didn't get very far before Hal interrupted me.

"Diego, look, I told them all this stuff already. Save the gas. This loathsome fuck has Tommy, wants to take this fine young woman's blood"—he pointed to Morgan—"would have the likes of us either sterilized or erased, and worst of all considers himself a patriot. We understand, bullets, mayhem, whatever. We're determined to whack this guy and get Schell back. Case closed. Why get maudlin?"

There was a huge round of applause, and I wasn't sure whether it was for the fact that he'd cut short my oration or had done such a fine job himself. I noticed even Isabel and Antony were clapping, so I hoped it was the latter.

"Okay, Okay," I said. "Before I get to the particulars, I was wondering if you had anything to add, Antony?"

Antony looked at me and nodded. He stepped forward and addressed the crowd. "Besides the guns, one thing I wanted to warn you all about is when we're in the middle of this, if you happen to see a huge white guy charging at you, drop whatever you're doing and run your ass off."

"Shit," said Captain Pierce, "I've been practicing that my whole life."

"This guy's the whitest guy you ever saw," said Antony, "and he's got a head like a fucked-up Thanksgiving gourd with teeth. He could break your neck with his bare hands."

"Is he single?" asked Miss Belinda.

It was close to midnight by the time I finally could explain what I wanted each of them to do. The second I was finished, though, like some magic trick itself, they snapped to and set about the various tasks I'd assigned.

Isabel and Hal started making gasoline bombs out of old jars and strips of cloth. Sal Coots instructed Peewee and Marge in the fine art of papier-mâché as he tore long strips from Antony's old newspapers. Morgan searched for a pair of scissors. Jack and Antony and Pierce planned a harness made of trouser belts for the spider boy. The house was a beehive of activity until well past four in the morning.

Once everyone had finally bedded down on the various couches and on blankets on the floor, I decided to go in and join Isabel for a few hours of sleep. Heading through the living room, I walked by the lounger that the Captain was sitting in. I thought he was asleep, but as I passed he reached out and tugged my shirtsleeve. He looked up at me with his clouded eyes.

"From one captain to another," he said, "when the battle is on, the only real enemy is Doubt." Having said that, he closed his eyes and leaned his head back.

It was crowded in bed. Besides Isabel on my right, lightly snoring, Doubt was to my left, tossing and turning, elbowing me in the ribs and talking in its sleep.

BREAK A LEG

It was midday and Antony and I sat at a table by the front window of a coffee shop that faced out on that main street that ran through the little town we now knew to be Fort Solanga. We were on a third cup of coffee each, silent as statues both, waiting for a sign. The street was empty save for an ancient Negro with a cane, sitting on a bench on the corner across from us, near the general store. We'd been there more than an hour, and the waitress was looking at us a little suspiciously.

"Here we go," Antony whispered.

I turned just in time to see a pigeon flutter down out of the sky and land directly on the head of the old man on the bench. It stayed perched there for nearly a minute before lifting off again. Then the man got up and headed west on the sidewalk. He was nearly out of sight when he passed a small shop. At that instant, an exceedingly heavyset woman, filling nearly the entire sidewalk, exited the place. She moved slowly eastward, stopping often for lingering looks in the shop windows.

A black Model A Ford appeared, heading west down the street. It stopped just past our coffee shop, turned around in the middle of the road so as to be heading east, and pulled up at the curb in front of the general store. Two men dressed in black suits got out of the car and went into the store.

The fat woman proceeded down the street toward the corner, still taking her time. There then appeared, passing by our window, a small disfigured fellow, a legless cripple. He was atop a makeshift dolly and pulled himself along the sidewalk, using his hands, heading west. Another man, with a scrawny physique and a bobbing Adam's apple, hat pulled down to cover his eyes, left a shop across the street from us, and passed the fat woman, heading east, his hands in his pockets, his lips pursed, whistling.

By the time the black-suited men exited the general store the heavy woman had reached it and was looking in its window. The two men got in the car, and the motor came to life. The thin man with the pulled-down hat turned around as if he'd forgotten something and began heading back toward the general store. As the Ford pulled away, the woman turned with a speed that belied her girth, took three steps, the last off the curb, and walked right into the front fender of the car. She went down with a thud that might possibly have cracked the asphalt. The car stopped, and the two men got out. The woman was lying in the road, writhing and screaming.

The woman's cries covered the rattling of the cripple's wheeled board as he crossed the street and headed for the scene of the accident. The two men in black, with a show of great exertion, helped the heavy woman to her feet. The thin man, who'd also come to the woman's assistance, reached down and picked up her pocketbook and hat. She put her hat on, took her pocketbook, and then, as if in answer to a question one of the men had asked her, nodded her head, drying her tears with the handkerchief she'd pulled from her purse. The thin man, seemingly satisfied that his help was no longer needed, broke away from the group and continued down the street.

By this time, the cripple had positioned his rolling board directly behind the Model A and lay down flat upon it. As the heavy woman stepped back onto the sidewalk, the thin man stepped down off the curb into the street as if to cross it, turned quickly, and with his right foot shoved the cripple on the dolly under the car.

The two men in black suits got back in the car. The thin man crossed the street. The Model A pulled away, revealing beneath it an empty board with wheels. Entering the coffee shop, Peewee took a seat at our table, "We're in," he whispered.

"Let's just hope the heat under the car doesn't set the dynamite off on the little guy," said Antony.

Late that afternoon, I sat by the phone in the office at the house, waiting for the call from Agarias. I'd already dispatched two cars, each with a ladder tied to its roof, to the street that the kid Jimmie lived on. From there, Isabel and most of our army would make their way to Agarias's compound, through the woods, past the sand dunes, and the ponds, carrying the ladders and a box full of gasoline bombs.

The minute the sun went down, the phone rang. I answered it, knowing it would be Agarias.

"Do you have her?" he said.

"I've got her, but she's reluctant to join you. I had to tie her up," I said.

"As long as she's not injured," said Agarias. "I knew I could count on you."

"I want to talk to Schell," I said.

"That's not necessary," he said. "I'm a man of my word."

"Either I talk to him first or the deal is off," I said.

There was silence on the other end. "Schell's a very tricky customer, as you well know," he finally said. "He's nearly escaped twice. I've had to chain him and sedate him."

"Sedate him?" I said, anger creeping into my voice. I'd decided I'd be as cold as ice, but my resolve was already breaking.

"Okay," said Agarias. "You've got thirty seconds."

Schell came on the line. "Don't bring her here," he said, his voice weak, the words slurred.

"We're coming to get you," I said. "The hell with her, she's been nothing but trouble. You don't know the whole story on her."

"Don't," he repeated. "You're not chained to this deal. I don't want you to lift a pinky to help me."

"It's going to be smooth," I told him. "Just like McLaren and the red balloon."

"Smooth," said Agarias's voice. I knew he'd be listening in.

"That wasn't thirty seconds," I said.

"You've got one hour to get here," he said. "Get ready to write down the directions."

I prayed the directions he gave would be to the place we'd staked out. If not, all would be lost. As he recited them, I was so nervous I missed the first part, but then the words *Fort Solanga* sounded, and after that the turns and street names fell into place.

When Agarias finished, I told him, "I want to be able to see Schell the entire time. An even exchange. I'll bring Morgan out of the car, you bring Schell to meet me."

"Of course," he said. "But you'd better hurry, because if you're a minute late, I'll start the transfusion, and I don't think Mr. Schell is in any shape to receive the pure blood of Merlin."

I hung up. Antony was standing in the doorway.

"We're on," I said.

"Did you talk to Schell?" he asked.

"He told me he's got a pin he can use as a key on whatever chains they have him in," I said.

I meant to get up then, but my determined cool broke like a dam, and I started to cry. My memory filled to bursting with thoughts of Schell, a swirl of scenes from my years with him. I owed him my life, and now his was in my hands. It took quite a few minutes for me to regain control of myself, and I was surprised that Antony didn't say a word. When I was done, I dried my eyes and stood up.

The big man put his hand on my shoulder. "Okay, you ready?" he asked.

"Yeah," I said.

"Let's go plug these fucks," he said.

Marge, who'd already risked life and limb for us and was going to stay behind and man the fort, grabbed me and gave me a spine-bending hug as we stepped out into the living room. "Break a leg, hon," she said.

I took Morgan's shoulders, Antony took her legs, and we lifted her bound, gagged, and squirming form off the floor. We followed Hal, who was dressed for battle in a baggy old suit and packing Pee-wee's derringer, as he led the way out to the car. Bringing up the rear was Captain Pierce, who was nearly knocked over as the rug covering the doorway fell back after we passed through.

"She's sure making a racket," said Hal as Antony and I laid her across his and the Captain's legs in the backseat.

"At least she's not singing," I said.

THAT SOFT ECLIPSE

It was so dark on the road past Fort Solanga that we nearly missed the turnoff for the dirt path that led to Agarias's compound. My heart started thumping as the Cord's headlamps illuminated the wall, the open gates, and, beyond them, the dim outline of the house.

"Everybody ready?" asked Antony.

My mouth was too dry to answer.

"Ready," said the Captain.

"Let me check my pants," said Hal.

I saw a guard with a machine gun just inside the walls as we passed through the entrance. Antony drove in about halfway to the house and stopped, cutting the engine but leaving the headlamps on. Directly in front of us, in the pool of light, was Agarias, standing on the porch next to Schell, who was in handcuffs. His head was down, and he looked unsteady on his feet. Agarias held a pistol, the end of the barrel resting against Schell's left cheek. Two black-clad men stood in front of the porch, one with a machine gun and one holding a pistol. Off to the right, the black Model A was parked where it had been the day before. Looking around, I saw two more of our friends in black suits, one off to the right side of the yard near the tree line and one off to the left.

Antony and I opened our doors and got out. He stood close to the car behind the open door, and I stepped clear of my door so that Agarias could see me.

"Where's Morgan?" asked Agarias.

"Right here," I said. I gave the sign to Hal and Pierce, and with no small degree of grunting effort, they carried Morgan's writhing form out of the car and laid her on the ground a few yards to the side of it. Her hair, her face, and arms were luminescent in the night. She twisted and turned, struggling against the ropes, crying against the gag. The two men who had been standing in front of the porch advanced as Agarias and Schell followed. Hal and the Captain each took two steps back.

When Agarias's men reached Morgan, the one with the pistol stuck his weapon in its shoulder holster and kneeled down to lift her. No sooner had he placed his hand under her shoulder than he said, "Wait a second . . ." That first indication of suspicion was the agreed-upon signal for Hal to yank on the length of fishing line that we'd attached to the chest of our Morgan. He did, and it ripped her wide open. The man with the machine gun lifted his weapon, and the other fellow stood, reeling backward, reaching for the handgun he'd just put away. A storm of pigeons, the squirming life and gagged voice of the effigy we'd made, rushed up out of the papier-mâché shell into their faces. The two instinctively stepped back, each bringing a hand up to cover his eyes.

Hal took the derringer out of his pocket, walked forward two steps, aimed, and shot the man with the machine gun in the face. He fell forward onto the dummy. His partner recovered, brought his pistol up to return Hal's fire, but stopped before pulling the trigger because he found his fingers no longer worked. There was a knife sticking through his wrist. He screamed, but that cry didn't last long, cut short by another knife that had just entered his throat and severed his spinal column.

Before the second man had hit the ground, Antony had already spun around, taken the Mauser from its holster, and squeezed off a volley of shots at the guard standing near the gate behind us. I peered through the shadows and saw his body jerk twice before going down. And that's when the Model A blew up, sending a roiling fireball into the sky, knocking Schell, Agarias, and me to the ground. Antony, Hal, and Pierce had already ducked for cover.

Shattered glass and chunks of hot metal rained down all around us. As soon as the shock wave of the explosion diminished, Agarias's men on either side of the yard started firing their pistols indiscriminately in the direction of the Cord. I could hear the slugs slamming through the car's chassis, and one or two kicked up dirt only inches from where I lay. Antony took down the gunman nearest him with the Mauser.

I could see the man on the right side of the yard in the light given off from the burning Ford as he backed in among the trees and continued firing. Hal gave a yelp, and a moment later called out in an anguished voice that he'd been hit in the leg. Two more shots rang out, one shattering a side window of the Cord and the other blowing out a back tire. Then the firing stopped. I waited what seemed an eternity for another shot, but none came. A few moments later a small shadow moved across the yard from the direction the man had been firing from. It was Jack Bunting, stumping along on his knuckles. When I could see him clearly, he said, "That cat's finished. I dropped out of the tree and slit his throat." Then I noticed a straight razor sticking out of his shirt pocket.

As we got to our feet, the first of the gasoline bombs crashed through the windows of the house, spreading their liquid fire. Flames and smoke leaped from the windows. Another crashed onto the porch and set it ablaze. As I scrabbled to my feet, I saw Antony stand up on the other side of the car. I called back to Hal, and the Captain, a veteran of battlefield surgery, said he had the situation under control. "God help me," said Hal.

That left only Agarias to worry about, and when I finally spotted him, he had Schell in front of him with the pistol to his back. In the midst of all the fireworks, I'd forgotten about Merlin, who was now standing next to his master. Agarias was looking the worse for wear. He'd lost his glasses in the explosion and his hair was wild.

"You still don't have Schell," he yelled. "Bring me the girl, and he lives. Anything else and I swear I'll shoot."

Merlin was obviously excited, his chest heaving, his nostrils flaring, his eyes wide with the desire to destroy something. It was a standoff. Antony whispered to me, "Do you want me to try to take down Agarias?"

I shook my head. The shot was too risky, and then what about Merlin? In a second he could be on Schell and snap his neck. As I stood there trying to decide, Isabel, Sal, Peewee, Belinda, and the real Morgan, her hair now close-cropped since donating her locks to the mannequin, approached from out of the trees. The house was an inferno, lighting the scene with a hellish glare. Belinda stopped to assist Pierce with Hal's wound, and the others gathered behind me, save for Morgan, who broke away from us and walked forward toward Agarias and Schell.

"Don't hurt him," she said. "I'll go with you."

As she drew close to them, Merlin crouched down and made a kind of whimpering noise. Suddenly Schell twisted his forearms in and out, and shook his hands. The cuffs slipped right off and fell to the ground. I could tell by the inelegant way in which he sloughed the chains that he was drugged. Agarias cocked the trigger of his pistol, still aimed at Schell's back.

Morgan stepped up to Schell and they put their arms around each other. Slowly they turned so that the barrel of Agarias's gun was now pointed at the back of her head instead.

"What are you doing?" said the doctor. His hand was shaking wildly, and his voice cracked when he spoke.

Morgan started singing, softly at first and then more clearly, the song "That Soft Eclipse." Schell hung on to her, and they moved slowly away from Agarias as if they were dancing, her back always to the gun.

"Stop," cried Agarias, spittle flying from his mouth. It was obvious he was straightening his arm, intending to shoot.

"Antony," I said.

The gun suddenly went off, its sharp crack startling me. A wave of panic surged through my chest. Isabel screamed, and Antony closed his eyes. Agarias looked surprised himself that he'd fired it. A second later, it was clear the shot had gone high. Schell and Morgan continued moving away from the doctor, who again lifted the pistol and aimed. Schell picked his head up, as if rousing from a long sleep, and seeing Agarias, bent his knees and pulled Morgan to the ground with him. As they fell, Merlin suddenly pounced at the doctor, and in the exact same instant, Antony lifted the Mauser and fired.

Agarias's shots slammed into Merlin's chest, and Antony's shots ripped into the broad, white back, forming dark, smoking holes in the smooth skin. The creature grabbed his father's head and twisted, and the dull sound of cracking bone was audible. Then the blood came from Merlin, and he staggered forward, still holding Agarias's lifeless figure. He dropped the body, tried to steady himself, and then toppled onto it.

I hadn't realized I'd been holding my breath, but as Merlin hit the ground, I heaved a sigh of relief and ran toward Schell. Antony was already there, lifting him with one hand and Morgan with the other. It took Schell a moment to get his bearings, and he shook his head, as if to clear it.

"Diego," he said in a weary voice, "I think you could have done without blowing up the car, but otherwise, nice work." Then he lurched forward, and for the first time in my life, he hugged me.

"Sorry to break in, Boss," Antony said to me, "but we got to move. I know we're out in the sticks, but somebody has to have seen this fire. The cops, the fire department, and the fucking French Foreign Legion'll be here in no time. Help me fix this tire and tell the others to scram."

"What do you mean, 'Boss'?" Schell asked Antony.

"Sorry, Boss," Antony said to Schell, "but the kid's the boss now, at least until this job is over."

"And he's welcome to it," said Schell.

I instructed Isabel, Sal, Jack, Peewee, and Belinda to get going back through the woods to their cars. Belinda gave the whistled signal that told her pigeons to fly back to their coop in the city. Isabel kissed me quickly and then they were off, fleeing around the burning house and through the trees, Jack riding on Sal's shoulders.

Although I wanted to stay with Schell, Antony and I jumped to and worked furiously to change the tire as quickly as possible. Captain Pierce had removed the bullet from Hal's leg, which had not gone in too deeply, and, using his own white shirt, made a bandage. By the time we were ready to go, Hal was able to hobble on one foot back to the car. We settled him up front, so he could stretch his leg out. Schell took a window seat in the back, the Captain crawled in, and I turned to look for Morgan.

She was kneeling on the ground next to her fallen brother. They were like a pair of ghosts in the night, and embers from the burning house fell around them. I ran over and pulled at her arm.

"We've got to go," I said. I dragged her back to the car and told her to get in on the Captain's lap, and then I squeezed into a space that was half of what I needed.

"Pray they didn't put one through the engine," said Antony. He turned the key, and the Cord, our reliable silent partner, came through one more time. Antony turned the car around and then floored it. We shot down the dirt path and out the end of the hidden entrance, onto the road, turning toward Fort Solanga. On our way, we passed the fire trucks and police cars.

We rode in a general silence, although Morgan still quietly wept until it was broken by Captain Pierce.

"I've seen that monster before," he said.

"Merlin?" asked Schell.

"No," he said. "That was a man. I mean the Monster. It never seems to die. We killed a lot of men tonight, but we didn't even wound the Monster."

"Well, we saved Tommy," said Hal. "I wouldn't have missed it for the world, bullet in the leg or not."

"I'll never forget it," said Antony, lighting a cigarette, "that's for sure." He rolled down his window, and smoke streamed out into the cold night air.

"The triumph of the shiftless," said Hal.

THE CON

When we came through the rug back at the house, Marge lifted Schell off the floor and spun him around. Antony made coffee for the drivers, and everyone congratulated one another on a job well done. To my surprise, Schell hugged us all. I was in a daze and just sat next to Isabel on the couch with my arm around her. I still couldn't believe we had pulled off the rescue. What had seemed doable the previous day now seemed foolhardy at best.

I was still staring, lost in thought, as the city gang was preparing to leave. Isabel nudged my arm and told me to get up and thank them. She followed me to the doorway and stood beside me. As each of them passed, they wished us well and told me I'd done a good job, and I felt as if we were standing in the reception line at our wedding.

Antony decided to sleep in the living room with the gun next to him just to be on the safe side. Schell told me that we'd talk in the morning, but that he had to lie down. Before he and Morgan went to his room, I tried to express to her how sorry I was about her brother.

She said nothing but leaned over and kissed me, and the strange thought struck me that she could someday very soon be my mother. My entire perspective on her changed in that instant.

For both Isabel and me, sleep came swiftly, but I woke in the middle of the night with Captain Pierce's words in my head, concerning the Monster and the men we'd killed. It struck me all at once that seven people had died as a result of my scheme, and the thought of it turned my stomach, making me ill. Finally I rolled out of bed and ran to the bathroom down the hall to vomit. When I was done, I was sweating like mad, but I felt much better.

Leaving the bathroom, I noticed that the door to the Bugatorium was open and the light was on. I peered in and saw Schell, sitting at the coffee table, working a deck of cards. When I entered, he looked up and smiled. All traces of the drug-induced exhaustion were gone from his face. "Come in and see if you can find a seat without pigeon shit on it," he said.

I sat down across from him, shivering slightly in the draft that seeped in the front doorway.

"I was just thinking," he said. "That con you came up with really showed a lot of promise."

"Thanks," I said.

"The only thing is, you've got to learn a little subtlety. A little subtlety goes a long way. Like I said, blowing up their car was a tad outlandish. I'm afraid you could have killed us all."

I nodded.

"And having poor Jack strapped to the underside of it all afternoon . . ." He made a face and shook his head. "Anybody other than Jack would have told you to jump in a lake if you'd asked him to do that. It just so happens I saved the little cocker's life one night when he got in over his head in a poker game."

"To tell you the truth, I think he would have done it anyway," I said.

"Maybe," said Schell. "Maybe. But as I was saying, not bad. The fake Morgan with the pigeons inside was a beautiful thing. I think you have potential."

"You guys going to make me a full partner?" I said.

"No, of course not."

"Why?" I asked.

"Because you're leaving," he said.

"What do you mean?" I asked.

"You're going to Mexico with Isabel."

I paused and then smiled. "You're right," I said. "I am."

"I knew it," said Schell. "It's the only way to go. Besides, we have to fly the coop here, no pun intended. Whoever Agarias worked for, they're never going to settle for us blowing up their lab and killing off their main mad scientist. Maybe not this week or next, but make no mistake about it, they'll be coming after us."

"What are you going to do?" I said.

"I'm sending Antony to California for a vacation. Morgan and I are going somewhere quiet and out of the way. We all need to lie low for a while."

"For how long?" I asked.

"Don't worry. I'll let you know when the heat's off. Tomorrow Antony can show you how to drive the car. You and Isabel will take the Cord to Mexico. I'll give you your cut of the money."

I thought about turning him down, but I had no good reason to. I needed his help now, he was offering it, and it all seemed perfectly natural in a father-and-son sort of way.

"You know," I said, "we didn't really accomplish much with this whole thing, did we?"

"We set out to find who killed Charlotte Barnes and we did. I have to contact Barnes and lay it out for him. Maybe with his connections he can really sound the alarm on this eugenics mess. My only hope is that he can get Kern off the hook. There's nothing I can do for him now."

"Do you really think it was the girl's ghost you saw in the glass?" I asked.

"I don't know. And at this point, it doesn't matter."

The next morning, Antony got me up early and took me out driving in the Cord. In broad daylight, the car looked pretty good, considering it had been in the middle of a shoot-out the night before. There were three bullet holes in the left side, a broken window, and the spare needed to be fixed. Antony said he'd take it later that day and get the work done.

"Kid, you drive like an old lady," he said when he finally deemed my driving abilities worthy of leaving the driveway and going out on the road.

I drove nervously, hunched over the steering wheel, eyes darting right and left. "I'm not used to it," I said.

"Takes time. This car knows the way to go, though. You just put it in gear and put your foot on the gas. Loosen up a little and let it roll."

By midday I was zipping along the roads of the North Shore.

"Okay," said Antony, "I'm bored. Take it back. You're not thrilling me with the short stops and gear crunching anymore."

"Antony," I said. "I'm leaving tomorrow for Mexico."

He took out a cigarette and lit it. "I know," he said.

"What am I going to do without you?" I asked.

"Fuck up, more than likely," he said.

"How am I going to contact you? Schell said you're going to California."

"Yeah," he said. "Before you go, I'm going to give you a phone number. If you ever need me, call it. An old woman will answer. Tell her who you are and leave a number and I'll get back to you."

"I'm going to miss you," I said.

"Don't worry, kid. You'll get over it." He said nothing else but just kept smoking his cigarette. When we pulled back in the driveway at the house, he got out without a word and went inside.

The next morning, the car was ready to go. Isabel and I packed it with blankets and food and whatever else we would need for the long journey. Schell suggested we cross the border in Texas in as remote a spot as possible. He handed me a huge wad of bills and told me it was my cut of all the jobs we had worked. I was dressed in one of Schell's best suits, and Morgan had given Isabel the paisley wrap to wear. We said our good-byes in the house. Morgan kissed us both and started to cry. Antony shook my hand and said, "Don't take any wooden nickels."

Schell followed us out to the Cord. He held the door for Isabel as she got in and kissed her through the open window. Then he came around to my side and said, "Once you get set up down there, I'll be in touch."

"How?" I asked.

"I have connections," he said.

"I want to tell you——" I began, but he cut me off by saying, "Time to go." He backed away from the car, and I started it. Pulling out of the driveway, I almost hit a tree but managed to right the back end at the last second. Then we were in the road and driving away.

The Cord didn't make it all the way to Mexico but crapped out somewhere around Phoenix, where we boarded a bus for the remainder of the journey. The trip was an adventure, worthy of a book itself. Isabel helped me relearn Spanish as we traveled across the United States. We saw a lot of places hit hard by the Depression, a lot of people scrabbling to survive, and we felt lucky to have money and a destination, a home to return to.

Antony was right, I'd gotten over leaving him and Schell behind as I fell, every day, deeper in love with Isabel. Sometimes, on those open country roads, while the Cord was still running, and Isabel's head lay on my shoulder, I'd open it up all the way, and heading straight into the future, with the wind rushing in the window, I'd feel like I was born anew, never having known anything about the con.

WAIT, THERE'S MORE

As Isabel had said, when she told me the story of the ghost in the silver mine and I thought it was just about over: "Wait, there's more."

We settled in Mexico City and got a small apartment in the Polanco section. It wasn't difficult to find work, as Isabel and I were bilingual, and we labored as translators for anything from business documents to minor literary works. Through relatives who still lived in the country, Isabel was able to locate her father, a mild-mannered and jovial old man, who came and lived with us in the city. He served as a witness and sole guest at our wedding.

Once we had established ourselves more securely, I took some of the money Schell had given me and whatever we could save and put it toward tuition at the University of Mexico. There I studied literature, and my early tutors would have been proud of my accomplishments. After many years of working and studying, with great support from Isabel, I managed to acquire a doctorate. Even better, I was offered a position at the university and wound up teaching all of those works I'd studied when I was younger and, even more satisfying, the great writings of my own people. It was a heady time for us, and life happened fast and happened faster. During these years Schell and Antony were never far from my mind, and sometimes I had the greatest longing to see them again, to know how they were, to tell them how happy I was. Every day when the post arrived, I'd search for a letter, even just a postcard, but nothing ever came.

World War II started. During those dark years and for many following Captain Pierce's words returned to me time and again. The Monster had risen. I knew, as many did not, that the grim protocols of Adolf Hitler, a horrifying program of genocide, had been germinated in the United States by "great men" the likes of Henry Ford and the disreputable, crackpot findings of the Eugenics Record Office. And as time progressed, I could see that even the scale of this atrocity would not satisfy the Monster, but that it would return time and again to haunt humanity.

In 1946, after Isabel herself had graduated university with a degree in mathematics, we had our first child, a boy we named Antonio, of course, after Mr. Cleopatra. Our second son, Diego, was born two years later. During this time of young parenthood, I'd wished to have some contact with Schell, as most people want to speak to their parents when they, themselves, become parents. I tried to locate him, but to no avail.

The years followed one after the other, like a string of scarves from the great Saldonica's breast pocket. One night in 1965, the year I turned fifty, the year my younger son was seventeen, the age I was when I'd left Schell, Diego was rummaging around our attic and found the suit Schell had given me to wear on the long-ago escape to Mexico.

He came downstairs and handed me a slip of paper folded in half, saying "I found this in the pocket." I opened the yellowed note and there was a phone number written out in Antony's oddly delicate hand. I remembered him saying, "Call it. An old woman will answer. Tell her who you are . . . and I'll get back to you." I smiled at the sight of it and had a halfhearted notion to dial until I realized that any woman who was old in '32 would now be long dead. Instead, I folded it and shoved it into my wallet behind a tattered and creased photograph of Schell and Antony standing beside the Cord, a lifetime ago.

Later that year, I was in California, at Berkeley, participating in a weeklong academic conference called Literature of the Americas. I spent the first evening drinking and gabbing with colleagues I'd not seen in a few years; by the second night I'd already begun to miss Isabel and our sons and stayed to myself in the hotel room, watching television and reviewing a paper I was to deliver the next morning. At one point I opened my wallet to retrieve my photo of her, clumsily knocking loose all of the photos, which scattered on the table. With them came that slip of paper. I don't know what got into me—curiosity? loneliness?—but I dialed the number. There were five rings, and I was about to hang up, when an old woman answered.

"What's your name?" she croaked.

"Diego," I said.

She asked for my phone number, repeating each numeral as I uttered it. Then, without another word, she hung up. I was bemused and never really expected to receive a call back. It was not until I was in bed, at around one in the morning, that the phone rang.

"Hello?" I said into the receiver, my mind fuzzy from sleep.

"What's up, kid," said Antony. I sat up straight, instantly wide awake, and burst out laughing to hear his familiar voice.

"Throw some sawdust under it," he said. "Where are you?"

I told him about the conference. He told me, "Ditch that bullshit and come see me." He gave me directions and a phone number, and then hung up without further discussion.

As soon as I finished my lecture the next morning, I ducked out of the conference and rented a car. He lived not too far away, up in the hills outside Berkeley. It was early afternoon when, after getting lost a few times, I pulled into the drive of a house that sat alone atop a wooded hill.

I knocked on the front door, and a young Mexican woman answered. She introduced herself as the housekeeper, Marta, and showed me to a patio set away from the back of the house, at the edge of the hill, which offered a breathtaking view of the valley below. Antony was sitting in a wicker chair, beneath a grape arbor facing the vista. In front of him was a glass-topped wicker table holding an ashtray, a pack of cigarettes, and a beer can.

"Antony," I cried, and he turned and smiled. Unlike most people who shrink with age, he was still a giant. His face was etched with wrinkles, and he'd lost some hair; what remained had gone white. But his eyes were still a piercing blue, as sharp and alert as ever.

"Kid, you gonna make me get up or what?" he said.

I walked over to him and gave him a hug. He enclosed me in one of his huge arms, and his incredible strength was still evident. He waved to the chair opposite him and I took a seat. The first words out of my mouth were, "What happened to you guys?"

He told me how he'd come out to California, decided the climate suited him just fine, and never looked back—except to send for Vonda the Rubber Lady, who joined him as soon as he said the word. Although they never married, they had a good life together, starting a profitable business cultivating marijuana. "Didn't I ever tell you I always wanted to be a farmer?" he asked. After Vonda died of cancer in 1956, Antony retired on the considerable sum he and Vonda had managed to stash away. Now, he said, he was just as happy to sit in the sun, sip a cold one, and daydream.

Next it was my turn to fill him in on what Isabel and I had done with our lives.

"That's great, kid," he said. "Schell would be proud of you."

"Antony," I said, "I'm fifty and you're still calling me kid."

"Fifty, Christ, that's child's play. Try out my age for a while. I feel like a three-hundred-pound meat loaf. My brain hasn't done an honest day's work in years."

"And Schell?" I asked.

Antony took a deep drag on his cigarette and shook his head. "I'm sorry, kid. Right after you left and I took off for California, he and Morgan bought the farm. They'd stayed too long at the old house. It burned to the ground one night, with them in it. The police said it was arson, because the fire was so hot the bodies were burned beyond recognition."

I hadn't been prepared to hear that Schell had died. I'd hoped that Antony would tell me where to find him. I felt like weeping, but I didn't.

Antony continued, his eyes gazing out across the valley, his voice oddly hollow. "No one was ever charged. I know who it was, though."

I knew he was referring to the Monster and the people behind Agarias. And I knew that even then, more than thirty years later, the Monster still lived. "Schell was a great guy," I said. "He saved my life when he took me in."

"Yeah," said Antony. "And luckily you were able to repay the favor that crazy night out in Fort Solanga."

"Have you ever wondered about the girl in the glass?" I asked.

Antony leaned forward in his chair. "I think about it almost every day," he said. "There's something I've wanted to ask you for years. The ghost Schell saw . . ."

"Charlotte Barnes," I said.

"You had nothing to do with that, did you?" he said and smiled.

"Are you joking?" I asked.

"Nah," he whispered and got that far-off look in his eyes again.

"So, I guess it was a real ghost."

"Maybe."

"What do you mean?" I asked.

"Do you remember the shape Schell was in just before that whole mess?" said Antony. "Moping around like he had a load in his pants? He was a good con man, but not a great con man. He wasn't ruthless enough. He had all the tricks, all the techniques, the facility for it. That part, if you'll excuse the expression, was in his blood. But he never really had the *heart* for it. He was trying so hard to convince himself that he was callous because that's the way his old man had been."

"Well if it wasn't a ghost, what the hell was it?" I asked.

He took a sip of his beer, squinted in the setting sun, and said, "Sometimes I think it was Schell."

"You mean he was seeing things because he was depressed?"

"Not exactly. When I left the East Coast he took me to the train station. It was the last I ever saw him. We were standing on the platform, waiting for the train to pull in, and I asked him about the ghost, 'cause, you know, it had never been resolved. Here's what his last words were to me before I got on board: 'The girl in the glass? She was always there, my friend. I just never had a good enough reason to notice her before.'"

"What was the reason?" I asked.

"I think it was you," he said. "I think it was you."

I sat in silence for a long time, stunned by the implications of Antony's theory, until I finally blurted out, "You mean he conned us?"

The big man wheezed with laughter and nodded. "He didn't want you to follow in his footsteps. He wanted something better for you. But he knew you wouldn't get it simply because he told you. So he mixed things up. The girl in the glass was the grain of sand in the oyster, the wrench in the gearworks, the mutation compounded over time, as he used to say about the spots on those fucking butterflies of his.

"Oh, I'm not sayin' he knew anything about Charlotte Barnes's murder before we all did. I think he must've made up the story about seeing the ghost of a little girl, just to toss the dice, and then BAM! Five days later . . ."

"He almost got us all killed," I said, smiling.

"Yeah, tell me that wouldn't have been a bitch. Sometimes, though, kid, you gotta do what you gotta do. That's the long and short of it."

By now the sun had nearly set; a sliver of orange stretched across the deep purple horizon before winking out. I didn't talk for a while but stared off into the twilight, trying to rekindle faded memories of the whole affair.

"Look, Diego, it's just a theory. No need to get morose. I'm half senile as it is."

All through the day Marta had been replenishing our beers. And although I hadn't had a cigarette in years, I smoked close to a pack that day. I stopped drinking at around eight o'clock and didn't leave till after midnight. By the time I got up to go, Antony had fallen asleep in his chair. I wrote out my address and phone number on an empty matchbook and gave it to Marta, telling her if he ever needed anything to call me. She promised me she would.

Before the year was out, Marta called me in Mexico. Antony had died suddenly, quietly, while sitting in his chair, overlooking the valley. I caught a flight, rented a car, and once again found myself lost in the hills. By the time I found the little funeral parlor where the wake was being held, the viewing hours were just about over. I jumped out of my car and ran up the steps. The last of the mourners were leaving, save one old man who sat, head bowed, in the last row of seats in the small room.

I stepped up to the large coffin and gave myself over to memories of my youth with Antony and Schell—the cons, the marks, the tricks. He lay there like he was carved from limestone, big and powerful even in death. Eventually, I touched his shoulder and said, "Okay, Antony," but before I turned away, I noticed something lying on the dark green satin liner, tucked in the corner to the right of his head. I leaned over and saw it was a playing card, turned facedown. My hand trembled as I reached for it. Flipping it over, I discovered the ace of hearts.

A sudden strong breeze, as if someone had thrown open a door, startled me, and I turned to see who was there, but the door was closed and the place was empty. That's when I noticed it fluttering above the center aisle, a simple pine white, like some ghost of a memory come to life.

ACKNOWLEDGMENTS

Whenever a writer delivers to his readers a novel that is set in a distinct historical period, as *The Girl in the Glass* is set in 1932 America, there is usually a good measure of research that has gone into the effort. Please keep in mind that I don't claim to be an historian. In other words, I never let the facts get in the way of following the fiction where it demands to go, but, that said, I did delve into many sources in the course of writing this book. I list some of them below, not to act the scholar, but I believe readers might be discovering one or two of the historical actualities presented herein for the first time and will want to investigate them further on their own.

Anyone interested in the concept of spiritualism as a con would do well to read the work of James Randi, internationally renowned magician and escape artist. He has a long list of very fine titles and is an engaging writer who rarely fails to amaze with his insight as to how less-than-reputable practitioners of the supernatural dupe their customers. The particular work of his I found most useful on this subject was *Flim-Flam: Psychics, ESP, Unicorns, and Other Delusions*. In addition to Randi, one can turn to the writings of the great Houdini himself, who penned a number of books, some of which remain in print, that dissect spiritualist techniques.

Before investigating the 1930s, I was unaware of the Mexican Repatriation that went on during that decade in the United States. In the 1920s and earlier many immigrants were welcomed into this country in order to serve as cheap labor for building the railroads and harvesting crops in western and southern states. With the onset of the Great Depression, though, the growing economic problems of the country and those in positions of power responsible for them found a scapegoat in immigrants. Many legal as well as illegal Mexican immigrants, along with children born in the United States, were forcibly deported back to Mexico. For an easily accessible and excellent essay on this subject, seek out Dr. Jorge L. Chinea's "Ethnic Prejudice and Anti-Immigrant Policies in Times of Economic Stress: Mexican Repatriation from the United States, 1929–1939" on the web at http://www.people. memphis.edu/~kenichls/2602MexRepatriation.html. For further reading, one can turn to the book *Decade of Betrayal: Mexican Repatriation in the 1930's*, by Francisco E. Balderramma and Raymond Rodriguez.

As someone who grew up on Long Island during the 1950s, 1960s, and 1970s, I was incredulous to discover the extent of influence the Ku Klux Klan once had in the area. During the 1920s it is estimated that one out of every seven people had some affiliation with the Klan. For a great essay on this phenomenon, seek out David Behrens's "The KKK Flares Up on L.I.," which can be found on the Web as part of a wonderful site constructed by *Newsday* that deals with many facets of the history of the island. There are also other fascinating articles to be found on this site written by *Newsday* staff reporters: http://www.newsday.com/community/guide/lihistory/ny-history-hs725a,0,7485380.story.

Unfortunately, the Eugenics Record Office is not a darkly fanciful invention but a true historical institution. Granted, my character Dr. Agarias, as well as his rogue experimental research supported by shady powerbrokers, is a fictional construct, but for coherent historical information about the ERO and its racist implications there are two excellent books for the interested reader—*War Against the Weak: Eugenics and America's Campaign to Create a Master Race* by Edwin Black and *The Unfit: A History of a Bad Idea* by Elof Axel Carlson. On the Web one can also find Image Archive on the American Eugenics Movement at http://www.eugenicsarchive.org/eugenics/ and "Carrie Buck's Daughter: A Popular, Quasi-Scientific Idea Can Be a Powerful Tool for Injustice" by Stephen J. Gould at http://www.findarticles.com/p/articles/mi_m1134/is_6_111/ai_87854861/print.

I believe the correlation that my character The Worm makes between Henry Ford's invention of the assembly line from his knowledge of slaughterhouses and Hitler's assembly line of genocide can be traced back to the controversial but interesting book by Charles Patterson, *Eternal Treblinka*.

On a lighter note, for a wonderful Web site teeming with information about the history of Coney Island and its denizens, the reader should investigate *Greetings from Coney Island* authored by Jeff Stanton at http://naid.sspsr.ucla.edu/coneyisland/index.html. For information pertaining to butterflies in Schell's bugatorium, I consulted a number of basic field guides, and also a charming book *An Obsession with Butterflies* by Sharman Apt Russell.

In addition to the textual references listed above, I had great help on this book by way of early readers—Rick Bowes, Michael Gallagher, and Bill Watkins. For a firsthand view of Long Island in the 1930s, I repeatedly tapped my old man, James E. Ford, who grew up in Amityville and lived his whole life on the island. And for the Spanish spoken by Isabel in the course of the story, a way of denoting the uniqueness of the culture represented by her and Diego without too badly confusing readers of English, I solicited help from my college Spanish teacher and longtime friend, Patricia Manley, and also my Spanish-language guru, Gabe Mesa.

I also owe a great debt of gratitude for the support and encouragement of my editor, Jennifer Brehl, and her indispensable editorial advice, which helped to make this book the best it could be. And last but by no means least, a thank-you to Howard Morhaim, my agent, for his steadfast and valuable guidance.

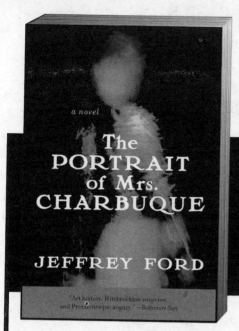

ALSO BY
JEFFREY FORD

THE PORTRAIT OF MRS. CHARBUQUE
A Novel

ISBN 0-06-093617-7

This mysterious and richly evocative novel tells the story of portraitist Piero Piambo, who is offered a commission unlike any other. The client is Mrs. Charbuque, a wealthy and elusive woman who asks Piambo to paint her portrait, though with one bizarre twist: he may question her at length on any topic, but he may not, under any circumstance, see her. So begins an astonishing journey into Mrs. Charbuque's world and the world of 1893 New York society in this hypnotically compelling literary thriller.

"Ford weaves a strange and affecting tale of obsession, inspiration, and the supernatural, with a dash of murder thrown in. . . . The twists and turns of Mrs. Charbuque's commission keep the pages turning." —*New York Times Book Review*

"A standout literary thriller." —*Publishers Weekly* (starred review)

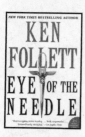